Sanctuary

Daughters of the People, Book 5

LUCY VARNA

Sanctuary

Daughters of the People, Book 5

LUCY VARNA

Bone Diggers Press
www.bonediggerspress.com

For Judy. Thank you.

Cover design © L.J. Anderson, Mayhem Cover Creations.

Published by Bone Diggers Press, Clayton, Georgia.

ISBN 978-1-943465-08-8

TITLES BY LUCY VARNA

THE DAUGHTERS OF THE PEOPLE SERIES
The Prophecy
Light's Bane
The Enemy Within
Tempered
In All Things, Balance
Sanctuary

THE SONS OF THE PEOPLE SERIES
Say Yes

THE CULLOWHEE HERITAGE SERIES
A Higher Purpose
A Wicked Love

THE PRUXNÆ SERIES
The Choosing

Notes from the Fab Four

Notes on the People compiled by Tom Fairfax, Phil Walters, George Howe, and James Terhune, known at the IECS unofficially as the Fab Four.

Aenkanien. A tattoo inked into the left-hand shoulder blade of a Son who becomes the husband of a Daughter. Once approval has been granted by the mothers of both parties and the tattoo is in place, a formal marriage ceremony is unnecessary; the two are considered married in the eyes of the People, though many couples choose to undergo a civil or, less frequently, traditional ceremony.

Amaetien. The tattoo Sons receive on their sixteenth birthday (the day they become men under the traditions and laws of the People) to indicate their maternal lineage. Usually inked onto the upper left arm, the *amaetien* is a symbol of the mother's eternal protection and devotion, and a warning to any who would harm the Son.

Ankana. Woman. Also refers to the Woman with No Face.

Council of Seven. The People's ruling body, consisting of seven women, one representing the line of each of the Seven Sisters.

Daughter. A direct descendant of one of the Seven Sisters, Daughters may be either immortal (if they have not yet broken their own curse) or mortal (if they have broken their own curse or are the daughter of a mortal Daughter).

Eternal Order. A supposedly mythical group devoted to undermining the ultimate goal of the People, to break the curse of immortality for every Daughter through the fulfillment of the Prophecy of Light.

High Guard. Seven Daughters devoted to eradicating the Eternal Order. A highly secret and deadly group.

Institute of Early Cultural Studies (IECS). Located in Tellowee, Georgia, USA, the IECS is the main historical research branch of the People and serves as a repository for much of its history.

Kaetyrm. Sister, usually used in a formal situation, though not always.

Maetyrm. Mother, usually used as a term of respect for an elder Daughter and not necessarily as a reference to one's own mother. Teachers, for example, are referred to as Maetyrm.

People, The. The name used by the descendants of the Seven Sisters to describe themselves. The People include all immortal and mortal Daughters, Sons, and the mortal descendants of all submitted Daughters to the second degree (i.e. through the grandchildren of Daughters who have submitted their wills and become mortal). Other descendants are not counted among the numbers of the People.

Prophecy of Light. Issued by an unknown person at some distant point in the past, the Prophecy of Light portends a way for the curse of immortality to be lifted from all of the People, and not solely the Daughters who submit their wills and become mortal. (See the Daughters of the People website.)

Seven Sisters. The progenitors of the modern People. The seven women, all sisters, avenged the deaths of their parents by killing the men of the People (the original band) and were cursed by the god An to live immortal lives without the ability to bear sons. The curse was tempered by the goddess Ki, who decreed that the curse could be broken by each one if she would submit her will, in whatever way (except sexually), to the man she loved. (See the Legend of Beginnings on the Daughters of the People website.)

Shadow Enemy. The traditional enemy of the People.

Son. Usually refers to the child of a Daughter who has broken the curse and become mortal, but may also reference the child of a Son or another male descendant of a Daughter.

Tellowee, Georgia, USA. One of the centers of the People, located in rural northeast Georgia.

One

THE KONYA ARCHAEOLOGICAL MUSEUM blended into the nearby buildings, distinguished more by the bold, yellow sign announcing its entrance than any architectural feature. The interior was by turns cluttered and stark, the whole covered in a fine layer of dust, but the exhibits were the focus, not their manner of presentation. The small museum housed a wide array of artifacts dating from the eighth century B.C.E. through the region's Roman period. Many were from the nearby dig at Çatalhöyük, Konya Province's most famous attraction.

Jerusha Mankiller knelt beside a marble sarcophagus and studied the reliefs carved around its sides. Half-dressed men and women twined around one another in a bacchanalian revelry fit for the god himself.

"Roman, second century A.D.," she murmured. "Beautiful."

A shadow fell across her. "It's a fancy casket, Jaybird, a hunk of rock. What's the big deal?"

Jerusha looked up and met the gaze of her companion, Drew Martin. He was a big man, easily six two, with broad shoulders and a burly frame. His blond eyebrows were furrowed over hard, cognac colored eyes in his rough-hewn face and the narrow scar at the corner of his upper lip whitened as his mouth thinned. She shook her head. He'd volunteered for this assignment. Why did he never remember that?

And her baby brother had assured her he would, that Drew had been a good soldier and a hell of an operator before he and Bobby, along with their friend Hiro Okada, had resigned from the military and formed BDH Security.

She stifled a sigh and rose to her full height, still a head shorter than Drew. "It's historic."

One corner of his mouth curled, twisting the lovely curve of his lips into a sneer. "It's a carved rock."

The security guard that had let them in clattered by, his scowl rivaling Drew's. He might or might not know English. That didn't really matter. It was the tone that was important. As far as the local populace was concerned, she and Drew were obnoxious, American newlyweds. Obnoxious, she could do. It was the newlywed part that was giving her fits.

She pasted a pleasant smile on her face. "I know this isn't as good as swords and armor, sweetie, but it's truly a beautiful piece. Indulge me?"

The strong lines of Drew's face softened and the sneer became a sensual smile, hot and maybe a little too knowing, all things considered. "Yeah, sure, baby."

She turned her back on him and resumed her study of the sarcophagus. That smile did things to her, naughty things she'd rather not think about, heating her blood and burning through her calm. Two of her immortal sisters had fallen under the spells of mortal men recently. As far as Jerusha was concerned, that was two too many. Damned if she'd be tempted by Drew's rough Southie charm.

He cupped his hands over her shoulders and brushed his mouth along her ear. "How come it is we're married and I still can't kiss you?"

Jerusha eased away from the hard warmth of his body. "A, we're only pretending to be married, and b, we're in public in the middle of a conservative Islamic culture."

"If I gotta wear a fucking ring, I oughta be able to kiss my woman."

"I'm not your woman," she said mildly, "and for the last time, would you watch your language? Your potty mouth is going to get us in trouble."

His voice dropped to a whisper. "I ain't the one with the potty mouth. We get back to the hotel, you gonna talk dirty to me?"

She bowed her head and turned partially toward him. "I'm going to kick your scrawny ass if you don't focus on our mission."

"Don't tease, baby." The guard's footsteps faded. Drew dropped his hands and shifted to her side, legs widespread, beefy arms crossed over his broad chest, fingers tucked against his ribs. "What's so important with the rock there?"

"It's historic." His sneer returned, and she grinned. "I'm getting a feel for their holdings. Begni's letter was smuggled out of here. I was hoping we could find something that might add some context to it."

"I know why we're here. Fuck, woman. You act like I ain't never done this before."

Jerusha tucked her hand into the crook of his arm and tugged him toward a wall of pottery displayed behind glass. "And *you* act like I'm the little woman."

"You are the little woman, Jaybird."

The raw humor in his voice tickled her own, that and the ridiculous nickname he'd given her. A code name, he'd said. More likely, he enjoyed trying to get her goat. "Technically, yes. Just remember who's the boss."

"That'd be me. Might makes right." He stared at the pottery and lowered his voice. "Guard's coming back."

Jerusha tilted her head, focusing on the guard's footsteps. The pattern of his shuffling feet coalesced and separated into the sounds of multiple people walking through the nearly deserted museum. "Somebody else is here, too."

"Sounds like three in all."

"Yeah." She rested her head on the solid width of Drew's upper arm and raised her voice slightly. "Come on, sweetie. Try to enjoy yourself. It's not like we'll get another vacation anytime soon."

Drew rested a hand over hers. "I'm enjoying it, baby."

The guard entered the room, followed by two men. One was middle-aged and nearly as tall as Drew, his frame lean beneath a black, wool coat. His eyes, frigid and impassive, scanned the exhibits under thick, dark eyebrows, and he seemed oddly familiar, though Jerusha would swear she'd never seen him before. The other man was bulldog stocky, from the square set of his shoulders to the awkward angles of his face. He walked slightly behind his companion and his coat fell at an odd angle over his muscled bulk.

The skin across the back of Jerusha's neck tightened. She met Drew's gaze and flicked hers toward the newcomers. "How about lunch? I can hear your stomach growling from here."

He dipped his head closer to hers. "Let's go back to the hotel and have dessert first, just you and me."

She hid her smile in his arm. Wasn't that just like a man? "Lunch first. I'm starved."

"Promise you'll make it up to me."

The low rasp of his voice scraped across her nerves, and she shivered. Oh, she'd make it up to him, all right, just as soon as she got him alone in a space big enough to deliver a good ass whooping. "You know I will."

He kissed her forehead and squeezed her hand. "I can always count on you."

Her skin tingled under the lingering caress. The way Drew was looking at her, so soft and warm, as if she were the center of his world. She sucked in a breath and guided him to the exit, chattering like the newlywed she was supposed to be. Blessed Ki, the man was good, maybe too good for her peace of mind.

She shook her head and followed him outside. Drew teased her, but he never followed through. Maybe he didn't feel the slow burn she did whenever he was around or maybe his focus was really that good. Either way, she had bigger things to worry about, like what a Greek tourist was doing in an obscure museum in Turkey accompanied by a bodyguard carrying a gun.

DREW YANKED his t-shirt off and tossed it on the bathroom floor. A full day undercover in Turkey had been enough to remind him why he'd quit doing it. The museum had been a bust. So had the ruins at Çatalhöyük. They'd been a shit ton more interesting than he'd let on, especially the archaeological dig, but the tedium of checking leads was not his cup of tea. Patience he had in spades. He just preferred using it tracking targets, not hunting down lost cities.

At least the company was good.

He eased the door open a crack and tuned an ear to Jerusha's phone conversation. Now, there was a woman he could respect. She was sharp as a tack, meaner than Satan on a three-day bender, and one of the best fighters he'd ever seen. She wasn't beautiful the way Bobby's other sisters were. Striking, yeah, with the kind of inner beauty that snagged a man from the get-go, but not conventionally pretty. Her tanned face was a little too broad, her nose, supposedly inherited from her long-dead Cherokee father, was a bit too wide, but her eyes were pure blue, the same color as a clear, cloudless sky. The first time those eyes had fallen on him, he'd shrugged off the heat skittering down his spine.

It was easy to ignore attraction when you thought the woman you were looking at was a hooker.

The second time he'd met Jerusha, he'd known she wasn't a hooker. Hadn't been so fucking easy to deny he felt something then.

He gobbed toothpaste on his toothbrush, stuck it in his mouth, and replayed their day in his head as he brushed his teeth. Something had happened at the museum, something she hadn't shared with him yet. He'd bet anything it had something to do with the museum's other visitors. The two men hadn't seemed like run-of-the-mill tourists. More like a high-end businessman and a stooge. The minute Jerusha had spotted them, her hands had tightened on his arm, and that from a woman who was loose as a goose.

Fuck all. If they were gonna work together, she had to trust him.

He spat into the sink and rinsed his mouth out. They'd been hand-selected for this job by her mother, Rebecca Upton, the director of the Institute for Early Cultural Studies and a bigwig among Bobby's people. It had taken three weeks for them to plan and begin the job. Drew had worked side by side with Jerusha during those weeks, ate with her, trained with her, shared space with her at BDH and at home.

The whole time, she'd treated him the same way she did her kid brother, matching Drew's smart ass remarks with enough snarkiness to float the Navy, taking him down in the gym like his bulk and brawn were nothing. He braced his hands on the counter and stared at his mug in the oval mirror hanging above the sink. Hell, they'd been sleeping together in the same bed for more than a week, were fixing to again, and she hadn't blinked an eye. That morning, she'd stripped down right in front of him like he was a fucking eunuch or something and her sweet little body didn't do a thing to him.

God's truth, he was having a hard time concentrating on the job they were there to do with her underfoot. Seeing her in all her glory hadn't helped.

He pressed the heels of his palms against his eyes and forced the memory of her smooth skin out of his head. Last thing he needed was for his dick to start leading him around.

Out in the bedroom, Jerusha said goodbye to her mother and hung up, then dialed another number. Drew raked his fingers through his hair, rolled his shoulders, and steeled himself for the night ahead. Another night sleeping next to her, behaving himself. He thumbed the underside of his brand new wedding ring, sliding the unaccustomed weight around his ring finger. This pretending to be married gig was for shit. Couldn't touch her, couldn't kiss her, couldn't even fucking cuddle with her at night without getting his head ripped off. One kiss, that's all he wanted, just one to see if the heat zinging through him was real, just one to see if she felt that heat, too.

He flipped the light off and padded out of the bathroom on bare feet. They'd been lucky enough to snag a room in a modern hotel, complete with a large bed, a TV, and enough hot water to do a man for a while. The room was small but comfortable, and a few steps up from some of the places he'd rested his head before.

Jerusha was propped up on the bed, two fluffy pillows cushioning her back, her long legs stretched out in front of her. She'd already changed into a set of oversized men's flannel pajamas with thin white stripes cutting through the dark blue fabric. She looked up and smiled, then curled her legs up, layering one bare foot over the other. He dropped onto the edge of the bed at her feet and waited. Sure enough, she wedged her toes under his thigh, exactly the way she did when she was around Bobby.

Her eyelids slid down, hiding her beautiful, sky blue eyes. "We're getting along fine, Bobby. Uh-huh." Bobby's barely audible drawl came over the line, and Jerusha snickered. "He's keeping his hands to himself. No, really."

Drew slid a hand around one of her ankles and rubbed. Her skin was warm and just as silky as he'd thought it'd be.

"I'll tell him that," she said. "Give Indigo my love."

She thumbed the call off and turned a piercing stare on Drew. "Bobby said if you laid a hand on me, he'd kick your ass."

Drew squeezed her ankle. "Yeah? Him and what army?"

"Wise ass. You ready for bed?"

"Whenever you are." He skimmed his hand up her calf over the lean curve of muscle. "You ready to talk about the museum now?"

"What about it?"

"Who were those men?"

7

She shrugged one shoulder and glanced away. "No idea."

He tapped the pad of his thumb against her shin. "Who were they?"

"Is this some kind of Delta Force torture? I don't tell you what you wanna know, you kidnap my leg?"

He grinned. "Yeah, that's it, baby. I'm torturing you. Now tell me who they were."

She rolled her eyes and scooted lower on the bed. "I think they might've been members of the Shadow."

"The People's enemy?"

"Yeah. The older guy with the nose?" She circled a finger in the air around her face. "Plus the accent spells Greek to me, and the other guy—"

"Had a gun. Yeah, I saw it."

She arched one black eyebrow. "You didn't even look at them."

"Security mirrors, Jaybird." He rubbed his hand down her leg. God, she felt good under his palm, firm and smooth. Good bet she felt like that all over. "You didn't see 'em?"

"I saw them. Just didn't think you had."

He tamped down on his impatience. Sooner or later she had to trust him to know what he was doing, surely to God. "The men?"

"You're a persistent bastard." She sighed and dropped her head back on the pillow. "They could've just been tourists."

"You honestly believe that?"

"No."

"So they were part of this Shadow?"

"Maybe." She grimaced. "Probably. We'll need to keep a sharper eye out. If it's the Shadow Enemy, no telling what they want."

"Any chance they're after the Lost City or maybe Sanctuary?"

"I don't know. Really, Drew, I don't." She sat up and cupped one hand over his shoulder, rubbing his bare skin gently.

"I wasn't deliberately keeping you in the dark."

"You can trust me," he said softly.

Her eyes shuttered. She flopped onto the bed and eyed the ceiling like it might disappear if she didn't watch it. "I'm trying to."

It'd have to do. He slid off the bed and hitched a thumb over his shoulder. "Bathroom's yours."

She flashed that carefree grin of hers, rolled off the bed, and strolled into the bathroom. He turned his back on her and stripped to his skin, wadded his dirty clothes up and dropped them near his suitcase. A woman like that was hell on a man's ego. Good thing he had plenty to spare.

Two

THEY HIT the rest of Konya's museums the next day, winding their way in an irregular pattern through the city. The tingling warning that had nagged Jerusha during their visit to the archaeological museum never returned, but her instincts jangled every time she thought about those men.

Maybe she'd been wrong about them. Plenty of Greek tourists had to visit Turkey each year, in spite of the natural enmity shared between the two countries. Turkey laid claim to at least as many Greek ruins as Greece did. That kind of heritage always drew interest.

Those men hadn't seemed like tourists, though. The museum's lone security guard hadn't treated them that way, either. For Drew and Jerusha, he'd been harried and rude. For the others, he'd been deferential.

After a grueling day wandering around the city searching for information, they opted to pick up takeout for supper and ate in their hotel room. Halfway through the meal, Drew tapped the table near Jerusha's plate. "Eat up, Jaybird."

She poked at her Iskender, a delicious blend of meat and sauce over bread served with tomatoes, spicy peppers, and yogurt. Maybe if she hadn't been so preoccupied, she'd enjoy it more. "I'm eating."

He snorted. "Tell me another one, baby."

She dropped her fork and glared at him. "Why do you keep calling me baby?"

"Because I can." He nudged her plate. "Now eat or I'm gonna come over there and feed you."

"Bully," she muttered.

"Partner," he corrected mildly. "It's New Year's Eve."

"And?"

"We could stay up late, count down the end of the year together." His blond eyelashes swept down, shading his expression. "Don't have to be on the road early, do we?"

"I guess not." She pursed her lips. "You're up to something."

His back thudded against his chair. "You ever gonna trust me?"

"You're a man."

"Yeah, I am." He leaned forward and his eyes went molten. "Remind me to remember that tonight when we're in bed."

"You wouldn't dare."

"I'm gonna do the time anyhow, fuck, yeah." He picked up his fork, stabbed it into his İzgara Köfte, and pushed a meatball into a mound of bulgur. "I figured as long as we're stuck together, we might as well have some fun. Don't mean I was up to something."

She stared at her Iskender. Well, didn't that just show her? Of course, he wasn't up to anything. He'd had plenty of opportunities to try something and hadn't so much as laid a contrary finger on her.

Bobby had called her a liar when she'd told him that.

She rolled her shoulders, shrugging off the disappointment crawling through her. "Sorry, Drew. It's kind of instinctive, not trusting men."

"The day you think I'm a man, you let me know."

"What's that supposed to mean?"

"You tell me." He pointed his fork at her, meatball and all. "Eat your supper or I'm gonna."

She huffed out a laugh. "First you're going to feed me, then you're going to eat it yourself. Make up your mind."

He grinned. "Just did. How about a little hand to hand after supper?"

"And that's your idea of having fun?" She clucked her tongue. "Well, if you really want me to kick your scrawny ass again."

"My ass ain't scrawny, Jaybird. Yours, now? Not much better than a handful."

"I'll have you know my ass is..." She sucked in a breath and pressed her lips tightly together. "I can't believe I let you goad me into that."

He leaned back in his chair and sprawled his mile-long legs out under the table, brushing his bare feet along her ankles. A smug smile twisted his mouth and the scar on his upper lip whitened. "I gotta win any way I can."

"Hunh. I thought you wanted me to trust you."

"We'll get there, baby. You'll see." He jerked his chin toward her plate. "Three more bites."

She picked up her fork and finished her meal, and damned if she didn't relax under his steady teasing.

After supper, Jerusha pulled out her laptop and reserved a room under their assumed names, Mr. and Dr. Willingham, at the Kelebek Hotel in Göreme, close to their next destination. Drew sprawled out on the bed beside her, his head close to hers, and prodded her into an hour of research on historic Cappadocia, the region where the underground cities they were scheduled to investigate were located.

He shifted on the bed, aligning his arm with hers, warming her through their clothing. She stifled a sigh and clicked on another link. "I thought you hated history."

"Not much on museums." He scrubbed a hand over his head and yawned. "Don't know how you stand it, either. Digging in the dirt seems like it'd be fun, though."

"Oh, yeah, loads," she said drily. "I love getting dirty."

He leaned back and flashed a wide grin at her. "Wanna wrestle in the mud with me?"

"Don't you have something better to do besides irritate me?"

"Not a thing, Jaybird. Got some cards in my suitcase, if you wanna play."

She closed the lid of her laptop with a firm click. "Anything's better than having you wallow on me. Honestly, Drew, you're worse than Bobby."

Drew's eyebrows snapped down. He slid off the bed and padded to his suitcase. "Think I'll go for a run."

"What? Wait." She shoved her laptop aside and sat bolt upright. "I thought we were going to play cards."

"Maybe later." He rummaged through his suitcase, strewing clothes everywhere, then stripped off his shirt. "Seems like we could both use a break."

"I didn't—"

He stalked into the bathroom and shut the door, cutting off her words. Jerusha snapped her mouth shut. Hard-ass, unflappable, steady as a rock Drew had just walked out on her. When was the last time a man had done that? She scrambled through her memory and came up empty. Men didn't walk out on Daughters. It just wasn't done, especially when the man in question was under said Daughter's protection.

The bathroom door opened. Drew came out dressed in ragged, cutoff sweatpants and a long-sleeved, skintight athletic shirt. He sat down on the edge of the bed with his back to her and pulled on socks and running shoes.

"You can't go out like that. It's freezing outside."

"It's called a gym, Jaybird."

She scooted off the bed. "I'll go with you, then."

"I'm a big boy." He stood and lifted both hands, palms out. "Look, Ma. I even tied my shoes all by myself."

She eyed his hard expression and the stiff set of his shoulders. "I'm not your mother."

"Yeah? Try to remember that once in a while, why don'tcha." He snagged his keycard and tucked it into the waistband of his sweatpants. "I'll be back in an hour, maybe two. Cards are in my suitcase, you wanna play."

"Drew, come on."

"You wanted space. I'm giving you space."

He pivoted on his heel and left, closing the room's door quietly behind himself. Jerusha sank onto the edge of the bed and stared after him. What the hell had just happened? One minute, they were needling each other the way they always did, and the next, he huffed off. She flopped backwards and slapped her hands over her face. Men. No wonder the Sisters had chained them up. Beat having to put up with their ridiculous emotional flip-flops, just when a woman was getting used to having them around.

THE HOTEL'S GYM was housed in a tiny room on the first floor and filled with outdated equipment. Drew glanced over the setup and settled on using the free weights. It wasn't the run he needed. Then again, running had just been an excuse. If he'd ever needed proof Jerusha put him on the same level as her kid brother, there it was, handed to him on a bluntly spoken silver platter.

He rolled his shoulders and set the weights up for bicep curls. Fuck that. Maybe his ego had taken a ding and maybe her last swipe was one too many. She didn't want him, there were plenty of other fish in the sea.

Margaret's steely-eyed gaze drifted into his head. He snorted and raised the weights, breathing out as he curled them toward his chest. He and Bobby's eldest sister got along fine, though come to think on it, she treated him a lot like Jerusha did, like he was another kid brother. Kinda put him off thinking on Margaret's womanly attributes, even if she had plenty to spare. Long, shapely legs, hands full of pale, blonde hair, and the lean body of a natural athlete.

Of course, she could bench press as much as he could, that on a bad day, and she was meaner than Jerusha ever thought about being. Twice as deadly, too.

He lowered the weights on a slow exhale. Hunh. Must be where Jerusha got it from.

For all her meanness, Margaret was controlled, steady. On the other hand, Bobby's next youngest sister, Moira, had the temper of a rattler on a hot, summer day and wasn't afraid to spew it on the unsuspecting. Drew figured that out about five minutes after she opened that Irish mouth of hers, him and everybody in a twenty-foot radius. God help her fiancé, Tom Fairfax. The mild-mannered archivist had helped discover the lead Drew and Jerusha were chasing down and fallen in love with the hotheaded Daughter in the doing. Poor guy was in for a lifetime of sharp tongue lashings with that one.

Charlotte, the next oldest after Moira, was one of the sweetest women Drew had ever met. Of course, she was married, had been for nearly a decade. He'd heard wedded bliss had a way of softening a woman up, especially one that had fully expected to live pretty much forever. Her kids were a hoot, too, climbing all over their *Uncle Drew* like he was part of the family.

Jerusha was the youngest of Bobby's sisters by blood, and then there was Dani, the Daughter Bobby's ma had taken in and raised as her own for the past eighty odd years. All of Bobby's sisters were attractive women in their own way, but Dani was something else. Tall and willowy, blonde curly hair, and those expressive green eyes. Drew finished his reps and reset the weights for overhead extensions. He'd been working his way around to asking her out when she'd met that fucker Dave Winstead and fallen head over heels for him.

Fucking FBI.

Losing that chance hadn't hurt nearly as bad as Drew had thought it would, and maybe that had a little too much to do with the woman he'd left in a hotel room twenty minutes earlier.

He cleared his mind and channeled his energy into a steady

workout, easing his way through a series of upper body lifts. An hour later, his frustration was gone and his muscles burned pleasantly. He put the weights away and jogged lightly up the stairs, and slipped into a darkened room. He eased the door shut and listened. Outside, cars sped down the street. Not many. It was late and Jerusha was right. Konya Province was a conservative region. People didn't live it up here the way they did in Istanbul.

Not that he'd ever lay claim to the way he'd lived it up in Turkey's capital, or any other place, for that matter. What Jaybird didn't know would save him from a helluva lot of jibes down the road.

He filtered out the street noise and focused on his surroundings, and finally caught the soft puffs of Jerusha's breaths. Asleep, then. He stifled a sigh and tiptoed into the room, heading for his suitcase.

"Hey, Drew."

He veered toward the bed and sat down on its edge, next to her prone form. "You're in bed early."

"Thought I'd get some sleep." She rolled toward him and curled her legs up behind him. "Do I need to apologize?"

Yeah, he'd love that. Just imagine, a slew of Daughters apologizing to men for treating them like their kid brothers. He rubbed a hand across his nape, wiping the idea away before he blurted it out and dug himself into a hole. "Naw."

"I feel like I need to."

"Forget it, Jaybird. I just needed some air." He caught himself reaching for her and curled his hand into a fist. No touching, no kissing, no cuddling, and now, no wallowing. That pretty much covered all the bases of keep away right there. "Gonna get a shower."

"I'll be here, waiting for the card game you promised me."

He laughed, couldn't help it. God, she was something. "Give me ten and I'm all yours."

"You and Go Fish," she retorted. "Hurry up. I'm bored as sin."

He scrounged clean underwear, slipped into the bathroom, and scrubbed himself down in a quick shower. When he walked out dressed in clean boxer briefs, Jerusha was sitting cross-legged on top of a freshly made bed playing Solitaire. She glanced up and smiled, seemingly completely unaffected by his near nudity.

Too bad for him.

He sighed and stretched out on the bed across from her. "Your deal."

She gathered the cards into a pile and shuffled them. "What are we playing?"

"Go Fish is fine."

A laugh sputtered out of her. "Seriously?"

"You scared I'm gonna beat you?"

"I'm shaking in my boots."

"That'd mean more if you were wearing boots."

She wiggled her bare toes and dealt the cards. "So, how does a manly man such as yourself end up playing Go Fish?"

He picked his cards up and sorted them by number. "What's wrong with Go Fish?"

"You went from being a muckity-muck in the Army to running a security firm to playing Go Fish in a hotel room in Turkey. Seems like a step down."

"Step up from where I was."

She tilted her head and eyed him over the top of her cards. "Boston?"

"The wrong side. Back when I was growing up, the neighborhood was a cesspool." He jerked his chin at her. "You got any threes?"

"Go Fish." She studied her cards while he drew one from the stock. "You ever go back?"

"I thought we were playing Go Fish, not Twenty Questions."

"I figure we can do both. We didn't have a lot of time before to get to know each other."

He snorted. "Yeah, you wanna get to know me."

"Why not? You're a pain in the ass, but you're a decent

guy." She pursed her lips and dropped her eyes to her cards. "Bobby thinks a lot of you."

"Bobby's like my brother. Hiro, too." And they treated him a helluva lot better than what was left of his own family did. "You gonna go or what?"

She huffed out a breath. "Do you have any Jacks?"

He plucked a card from his hand and slid it over. "What about you?"

She laid four Jacks down on the bed in front of her. "What about me?"

"You do this kind of thing a lot? You know, chasing down dead people and shit?"

Her eyes went round. "I never chase down shit," she said solemnly.

"Wise ass. What about the dead people?"

"It kinda comes with the territory. The People and history go hand in hand. Do you have any eights?"

"Go Fish. So, you spend a lot of time in the past."

She drew a card, frowned at it, and tucked it into her spread. "I study the past. Big difference."

"Not as I can see. You got fours?"

"What, are you working your way up the numbers?" She shook her head and pulled two cards out of her hand. "Your fours, Sir Drew."

He grunted and stacked his fours with hers on the bed in front of him. "Ain't no sir."

"You work for a living," she murmured.

"Damn straight, least it was before I got into Spec Ops." She opened her mouth, likely on another question, and he wagged a finger at her. "You know I can't talk about it."

She snapped her teeth together. "I'm curious."

"You and everybody else. Give me all your sixes."

"You really need to find a different strategy."

"You got any or what?"

"Go Fish," she said, her words precise and sharp. "Are you

really going to keep me up until midnight playing cards?"

He bit back his first response. If he couldn't kiss her, teasing her about a New Year's kiss was probably off limits, too. "Only if you wanna."

"I guess it'll do. Do you have any tens?"

He swore under his breath and handed over his lone ten. "You're cleaning me out here, Jaybird."

She grinned. "That's the name of the game."

Wasn't it just. "So, tell me about this Shadow Enemy."

The happiness in her expression faded. She placed her cards face down on the bed. "You were briefed on them."

"Only what the director wanted me to know." He tossed his own cards down and folded an arm under his head as a pillow. "You're the history nut. Tell me how the People and the Shadow became enemies."

"It was a long time ago."

"Figured that."

"No, a really long time ago. You ever hear of the Minoans?"

He sorted through the research filed away in his head, done in the weeks leading up to their trip. "Early Greeks?"

"A proto-Greek civilization. Very advanced, beautiful artwork, culturally rich." She tilted her knees up and wrapped her arms around them. "We only know pieces of what happened, and even then, we can only guess."

"So give me your best guess."

"Best guess, a group of Daughters found a way to coexist with men during an early Minoan period. They interbred with them, had children. We have a single textual fragment in the Archives referencing what happened next."

"Nothing good," he guessed.

"The Minoan men decided to sacrifice their own children."

"Shit. Helluva thing to do."

She lifted one shoulder, dropped it. "We only have one side of the story. When the Daughters found out what had happened, it was a bloodbath, not the first one in the People's history."

19

Her voice was so soft, so full of sorrow, so tired. He rested a light hand on her feet and rubbed gently. "I read a translation of the Legend of Beginnings."

She sighed and rolled her head back, staring at the ceiling. "You think things like that are justified when you're a kid, that whatever the People had to do to survive was right and good. I sometimes wonder what would've happened if the Daughters living with the Minoans hadn't carried their vengeance so far."

"They were bringing justice to the men that killed their kids."

"Yeah, but at what cost? Thousands of years of war between us and the survivors. Millennia, Drew. Do you know what that's like? Do you know how hard it is always looking over your shoulder, never knowing when your enemy will strike, always worried they'll find you and kill your family, no matter how hard you work to protect them?"

He squeezed her feet. "I know what it's like to have enemies."

She lowered her head and met his gaze evenly. "Yeah, I guess you would."

"Come on, baby. No more worrying, not tonight. It's almost midnight."

A slow smile lifted the corners of her mouth. "You're trying to wiggle your way into a kiss."

Maybe he had been earlier, but after that wallowing comment, he'd be damned if he'd try it again. "Nope. Just a countdown and a Happy New Year."

"Seriously?"

"Serious as a man can be." He swept the cards into a pile and sorted them out. "Bathroom's yours, if you want it."

"I was winning."

"And you can win again tomorrow night."

"Fine, then." She flounced off the bed and sashayed toward the bathroom. "You know, maybe I wanted a kiss."

"You want one, you can take it."

She shot a narrow-eyed glare over her shoulder. "Never challenge a Daughter to take what she wants, Drew. She just might do it."

Said the woman who thought he was a kid. He sat up and stuffed the cards back in the pack. "I'm shaking in my boots."

"As if."

The bathroom door clicked shut. He tossed the pack of cards into his suitcase, clicked off the lamp on his side of the bed, and slid under the covers. Not in a million years would she ever try anything with him. That was a bet he'd place any day of the week.

Three

I N SPITE OF their late night, they woke early the next morning, packed, and checked out of their hotel, stopping long enough for a quick breakfast in the hotel's restaurant. Drew drove, consigning Jerusha to the passenger's seat of their rental car. She stretched her legs out and studied the view of Konya as they passed through the city, the sameness of the buildings, the people scurrying along the sidewalks, the snow spurting out of a leaden sky.

"You sure you know where we're going?" she asked.

"There's this thing called MapQuest. Gets you where you need to go every time."

The Alaeddin Mosque slipped past his window. She swiveled in her seat and studied it through the rear window. "That's the second time we've passed that mosque."

"Ya don't say."

"And we're not lost?"

"Nunh-unh."

She shifted in the seat, facing him. "Trust goes both ways, Drew."

"That it does." He signaled for a right turn and eased the car onto a perpendicular street. "You said those men might've been members of the Shadow. I'm taking a precaution or two, just in case."

"By getting us lost," she said flatly.

He shot a side-eyed glare at her. "I know where we're going."

"Don't be such a man, Drew. If we're lost, just say so."

His hands tightened on the steering wheel. "You wanna drive?"

"As a matter of fact."

"What's the road number from Konya to Nevşehir?"

"Er, the road number?"

"Yeah, the road number. It's D300. D'you know the speed limit? How 'bout the driving regulations?"

She flopped back against the seat and crossed her arms over her chest. "It's not like it's hard to find those things out."

"Yeah, uh-huh." He shook his head and made another turn. "It ever occur to you I might know what I'm doing?"

"Bobby said—"

"Fuck that, Jaybird. You can't trust his word forever."

"It's all I've got to go on," she gritted out.

His shoulders rose and fell on a noisy sigh. "Yeah, sure it is. We been living in each other's pockets for nearly a month now and that's all you got?"

She hunched down in the seat and stared out the windshield. When he put it like that, it seemed ridiculous for her not to have formed her own judgment about him, independent of Bobby's.

"It's like you said," he continued. "Trust is a two-way street. Far as I can tell, you ain't even on the fucking road."

"I'm a Daughter."

"Can't hide behind that forever." He jerked his chin toward a road sign. "Wouldja look at that? Nevşehir's straight that way."

"You don't have to rub it in," she muttered.

"I'm gonna do the time, baby, I might as well get something out of it."

Like the kiss he'd never claimed the night before. When she'd come out of the bathroom, he'd already been lying on his back under the covers, bedside lamp off, one arm under his head. His watch had beeped at midnight and all she'd gotten was a softly spoken *Happy New Year* in that flat, nasal twang of his.

She sneered at her reflection in the passenger's side window. He'd challenged her to take a kiss. It would serve him right if she did.

She closed her eyes and drifted, filtering through everything she knew about the underground cities in the Cappadocian region. One of them could be the City of the Sisters, the Lost City she and Drew were searching for, most likely not one of the larger touristy ones. Gaining access might be a little tricky. Good thing she'd spent most of her life building credentials under one name or another. Those should help them gain access when they needed it, and if not, they'd do things the old-fashioned way. It had been a while since she'd played cat burglar. Drew would probably enjoy it, too, if Bobby could be believed.

She frowned and shunted thoughts of her brother aside.

Any plan they made hinged on the city having been rediscovered and explored in the last century or so. If it hadn't been, the People would need more than her and Drew to find it, and a helluva lot more time than they'd allotted for their initial foray.

Drew muttered a curse under his breath, jolting Jerusha out of her thoughts, and the car slowed fractionally.

"What is it?" she asked.

"We're being followed."

She sat up and glanced behind them, searching the sparse traffic for signs of a tail. "I thought you took precautions."

"Yeah, I did. Fuckers must've been lying in wait at the major decision points, one team per outgoing highway. Who the hell does that?"

"People who really want to track us. Will you try to outrun them?"

He snorted. "In a Volkswagen Golf?"

"Right. Sorry."

"You shoulda let me get the BMW Z4."

She snickered and settled back into her seat. "We're on a budget."

"Tightwad."

"Realist. Besides, the Z4 would've stood out more."

"The Z4'll outrun nearly everything on the road." He ran a hand over his hair, ruffling the short strands. "Ok, we got a coupla options."

"Try to lose them."

"Gonna be hard on a straight road in the middle of fucking farmland. We could wait until we reach Aksaray, maybe lose them in the streets, maybe find a hidey-hole and wait them out. It'd be easy to switch cars unnoticed, as light as we're traveling."

"That's assuming they don't cut us off before we get there." Jerusha tapped one finger against her thigh as she turned their options and the possible outcomes over in her mind. "We could let them follow us, see how it plays out."

"You really think that's a good idea?"

"Well, if we did, we might get a chance to turn the tables, maybe figure out who it is and why they're following us."

"Wouldn't be hard to corner at least one car, even in a Golf." A sly smile tilted one corner of his mouth. "Been a while since I played hide and seek."

She bit her lip, hiding her own smile. "You're enjoying this way too much."

"Your ma's paying me the big bucks to enjoy it."

"She's paying you to help me track down the City of the Sisters and Sanctuary."

"Same thing. Anyhow, I'm just the hired muscle. Maybe it's time you took advantage."

She eyed the smile lingering on his mouth, the gleam in his cognac eyes. "You've got a plan."

He flashed a grin at her. "Baby, I've always got a plan. Pit stop?"

"We're barely out of Konya."

"Roll with it, Jaybird. I need you to play along."

Like they hadn't both been doing that the whole time. "Give me the deets, Drew."

"That's my girl."

Her heart flipped over. His girl. He'd said it so casually, as if she really were, as if for a moment, he'd forgotten they were virtual strangers playing roles they'd been assigned by her mother. Jerusha inhaled slowly and focused on the plan he was sketching out, and not on how it would feel to really be his.

DREW PARKED next to the petrol station, got out, and slammed the car door. Jerusha did the same and followed him around the side of the building. He stopped in plain view of the gas pumps, his back to her, his bruiser hands curled into fists.

She took half a second to admire this view of him, his broad, muscular shoulders tapering to narrow hips, the strong curve of his ass, the long length of his legs. It wasn't as nice a view fully clothed as it was when he walked around their hotel room without a stitch on, but by Ki, it was close.

She sucked in a breath and prepared to play the role he'd assigned her: Bitch Wife. "I can't believe you didn't tell me about her, Drew, and now she's calling you? We're on our honeymoon, supposedly celebrating the start of our life together, and you're making time with your ex."

He whirled around, eyes narrow slits, and jabbed a finger at her. "You need to let that go."

"She called you on our *honeymoon*," Jerusha gritted out. "In the middle of sex, and you answered the phone."

"I've got a kid with her. What else do you expect?"

"I expect you to let me know you had a fucking kid, for one."

A car pulled up behind her, right on schedule, and Jerusha bit back a smile. She'd forgotten how fun reeling in the unsuspecting was. Car doors slammed and her curiosity got the better of her. She pivoted toward the gas pumps, crossed her arms over her chest, and hunched her shoulders as she mentally calculated the age, height, and weight of the two men hovering near the sedan that had been tailing her and Drew.

She pitched her voice just loud enough to be heard across the distance between her and the gas pumps. "When I said I wanted kids, you told me you didn't want any, that you'd had enough of that when you were a kid, helping your parents raise your siblings. You never told me you already had one yourself."

"Jesus, Jaybird. I didn't know how. You get so goddamn jealous every time I even look at another woman, and fuck. I didn't want another argument."

"Yeah? Well, you've got one now."

She whirled around, another angry retort at the ready. He was standing right behind her, so close she nearly flinched back. How the hell had he gotten that close without her hearing him or at least without him setting off her internal alarms?

He wrapped his hands around her upper arms and yanked her close, and dropped his voice to a low murmur. "Helluva temper you got there, Jaybird."

She curled her lips into a smirk. "Helluva crap argument, if you ask me. You couldn't come up with a better scenario?"

"I was working on the fly. You got into it well enough."

"What can I say? I like yelling at you."

"Yeah, I figured." He lowered his head and brushed his mouth across hers. "Mmm. You sure you're ok with this?"

"It's just a kiss, Drew, and besides. It'll be more convincing."

"Yeah." His hands tightened on her arms and he inched her closer, molding their bodies together. "Hold on to your knickers, baby."

She meant to snicker, meant to make light of his phrasing. His mouth came down on hers, claiming her in a gentle kiss, and her humor died as quickly as it had risen. His lips moved over hers, coaxing her into a response, and she gave it to him, opening her mouth, sweeping her tongue across his, tangling her fingers in his jacket and holding him as close as he held her. Heat swept through her in a blazing rush of light and flame, and she rose on her tiptoes, aligning their bodies together in a perfect melding of male and female.

He yanked back, his breath harsh, and stared at her, his cognac eyes hot. "Jaybird," he whispered, and then his mouth was on her again, demanding and hard, his rough need a welcome relief. Oh, she'd missed this, missed kissing a man, missed feeding his need with her own, and Drew was so perfect, so good. He sucked her lower lip into his mouth, scraped his tongue across hers, and she moaned, melting into his solid strength.

Quiet footsteps came from behind her, and Jerusha nearly cursed. Right. They were reeling in their tail, trying to gain information. Making out was just a fringe bene, not the main event.

She pushed against Drew's chest and jerked her head to the side, breaking the kiss. "You ass. What right do you think you have to treat me like that?"

"We're married, that's what right I have." He shook her, hard enough to jostle her good, and his expression morphed from passion into thunderous anger. "If I wanna fuck you in the middle of a parking lot, I by God will."

"You try that and I'll saw your dick off with a dull knife and offer it up as a sacrifice to the god of war."

"Yeah? You and what army?"

She nearly laughed. Blessed Mother, he was adorable. Instead, she gritted her teeth and played her part. "Let me go, you cretin."

He released her arms and held his hands up. "You want me to let go? Fine, I will. I'm gone, baby. You can find your own way back to the States."

"Anything's better than being tied to a liar. I'll never trust you again."

She pivoted away and marched into the petrol station, and worked on faking an emotional meltdown. When was the last time she'd cried? She searched her memory, hoping to find something, *anything* to draw on, and snorted. Nope, not a thing came to mind. Not even Bobby's recent kidnapping had earned tears, though it had pissed her off plenty. Nobody fucked with her baby brother, nobody. She loved the little brat too much, and that would have to be enough.

She channeled her anger and frustration over the incident into her Bitch Wife character, and soon enough, her hands trembled. Suppressed rage would do that and the adrenaline rush that followed would aid the anger along.

She opened the door, slid inside, and went to the counter, sniffing for good measure. One of the men tailing her and Drew was on the other side of the store, his attention apparently focused on items stacked along the shelf in front of him. Jerusha turned her back on him and faced the man behind the counter, a native Turk with nearly black hair, a drooping mustache, and olive-toned skin.

"Do you have a restroom? Ah, a bathroom?" She laughed, adding a touch of hysteria for effect, and pressed shaky fingers to her forehead. "I can't remember the Turkish word. Toilet? Come on, you have to know some English."

The man shook his head at her, but he pointed outside and around the corner, toward the area where she and Drew had staged their fight. She nodded and hoped against hope that the clerk was actually sending her to the bathroom and not back to her fake husband.

When she went outside, Drew was gone. Probably to the men's room or around the back of the building, depending on what was convenient as a hideaway. She rounded the corner and nearly sighed. One of the doors embedded into the side wall was posted with the universal sign for a women's bathroom. She entered, locked herself into one of the two stalls, and waited.

Three minutes later, the outside door opened and a man's booted feet came into view under the door. "Miss, you ok?"

"I'm fine." She sniffed out a fake sob and winced. Man, she

29

really needed to work on the crying thing. "I just need a minute."

"I wait here, take you to bus station?"

She rolled her eyes. Like anybody in their right mind would fall for that. The first thing an American woman always asked a man in the women's room was, *What the hell are you doing in the women's room?* Thankfully, whoever was on the other side of the door hadn't met any American women before or he'd know that.

"Oh, that'd be great," she said. "I'll be right out."

"I wait."

His footsteps receded, the door opened and shut. Jerusha counted to thirty and opened her door, and sure enough, there he was, waiting for her. He was a big man, not quite as tall as Drew, but solid, muscled, and a great deal larger than his absent companion.

She smiled, let it waver a bit. "I thought you were outside."

"No, miss. You know I'm not."

"True." She dropped the emotionally distraught wife act and sneered. "And now, we're going to have some fun."

He nodded and pulled a gun out of the back of his pants, his dark eyes steady. "I have fun. You, maybe not."

She shrugged. "If that's the way you wanna play it."

He leveled the gun on her, and she ducked, launching herself across the room at a speed mortal humans had a hard time tracking. She was on him in a flash, one hand around his wrist pushing the gun away, the other buried deep in his stomach in a hard punch to his gut. His eyes widened, the breath whooshed out of him, and he doubled over with a muttered *oomph*.

She tangled the fingers of one hand in the short strands of his dark hair and yanked his head up. "Rule number one? Never underestimate a Daughter."

She cracked her knee into his nose, and down he went, crumbling into a heap on the floor, his broken appendage cradled in mitt-sized hands. She disarmed him, tucked the gun behind her back into the waistband of her jeans, and grunted as she dragged the man into the corner away from the door. He was a heavy son of an Ottoman. Why did the big ones always come after her?

A minute later, Drew pushed the door open, one arm around the neck of the second man that had been tailing them. "Looky what I found, Jaybird."

She hooked her hands on her hips. "Mine's bigger."

He flashed a crooked grin at her and yanked his fishy all the way into the bathroom. "You want, we can compare sizes when we go to bed tonight."

She rolled her eyes skyward. Why had Bobby sent the smartass with her on this mission? She could've had Hiro, nice, steady, reliable Hiro, but no. Bobby had given her the Southie with an smart attitude and a mouth to match. "You learn anything?"

"Not yet. Wanted to wait on you." Drew dropped his guy onto hers and brushed his hands off against his thighs. "I keep hearing all this shit about how the People have special interrogation squads. You know anything about that?"

Bless him. When they got to the hotel that night, she'd be sure to reward him with an extra big slice of the first dessert she could find. Baklava, maybe. If that didn't satisfy Drew's sweet tooth, nothing would.

She squatted in front of the smaller man, and he scrambled away from her and propped his back against the cold, concrete wall.

"As a matter of fact," she said, "*I* was on one of those squads. Had to give it up so I could dig in the dirt. Sure do miss it, though."

"Yeah?" Drew fished a pocketknife out of his front pocket and handed it to her. "Don't see why you can't practice on one of these poor fucks."

The smaller man blanched and launched himself into a wobbly run, scrambling past Jerusha in a futile bid for freedom.

She caught his arm and hauled him back, tossing him onto the floor with as much effort as a pitcher throwing a baseball.

The man cowered on the floor, one hand held palm out. "Please don't kill us," he said in thickly accented English. "We're no good to you dead."

"Yeah?" Drew nudged the side of the man's foot with the toe of his boot, none too gently. "You want to keep your skin, maybe you should talk."

The man shook his head. "I can't. He'll kill me."

Jerusha leaned forward and pinned the man with a hard stare. "You don't talk and *I'll* kill you, very slowly, very painfully, right here in this bathroom if I have to."

"Then you'll have to kill me." A bead of sweat slid down the man's temple and onto his cheek. "I tell you anything and I'm as good as dead."

The larger man stirred and pushed himself onto all fours. "No talking. He'll kill us."

Jerusha snapped the knife open and tested it's balance. Hunh. Not bad for a pocketknife. "He, who?"

"*Him*," the smaller man said.

A chill grated down her spine and she hesitated. Could the Shadow be behind this or was the little guy just being coy in the hopes of stalling her? Only one way to find out. "You're tailing us for Alexiou."

He clamped his lips together and scooted farther into the wall.

"Why?" she asked. "What does he want?"

"I don't know," the man whispered.

Jerusha flipped the knife in her hand and stabbed it point down into the man's shin through his thin slacks, just missing the bone. He screamed and clutched his leg, and the larger man muttered and slunk into the corner, well out of her immediate reach.

She wiggled the blade out one millimeter at a time. "Tell me what I want to know."

"I can't," the man sobbed.

Jerusha raised her arm, and Drew caught her wrist, holding her hand suspended in mid-air. "Hold on there, hotshot. Maybe we don't need to know the whys."

She twisted around and gaped at him. "Are you kidding me?"

"Hey, all I'm saying is, sometimes the whys aren't as important as the whos." He jerked his chin at the sobbing man. "Besides, he's making enough noise to break a junkie out of a high. You think that clerk's gonna wait to call the police?"

"If I'd known he'd be a baby about it..."

Drew heaved a sigh and shook his head. "Come on. The clerk got a good look at you. If we're lucky, he won't think to check our tags and we can be miles away before the coppers show up."

"The coppers?" She snorted and wiped Drew's blade on the smaller man's trousers, scraping off most of the blood. "Good thing I got what I needed, huh?"

"Good thing," Drew agreed. "You wanna kill 'em or throw 'em back."

She pushed herself into a stand, folded the knife, and tucked it into her pocket. "Throw 'em back. I hate cleaning up blood."

"What if they ID us?"

"They try and they'll be dead before the end of the day." Lightning quick, Jerusha leapt forward, grabbed the larger man's jacket collar, and yanked him off the floor. "You understand that?"

He nodded gingerly, and she let him go.

She dismantled the large guy's gun and threw the pieces into the fallow fields surrounding the petrol station. They were on the road minutes later, easing out of the parking lot and onto the highway at a normal speed, just two American tourists minding their own.

Drew adjusted the rearview mirror. "You think we're clear?"

"Yeah, I think so." She slouched lower in her seat and rubbed a finger across her forehead. "Kinda worries me, though. If it's Alexiou..."

"You sure it's him?"

"Pretty sure. You saw how that man reacted, and if I'm right and the Shadow really is after us, there's no place we can go that they won't find us, not here, not if they really want us found."

His thumb tapped against the steering wheel. "You don't sound worried."

"I've been in this situation before, back when Alexiou Senior was still alive. Best thing we can do is stay on target."

"Even when we're the target?"

She rolled her head toward him along the back of her seat and grinned. "Come on, Drew. That's half the fun. We find the Lost City, maybe dig up some clues to Sanctuary, and in the meantime, we tweak Alexiou's nose by doing it in plain sight."

"And that's your idea of fun?"

"Beats comparing the sizes of our reproductive organs."

"Hey, you brought size up first." He slid a sideways glance toward her. "Not that it matters. I'm bigger."

She laughed and laid her hand on his thigh above his knee, and squeezed the toned muscle for good measure. "I'll give you bigger just this once, but only because you let me borrow your knife."

"I want it back, too. It's a family heirloom."

"Really?"

"Yeah. My grandfather gave it to me before he died. Only thing I got left of him." He covered her hand with one of his, holding it against his leg. "So, Aksaray to Nevşehir or do we plot a new course?"

"This course is fine, Drew," she said, and it was. She hadn't spotted a single police car on either side of the road and Drew's hand warmed her skin. She relaxed into the seat and kept her hand there, cushioned between his thigh and his rough palm, and let her mind drift back to their kiss. Next time, it wouldn't be a fake scenario played out for their victims. Next time, it would be real and she'd do exactly what he'd challenged her to do last night. She'd take what she wanted the way Daughters had been doing for nearly ten thousand years, and before she was done, he'd beg for more.

DREW STRETCHED OUT on the bed with the remote and flipped through local TV channels. God, he needed a diversion. That kiss with Jerusha, her mouth moving under his, hot and slick, her tongue stroking into him like she wanted so much more. His dick stirred and Drew shifted on the bed. Fuck. He couldn't even think about it without his body going haywire. How the hell was he supposed to function with her hanging out in his head?

The shower cut off in the bathroom and he slung an arm across his eyes. That kiss had been one thing, seeing her in action something else entirely. He'd known *exactly* what she was going into the mission. Bobby had explained the People to him and Hiro two months ago, and after, Drew had done his own digging. Immortal, tough as nails women cursed to immortality, and Jerusha was one of them. He'd known that, admired it, but it hadn't sunk in until that morning. Watching her handle a man twice her size like he was nothing? Shit, yeah. Made him want her hands on him, all over him, those nimble little hands of hers.

He dug the heel of his hand into the base of his dick, trying to tame it, what good it'd do. Thing had been at half mast since she'd smiled sweetly at him and laid her hand on his thigh. How was a man supposed to resist those blue eyes of hers? Why the hell would he want to?

He slapped the remote onto the mattress and scrubbed both hands over his mug. The mission. He had to think about the mission. He'd made a promise, BDH had taken money. If his focus was shot, he'd be no good, and if he was no good, he might as well hang up his hat and call it a night.

Fuck that. He hadn't blown a mission *ever* and he sure as

hell didn't intend to now, so he'd find a way to deal. If that meant jerking off every time Jerusha's back was turned, well, it beat the alternative.

The bathroom door opened, and a minute later, she sashayed into the room wearing a thin, white camisole and barely-there bikini panties with her straight, black hair loose around her shoulders. He bit back a moan and focused on the TV. The one night he needed her to wear the men's pajamas she preferred, and she came to bed in a whole lot of skin and not much else.

She slid under the covers, scooted over to him, and rested her head on his shoulder. "What's on?"

"Ah, no idea." He snagged the remote and ignored the warmth of her skin so close to his. "Anything you wanna watch?"

"I'm game for whatever."

His mind flashed to their kiss and he winced. Yeah. He needed to get himself under control if an innocent comment stirred him up.

She rubbed her cheek against his arm. Her hand crept across his abs and she fingered the waistband of his boxer briefs. "What's this?"

His stomach muscles drew in, away from the soft rub of her fingertips along the edge of his underwear. "Figured you might be intimidated 'cause I'm bigger than you."

She laughed and her fingers inched a little higher, meeting bare skin. "Come on, Drew, be honest. You haven't worn underwear to bed the entire time I've known you."

Busted. "Ready for bed?"

"Mmm." She scooted away from him and curled up on her side facing him. "You coming?"

He rubbed the fingers of one hand over his eyes, but the image was already branded into his brain. Him buried deep inside her, her arching into him, his cum splashing into her womb as she moaned and writhed and her pussy pulsed around him. Fuck. Maybe jerking off wasn't gonna do the trick. Maybe he needed to find a woman and burn off some of the need, or maybe he needed to do something to get Jerusha out of his system, like yank her clothes off and see if she tasted as good as he remembered.

Her hand skimmed over his bare thigh. "You ok?"

"Uh, yeah." He let his hand fall away and flipped off the bedside lamp. "You mind if I watch TV for a little while?"

"Go ahead. Would you get under the covers with me, though?"

He bit back a sharp retort. One day she wanted her distance and the next she wanted him close. That was just like a woman, wasn't it, dragging a man back and forth according to her whims. He picked a channel at random, set the remote on the nightstand, and slid under the covers with his head and upper back propped up on a pillow. She sidled over and draped herself over him, her thigh across his, her hand low on his abdomen, her head on his chest. He tucked the covers around her shoulders and nestled her close. Hell, she wanted to cuddle, he had no objections. He'd wanted to for a while, hated having to restrain himself when gut instinct demanded he get close to her.

She pressed a chaste kiss to his chest and sighed. "Do you really have siblings or was that part of the act?"

He tucked his free arm under his head and stared at the light from the TV flickering across the ceiling in a futile effort to keep his body under control. "I had a brother. He died when I was a kid, and my sister ran away not long after. Drugs. She fell in with a gang, stayed wasted all the time." And their ma had blamed Drew for both, like he could've done anything about either. "Why?"

"It seemed to touch a nerve."

"Sometimes, yeah, it does. Not everybody's got the family you do, Jaybird."

"I know how lucky I am, Drew, trust me." Her fingers toyed with the hair under his navel, unknowingly ratcheting the desire scorching his blood higher, and her thigh shifted over his. "Do you have kids?"

He laughed, nearly startled out of the spiraling need gripping him by the absurdity of her question. "Do I look like dad material to you?"

"You kinda do. My nieces and nephews adore you. Soon as Charlotte's oldest found out we were coming out here together, she begged me to bring her along so she could spend time with her Uncle Drew. What did you do, bribe her?"

"Naw, I just treat her like a person." The way he'd always wanted to be treated, like he mattered to the people around him. First time he'd found that kind of belonging was in the Army, but it wasn't the last, and it wasn't the best, either. "What about you?"

"Not yet, but I'm young still."

And that was something that had never come up before. He cleared his throat and adjusted his hold on her back, cupping her ribs through the silky camisole. "How young is that?"

"Young," she said, sly humor tingeing her husky voice. "A hundred and sixty-one in April."

He sucked in a breath and bobbled his grip on her. "Holy shit, Jaybird."

She laughed, long and hard. "Oh, Drew, honestly. What did you expect? You had to know I'm a lot older than you."

"Yeah, but not that much." He shook his head. No, that wasn't true. He'd known Dani was in her eighties and Margaret older by centuries. He just hadn't followed the logic of birth order and applied it to Jerusha. "Kinda taking *old maid* to the extreme, ain't it?"

She tilted her head up and narrowed her eyes at him. "I'll show you old maid."

"You think so?"

"Oh, yeah." She pushed herself up and stretched out on top of him, straddling his stomach, her mouth inches from his, the blunt ends of her inky hair sliding across his skin. "Now who's bigger?"

"I'm still bigger, Jaybird," he murmured.

"Yeah, but I'm on top." Her hips slid down his torso and

back up again, spreading aching need wherever she touched. "I think I like being here."

Hell, he liked her being there, too. In fact, he absolutely fucking adored it, but that didn't make it right. He cradled her hips between his hands and dug his fingers into her skin. "What're you up to?"

"Last night, you told me if I wanted a kiss, I'd have to take it. You challenged me, Drew. You challenged a Daughter. Did you think I'd just let that pass?"

He sure as hell hadn't thought she'd take him seriously. Her hips slid inches lower and her pussy settled over his erection. Heat shot through him so fast, he couldn't stop it. His hips arched into hers, and she ground into him, a hard tease through the layers of their underwear.

"Come on, Jerusha. Don't wind me up."

"Is that what I'm doing? Am I winding you up?" She braced her palms on his chest and threw her head back, eyes closed, body arched. Her hips undulated over his, harder, faster, and she gasped. "Touch me, Drew. Make me feel."

Panic ripped through him. Much more of that and he'd come all over her, whether she meant him to or not. "Jerusha, wait. Just wait a minute."

"Drew, please," she breathed. "You feel so good."

His body pulsed and everything in him rushed into the place where their hips met. He clamped down hard on her hips, directing her grind, and gritted his teeth. Just a minute. If he could hold on for a minute more, she'd come, and he could let go. God, he wanted to be in her when she came, but there was no time. He was too close, so fucking close, and just the thought of being inside her slick heat pushed him past what little control he had. He curled his fingers into the waistband of her panties and yanked, ripping the seams apart.

She shuddered and her head fell forward, her eyes so hot, they glowed. "That's it, Drew. Take what you want."

"I'm giving, baby," he said, and he did. He slid his thumb

into the folds of her pussy and found her clitoris. She was wet and hot and felt so good under his skin, it was all he could do to let her have her way. Next time, he'd have his mouth there, sucking her in, pushing her so far so fast, she wouldn't have time to do anything except breathe his name. He flicked his thumb across her clit, once, twice, and she moaned, the sweetest sound he'd ever heard.

There was no need to hold back any more, no need to restrain himself. He brushed the pad of his thumb over the nub of her sex, timing his touch to her panted moans, and pushed into her, grinding into her pussy, imagining he was buried deep inside her tight little body.

She sank her nails into his skin and jerked her hips against his touch. "Drew," she said, sharp and low, and her body sagged on top of him, her heart hammering against his where their chests melded together. "Mmm, Drew. Don't stop. I know you're close."

He yanked his hand away from her sweet pussy and rolled her over onto her back, bracing himself above her with his hips cradled between her thighs. "I want your hand on me when I come."

A slow, seductive smile spread across the sensual curve of her mouth. "I want you naked when you come."

"Fuck, yeah." He slid off the bed, shucked his boxer briefs, and returned to exactly where he wanted to be. "Touch me," he said, and nearly winced. God, he hadn't meant to say it like that, rough and demanding, but her hand was already skimming down his skin, encircling him like she knew exactly what he needed. She caught a smooth rhythm up and down his dick, and her touch was so sweet, he nearly came on the first downward stroke.

His hands curled into the sheet next to her and he met that hot, knowing gaze. "So beautiful," he murmured. "God, you're so beautiful, baby."

He claimed her mouth in a desperate kiss, devouring her in greedy sweeps of his tongue across hers, tasting her, breathing her in. Her hand slackened on his dick, and he wrapped his around it and pistoned his hips into their combined strength, riding the frantic edge of need. Her free hand slipped up his side and her nails cut into his back, and he broke the kiss and buried his face in her throat. The need spilled over into a hard orgasm, shuddering through him as he came in hot waves, and his cum shot onto her skin over and over again.

He sucked in a breath, let it out on a bark of laughter. "God, Jaybird. When you say you're gonna take what you want, you really mean it."

The laughter he'd expected never came. He summoned what little strength he had left and braced himself above her. Her face was a tight mask, so different from the desire-softened expression she'd worn earlier, it might as well have belonged to a different person.

"What's wrong, baby?" he asked.

Her lips pressed together in a thin line. She shook her head and glanced away, and his thudding heart froze in his chest.

He'd gone too far. Somehow during the time between her coming and him following, she'd changed her mind or he'd hurt her or done something equally stupid, God only knew what. What a fuck up he was.

He released her hand and levered himself off of her. "Let me clean you up."

Her eyelids fluttered shut and she nodded, and the pressure in his chest eased a fraction. He padded into the bathroom, swiped a wet washcloth over his softening dick, wet another in warm water. She was lying exactly the way he'd left her when he came back in, staring up at the ceiling, sniffing back tears.

His heart twisted in his chest. God, he hadn't meant to hurt her. Tease her, please her, make her laugh, but never wound. He sat down on the edge of the bed and cleaned her as gently as he could. "I'm sorry, Jaybird."

Her eyes widened. "What for?"

He shrugged and tugged the remains of her panties off, and

41

his gut twisted into a sick knot. He'd treated her like an animal, ripping her clothes away, forcing her to finish him off. If he'd realized she'd wanted to stop when her hand went loose, he would've. He just hadn't thought that. She'd been so into it, rubbing herself all over him, urging him to take what he wanted. Fuck. Why hadn't she told him to stop? Why had she let him keep going?

He tossed the washcloth into the bathroom on his way to her suitcase and rummaged for her manly pajamas.

"What are you doing, Drew?"

"Getting you some clean clothes. Least I can do after ruining yours."

"I didn't mind." The covers rustled and the mattress squeaked, and when he looked around, she was sitting up on the bed with her knees bent close to her chest and her arms around her legs. "Pissed me off a little when you lied to me."

He whirled toward her and jabbed a finger at her. "I ain't never lied to you, Jaybird, not one goddamn time."

Her dark, straight eyebrows veed over a glare. "Yeah? What was that about me being beautiful, huh? You think you needed to lie to me, that I needed flattery to keep going?"

He slung her clothes onto the bed at her feet. "You ever think maybe you're beautiful to me?"

"You're *lying*," she hissed, and tears sprang into her eyes. "I can't believe you'd do that to me after I—"

"After you what, Jerusha? After you teased me into a hard-on? After you threw yourself at me and took what you wanted, even after I asked you to wait? We're on a fucking mission, not in the middle of a goddamn safety zone. We can't afford to get distracted." He laughed, hard and raw, and frustration trembled inside him, pushing out words before he could think them through. "Hell, Jerusha. I can't afford to have you screwing with me like that, can't afford having my head tangled up while you yank me back and forth. Come here, go away, fuck me now, Drew. What the hell were you thinking?"

She blanched and bowed her head. "That's enough, Drew."

The anger bled out of him as fast as it had come. He scraped an unsteady hand over his mouth and sank onto the edge of the bed beside her. "Yeah, I guess it is, especially when I didn't mean it."

"No, you were right. I was, not playing you, not using you, but I wanted you and I didn't consider that maybe you weren't really interested." Her forehead dropped to her knees and a breath shuddered out of her. "Don't hate me for it."

"I don't hate you." Far from it. He wrapped his arms around her and pulled her into his lap, comforting her as much as he could. "Didn't mean to hurt you, either. You don't deserve that."

Her arms crept around him and she sniffled into his chest. "You really think I'm beautiful?"

"Yeah, I do. Not pretty, exactly, not like Dani and Moira, or sweet like Charlotte, and sure as hell not as mean as Margaret, but yeah. You're one of the most beautiful women I've ever met. It shines out of you so bright, even an idiot like me can see it."

"Drew." She breathed out a laugh and her fingers dug into his ribs. "I can't believe you just compared me to my sisters."

"Hell, Jaybird, I'm a soldier, not a poet. I ain't got enough tact for spit. For the record, though, there's no comparison." He rubbed his cheek across the silky strands of her hair, pressed a kiss to the top of her head. "Let's get some shuteye. We can argue some more in the morning. I'll even let you get in the first dig."

"Will you hold me tonight?" she asked, and her voice was so soft, so uncertain, he couldn't deny the simple request.

"As long as you need me to, baby." Anything to make up for the way he'd treated her, anything to bring that light back into her beautiful, sky-bright eyes.

He helped her into clean pajamas, cut the lights off, and slid into bed beside her, snuggling with her until her body relaxed into his and they both fell fast asleep.

Four

REBECCA UPTON released the edge of the living room curtain and stepped away from the window. Peeking outside every five minutes wouldn't hurry her youngest daughter along and it only fueled the worry lodged in Rebecca's gut. Dani would arrive exactly when she intended to, hulking fiancé in tow, and that's all there was to it.

The college bowl announcer's voice on the television rose to a fevered pitch. The University of Nebraska's quarterback fumbled the ball. A Georgia linebacker picked it up and plowed through Nebraska's line toward the goal, and half the people in Rebecca's living room jumped to their feet, shouting over one another as they cheered one of the two teams along and jeered the other.

Robert's hand circled her forearm. "She's just running late."

Rebecca relented and sat on the edge of the armchair next to her husband. "She's always running late these days."

"So did we when we first met." His smile widened and a familiar spark lit his hazel eyes. "Do you remember how it was back then? We could barely keep our hands off each other."

She bent down and pressed a soft kiss to his mouth through the beard and mustache he insisted on growing in the winter. "I still can't resist you, darling."

"And you don't have to." He waggled his eyebrows. "I'm

feeling a mite frisky. What say we sneak off and head into the bedroom, just you and me and that bottle of Boërl & Kroff Brut Rose champagne Margaret gave us for Christmas?"

"As soon as this crowd leaves, I'll take you up on that." A car door slammed outside. Rebecca sat up and twisted toward the curtained windows. "They're here."

"Damn it," Robert said, wry humor rich in his voice. "I was this close."

"I'll make it up to you."

"I'll hold you to that, lover."

She stood and wended her way through the bodies of her children and grandchildren, occupying whatever space they could carve out in the crowded living room. The front door opened and Dani stepped through, her cheeks rosy, her blonde curls piled in a messy knot on her head, a small, cloth bag in one gloved hand. David followed close on her heels, his silent bulk hovering half a pace behind her.

Rebecca held her arms out and accepted a quick hug from Dani and a peck on the cheek from David. "I was getting worried."

Dani's bright green eyes slid to her companion. "We had an emergency."

One corner of David's mouth tilted into a half smile. "Gonna have another one when we get home."

Rebecca stifled a smile. Honestly, had she and Robert ever been that bad? "Did you bring it?"

"Yeah." Dani unwound her scarf and gave it to David, then handed Rebecca the bag. "Can we go some place quiet?"

"Of course, darling. We can use the library."

"That'd be great." Dani stood on tiptoe and bussed David's mouth. "Go be a man."

He grunted and slipped his thin jacket off his broad shoulders, revealing a moss green, hand-knit mock turtleneck. Dani tucked her hand into the crook of Rebecca's arm and drew her down the hallway, away from the rowdy crowd. "Sorry we were late. We didn't get in from Kansas until late last night. Big lug insisted on sleeping in, no matter how many times I told him we needed to get here early."

"A premonition?"

Dani shook her head, sending blonde wisps of hair swirling around her oval face. Her lips pressed into a thin line and her hand cupped her stomach. "I don't know. Maybe. There's something coming, something dark. I wanted to spend time with y'all before it gets here."

The skin along Rebecca's spine tightened. The vision the Woman with No Face had shared with her just before Thanksgiving popped into her mind, the roiling shadow, the blade shattering. Had Dani witnessed Rebecca's coming death? Surely fate would never bestow those images on a daughter, no matter how pressing the need.

She led Dani into the library, shut the door quietly behind them, and settled on the couch next to the child given into her care by the very woman that had predicted Rebecca's demise. "Can you tell what it is?"

"No, just...shadow, but nothing I've ever felt before." Dani frowned and cocked her head. "If I didn't know better, I'd think it was Alexiou, but I'd swear it's not. He, I don't know, feels different than this. I just don't know. Could be just my imagination."

"I doubt that very much." Rebecca stroked a soothing hand over Dani's arm. "Perhaps you shouldn't push so hard. You're still quite young, nowhere near the age when most of Kiya's descendants begin to receive the Lady Ki's blessing."

Dani's expression twisted into a grimace and she slumped into the couch. "I can't believe you called it a blessing. Do you know how awful it is to get this sick feeling in your gut and never know what's coming behind it?"

"I'm sorry, darling. I didn't mean to make light of your gift."

"You didn't. It's just..." Dani blew out a breath and her gaze fell on the bag. "The whole time we were in Kansas, I had this feeling, this odd, insistent pressure that kept prodding me. Something wasn't right, something was off. I thought it was his mom. She pretty much hated me on sight."

"It couldn't have been that bad."

"Oh, yeah, it was. Trust me. Nobody's good enough for that woman's baby boy." Dani curled her legs up onto the couch and faced Rebecca. "But then Christmas morning, she handed us this gift, and I knew. *That* was the source of my unease, *that* was what I was there for, and Blessed Mother, was it a doozy."

"And you made me wait until you got here to find out what it was."

Dani grinned. "Well, I'm not a saint. Besides, anticipation's half the fun."

Rebecca clucked her tongue. "I keep waiting for you to outgrow this urgent need you have to seek fun wherever you go."

"Maybe in another coupla decades." Dani nudged Rebecca's arm. "Go on. See what it is."

Rebecca set the bag in her lap, and now that it was there, she hesitated. Perhaps this, like the vision the Woman had shared, was something she didn't want to face. Perhaps it would be better to return it to her errant daughter and allow someone else to deal with it. Did passing off that duty make her a coward or was it centuries of accumulated wisdom staying her hand now?

"It won't bite," Dani said gently, and Rebecca steeled her nerves. She reached into the bag and pulled out an intricately carved wooden box, and opened it before her courage failed. Inside rested a single armlet crafted of hammered copper, its surface coated with a fine patina.

The Eye of Marnan peeked at Rebecca through layers of age and wear.

Her heart leapt into her throat. She pressed trembling fingers to her sternum, her gaze caught on the twin to the armband uncovered in a Swedish archaeological dig during the past summer. "Dani, where...? How?"

"Dave's mom." Dani stroked a finger along the edge of the

copper. "From what I can make out, her grandmother several times removed was the Daughter buried at Sandby borg. That woman's daughter, her only daughter, was named Frigda, and she gave this to her mortal granddaughter and so on, and that's how Katherine came to have it. A line of only children, all daughters."

"It could've been lost, so easily."

"Yeah, that's what I was thinking. But they held on to it and now, it's returned to the People." Dani hissed in a sharp breath and placed a hand over her stomach, and her green eyes darkened. "The pieces fall into place, Rebecca of the Blade, and to your line falls the greatest burden."

Rebecca set the box hastily to one side and cupped Dani's shoulders. "Dani, are you ok?"

Dani hunched her shoulders, her skin two shades too ashen under her tight expression. "Damn visions. At least that one was kinda clear."

"Your voice went flat."

"Yeah, it happens." Dani pressed the heel of her palm to her forehead and her lower lip trembled. "Sorry, Mom. Can you get Dave? I really need him right now."

"Some water, too, darling. I'll be right back."

Rebecca hurried out of the library into the living room and fetched her son to be, then scrounged a glass of water for her youngest daughter. The visions were coming too hard, too fast, and at far too young of an age. She closed her eyes and breathed a quiet plea to the Lady Ki, praying the goddess meant no harm to the woman Dani had become.

JERUSHA WOKE UP surrounded by a furnace, tangled together with Drew. One of his massive thighs was wedged between hers, her thigh was slung over his hip, and her arms were trapped between them. She eased her head away from Drew's chest and heat surged into her cheeks. She'd all but begged him to hold her last night, and he had, apparently never letting her go even in sleep. How embarrassing was it that she, a Daughter of the line of Abragni, the youngest natural child of one of the People's fiercest warriors, had needed a man's comfort? How much worse was it that she didn't want him to let her go?

If her sisters found out, they'd never let her live it down.

His arms tightened around her. "Where do you think you're going?"

"Ah." That was a good question, and she had an answer for it, surely she did. She scrambled through her suddenly empty brain and landed on the first excuse she came to. "Bathroom."

"Hunh." His hips surged forward and the head of his thick erection slid along her belly. "Thought maybe you were running scared."

She scowled at his chest. How the hell had he known that?

His hips shifted again and he *mmmd*. "Too bad we got a full day. Wouldn't mind tasting your sweet little pussy."

Heat shot through her and her inner muscles clamped together on a hard throb. Drew's mouth on her skin, his tongue rasping across her clit, his fingers pushing into her? She closed her eyes and struggled to breathe through the wanton need boiling into her blood. Last night, he'd accused her of playing him. Was that what he was doing now, getting a little payback, teasing her into losing control the way she'd teased him into losing his?

"Drew." The word croaked out of her and she winced. It was bad enough that she needed him. Was she going to let him know it, too? She cleared her throat and tried again. "You said we needed to focus on the mission."

"Mm-hmm, I did." His hand slid down her back and across her hip, and his fingers delved into her panties, strumming her clit as if he knew exactly what was on her mind. "And we can, soon as I make you come."

"Drew, um." The pad of his finger circled around the sensitive nub between her thighs, stroking hot pleasure into her. "Oh," she breathed, and he laughed.

"Want me to stop?"

No, not for one blessed second did she want him to quit, and he knew it, too. She scraped her nails down his abs and wrapped her hand around his erection, sliding it up and down the hard, silky length. "Only if you want me to."

"Oh, hell, Jaybird."

She laughed softly and nuzzled the tip of her nose into the mat of crisp hair covering his chest, breathing him in. The faint hints of soap and cologne and man tickled her nose. Mmm, so good.

His fingers shifted on her sex and the tip of one finger prodded her pussy, twisting in and out of her. "God, I wish we had more time."

"Later." She wiggled away from him, stripped off her panties, and pushed him flat on his back, straddling him. "I can please us both."

He tucked a hand behind his head and grinned. "Yeah?"

"Oh, yeah." She slid her wet pussy over his hard length, back and forth, slow and easy, and braced her palms flat on his chest. Desire throbbed through her, demanding and greedy. She wanted him inside her, every single inch, filling her, stretching her, but not yet. Not until she could trust him. In the meantime, she ached and seethed and yearned, and she refused to let the thirst she had for him go unquenched. "Hold on, lover. It's gonna be a bumpy ride."

His cognac eyes went hot and a little wild, and the grin slipped off his face. "Take your shirt off."

She shook her head and smiled as her hips skidded over his, rubbing her clitoris across the underside of his cock where it was pinned between their bodies. "You want it off, you take it off."

His hand came out from behind his head and the fingers of both his hands caught in the hem of the men's pajama top she wore. "You sure about that?"

He didn't give her a chance to answer. His hands yanked

apart, taking the two sides of the front of her shirt with them. Buttons popped and spun through the air, and he spread the thin cloth wide, baring her torso to his gaze. His hips flexed into hers and his palms dragged over the tips of her breasts. "Gorgeous."

The word twisted through her and some of the heat died. She wasn't beautiful or gorgeous or even passably pretty. Why did he keep telling her that when they both knew it wasn't true?

His hand came down hard on her ass in a near slap. "None of that. I say you're gorgeous, you better believe me."

She rolled her eyes and her hips stilled. "Come on, Drew."

His eyes narrowed into slits. "You calling me a liar?"

"No, but—"

"That's what I thought. Your body is a fucking work of art." He dug his fingers gently into the skin over her hips and ground into her. "What was that you said about being in a hurry?"

She laughed and undulated her hips, and passion rose, as swift and sure as the rising tide, engulfing them both, carrying them into sharp orgasms under the slide of her pussy along his dick, releasing in muted gasps and thudding heartbeats.

After, he pulled them both into the tight confines of the shower and soaped her skin with his hands. "What's on the agenda today?"

She leaned her head back under the spray, wetting her hair. "I thought you hated it when I reminded you what we're doing."

"Hey, talk or sex. Your choice."

The light humor in his voice tickled her own. "I take it you want sex."

"I'm a man and I like sex, so yeah."

His mouth clamped into a thin line and a faint tinge of pink colored the skin over his cheekbones.

She tilted her head and considered him. "Liking sex makes you blush?"

"Uh, no." He handed her the soap and turned his back to her, effectively hiding his expression. "I was just remembering the first time we met."

"Reno, a few years ago."

"Yeah."

A slow smile curved her mouth. "Where I was working undercover as a prostitute."

His shoulders tensed so slightly, she would've missed it if she hadn't been watching for a reaction. "I didn't know you were Bobby's sister. He never said. We were there on vacation, and I guess he wanted to see you."

"Possibly."

"I didn't recognize you." He rolled his shoulders and bowed his head. "I mean, I knew you were his sister. I saw all the pictures behind his desk, but I didn't put you with her or, um."

She soaped a washcloth and eyed his back. There were scars there, some shallow and thin, others jagged and raw, as if they hadn't healed properly. She chose one and ran the cloth gently over it, easing away a long-gone hurt. "Are you trying to tell me something, Drew?"

"I thought you were a hooker."

"And? I was playing one, so thinking I was a hooker won't hurt my feelings."

"It's not that." He cleared his throat and brushed a thumb over the tip of his nose, and his voice lowered to a husky whisper, barely audible above the steady rush of water falling down around them. "I was kind of attracted to you."

"When you thought I was a hooker."

"Fuck. I know that sounds bad."

"Actually, I'm kinda flattered."

He jerked his head around and stared at her, his expression inscrutable. "Go ahead, Jaybird. Make fun of the Southie."

"Seriously, Drew." She shook her head and concentrated the washcloth on the skin stretched across his ribs. "When a man like you wants a woman, trust me. She's flattered."

He snorted and twisted back around, muttering under his breath.

"What was that?" she asked. "Couldn't quite hear you."

"Yeah, yeah. Just tell me what we're doing today, will ya?"

She wanted to press for answers, wanted to delve a little more deeply into the whole *I was attracted to you the first time we met* thing he'd just admitted to, but she knew better. If she pushed, he'd clam up, and then she'd never get any answers.

So talk about work it was, and that she could do in her sleep. "Derinkuyu was entirely too big for the two of us to search it on our own."

Though it had been worth the tediously long hours they'd spent there just to marvel at the structure, even if they hadn't found hide nor hair of the Seven Sisters in the eighteen-story underground city. Of course, they'd only been through a fraction of that, not that it mattered. If signs of the People's presence had been found in Derinkuyu in the fifty odd years since its rediscovery, chances were good they would've been part of the body of published research. Jerusha had, with a lot of help from volunteers her mother had drafted, already scanned the literature and scoured the web and other sources, and found diddly squat. Still, she and Drew were in the region. Though she hadn't expected to find anything in Derinkuyu, it had felt right to at least pay it a visit.

She slid her fingers over the scars on Drew's back, the pucker of a gunshot wound along his right flank, a thinner, smoother scar marring the skin over his left ribcage, and others. So many stories, trapped in his skin. She kissed one, just because she could. "We'll work our way through the other, more well-known underground cities over the next few days, concentrating on the ones where tombs were found. If none of those pan out, we'll start on the less accessible ones and hope the one we need is open to tourists."

"That ain't gonna stop us, Jaybird."

No, it wouldn't, but they'd cross that bridge when they came to it. "I do have a couple of friends I'd like to see while we're here."

He turned around and took the washcloth from her. "That

wasn't on the agenda."

"These kinds of friends never are."

"Would these friends be immortal by any chance?" He tossed the washcloth over his shoulder, snagged her hips, and bumped their bodies together. "More importantly, do they have guns?"

She clucked her tongue and rubbed her fingertips into the hair covering his chest, away from the temptation of his smooth skin. "What is it about soldiers and guns?"

"What can I say? We like things that go boom. Speaking of." He rubbed his growing erection across her stomach. "I've got a gun for you."

"I bet you do."

"Tonight, I'm gonna let you pull the trigger."

She groaned and dropped her forehead to his chest. "I can't believe you just said that."

"Believe it, baby." He smacked her ass, kneaded the skin over the heat he'd raised. "Kiss me quick so we can get to work."

She stood on tiptoes and claimed his mouth in a tender kiss, only their second real one. The knowledge jolted through her. They'd barely kissed the night before. It was a lack she intended to remedy as soon as she could get him alone again.

His hands wound around her back, holding her snug against his chest, and he devoured her, as thoroughly as a man with all the time in the world to spend on the woman he was with. Slow pleasure threaded its way through her blood, not the heat of passion, but the gentle sweep of happiness. She turned the idea over in her head, testing its depth, measuring its value, and eventually discovered a kernel of truth. She was happy being with Drew. For the first time in her long life, a man's presence actually brought her joy outside of sex. She tucked the knowledge away in her heart and gave herself over to the leisurely exploration of his mouth on hers.

Five

THE MUTED conversation between Jerusha and the Turkish archaeologist she'd cornered drifted to Drew, magnified slightly by the cavern's rock walls. He tucked his fingers close to his ribs and carefully scanned those walls, searching for any detail that might indicate they'd stumbled on the right underground city.

It was the third one they'd been in that day, and already, he'd forgotten its name. Not that it mattered. Jerusha had a mind like a steel trap. Nothing escaped her attention, not the names of the cities they'd visited or the embarrassment scalding his cheeks during their shower.

He should never have admitted the hooker thing, even if it had tickled her pink.

He shifted his stance and trained his gaze on another patch of the ceiling, working his way down to the cavern's floor. She'd gone a little cold on him again, soon as they'd left the hotel, and that was fine. Things had heated up pretty fucking fast between them last night. Slowing down now seemed like a good idea, though looked like his idea of slow and hers were worlds apart, pretty much like him and her.

He thumbed the underside of his wedding ring and stifled a sigh. They still had to act like a married couple out in public, though. Hadn't been a hardship after having her grind him into two orgasms. Hell, it'd never been a hardship playing nice with Jerusha as long as she played back, but when she didn't? Yeah, that fucking sucked. It'd only taken one cold, side-eyed glance out of her blue eyes for him to get the message that morning.

Back off, Southie.

So he had. Maybe it rankled a little, having her blow cold on him after the way she'd sidled up to him last night. Maybe he'd wanted to hold on to the heat a little longer before having to give it up to their mission. He rolled his shoulders and clamped down on the knot of emotion riding low in his gut. Maybe he'd wanted a helluva lot more out of her than them getting each other off.

At least he knew now that she felt the insistent tug of attraction, too.

The section of wall he was scanning turned out to be a whole lotta blank rock. He shifted again and worked his gaze up the next section. Nearly four cities down and a shit ton left to explore. The rate they were going, it'd take weeks to search them all, and that was assuming they had easy access. If they had to hoe the hard row, it'd take a lot longer. He didn't mind that a bit. Wasn't the first time he'd broken into a place he wanted to explore. Probably wouldn't be the last, either.

Footsteps scuffed behind him and a narrow hand slid along his back above the waistband of his jeans. Jerusha peeked around his arm and smiled up at him. "Ready to go, sweetie?"

"Yeah, sure, baby."

He forced his muscles to relax and slung an arm around her shoulders, gathering her closer than was probably proper. Tough shit. He needed something to tide him over until he could get her alone and figure out why she was pushing him away again. Maybe it was the trust thing or maybe she was just being a woman. Either way, he needed to know.

"You have a good talk?" he asked.

"An excellent one." Her other hand slid across his abs and rested above his bellybutton, and heat shot in a predictably straight line into his dick. "They're closing soon. Why don't we call it a day and grab something to eat?"

"Hey, I'm always up for food."

She patted his stomach and grinned. "You're so easy."

"You would know."

They trailed behind the archaeologist, winding their way out of the underground city into the open air and down the rock lined walkway to the parking lot. Theirs was one of the few vehicles sitting there, but it wasn't the one his gaze fell on. Fuck all. After the little talk Jerusha had had with the sedan's occupants yesterday morning, it shouldn't have been anywhere near them.

He dropped his hold on Jerusha's shoulders. "Son of a bitch. Looks like we got a problem."

She followed his gaze and scowled. "You know, when a Daughter warns you off, you're supposed to listen. I friggin' hate repeating myself."

"Yeah? Apparently Mutt and Jeff are too stupid to get that."

She sputtered out a laugh. "Mutt and Jeff?"

"What? It fits."

The car's engine turned over. Drew broke into a run toward it, Jerusha right beside him, her long strides nearly matching his. He got close enough to make out the driver's eyes, the small guy Jerusha had skewered. The guy met Drew's gaze evenly, then backed out and sped out of the parking lot, dirt spewing away from the tires on the way out.

Drew slowed his pace and stopped, hands hooked low on his hips. "I shoulda let you kill 'em yesterday."

"Then we would've had to clean up the mess." Jerusha crossed her arms over her chest and stared after the sedan. "Anything about that strike you as odd?"

"Pretty much everything." He glanced over his shoulder at the entrance to the underground city they'd just left. "They could've cornered us inside, could've waited at another pit stop and picked us up there, but they were just sitting here in plain sight."

"Right where the exit dumps out, like they wanted us to see them."

"Yeah, exactly." The skin along his nape prickled and he rubbed a hand across it. "I don't like it."

"Me, neither, not a bit." She shook her head and the end of her braid twitched across her back. "Let's get some food in us. Maybe we can figure it out with our bellies full."

A full belly didn't help much, though. Drew's brain wrestled with the curious incident of their not-so-subtle tail the whole time without shedding any light on the problem. Jerusha reverted to her usual snarky self during the meal, and some of his tension eased away. It was a relief to have her back to normal, needling him the way she always did. During the walk between the restaurant and their car, she tucked her hand into his like it was no big, and he held her lightly, too worried about scaring her off to do more.

They made it back to the hotel around seven local time. As soon as they walked into their room, the hairs on the back of Drew's neck stood at attention. He threw an arm out, holding Jerusha back, and scanned the room. What was wrong, what was wrong...

His suitcase was an inch out of alignment on the chaise. Hers wasn't zipped all the way closed when he knew for damned sure she'd left it that way. He went over the room again. A sheen of mud smudged the carpeting near the end of the bed, the shade of the lamp on his nightstand was perfectly level when it hadn't been before they'd left.

Fuck. Somebody had been in the room.

Jerusha's hand knotted into a fist against the back of his jacket. He tapped his ear, then pointed to the discrepancies, and her mouth slowly thinned into a firm line. She circled her finger in the air, and he nodded. Search the place it was.

"What did you think about the restaurant, sweetie?" she asked.

God, she was good. Silence was a dead giveaway that

something was wrong. Conversation? Business as usual. He dropped a hard kiss to her mouth. Who would've thought a rough and tumble Southie and his best friend's sister would fit so well together, on the clock and off?

He closed the door and ran his fingertips lightly across the top of the carved doorframe. "Lamb chops were a little tough."

She waggled her eyebrows and grinned. "You should've had the Beyti."

He took the left-hand side of the room, her the right. They worked their way around it, checking behind picture frames, sliding their fingers into hidden crannies and along the wrought iron fixtures scattered throughout the room, bantering enough small talk between them to bore anybody listening. Drew found his first bug on the back side of a vase of flowers near the entrance. He left it there and continued to search, and found a second one stuck to the base of the lamp next to his side of the bed.

A slow burn heated his blood. Wasn't it bad enough they were being tailed? Did the Shadow have to listen in on their pillow talk, too?

He met Jerusha at the bed's intricately wrought headboard. She slid her hand over the top and into the back while he lifted pillows and prodded the mattress and bottom of the headboard. They both explored the curved metal spokes holding the top and bottom together. Her hand came away with a tiny listening device. "I'm feeling a little sticky, sweetie. How about a shower?"

His mind shot straight to the shower they'd taken that morning, her soapy hands running over him, his over hers, and his dick perked up. He backed off the bed and scrubbed a rough hand over his hair. "Sure, baby."

Inside the bathroom, she flushed the bug and flipped the faucets in the shower and sink on full blast. He pulled her into a hug and placed his mouth near her ear. "I found two."

She lifted onto her tiptoes and curved her hands around his waist. "Three, including the one on the headboard."

"Fuck. Reckon that's why Mutt and Jeff were so obvious?"

"Maybe. Leave them or ditch them?"

He turned the two options over in his mind, weighing possibilities. "We ditch 'em, chances are good they'll just put more back. Next time, we might not be able to find 'em all."

"Not sure we did this time. We need to check the bathroom."

"Yeah, I know. Damn it." He sighed into her neck. "No more sex."

"What?" She dropped onto her heels and leaned away from him, her blue eyes wide. "You're kidding, right?"

He shook his head, then rubbed his cheek along hers, aligning his mouth with her ear. "I don't share, Jaybird, not even the sweet little, sexy moans you make when you're really into it. Those belong to me, not the dweebs following us. No sex until we figure out how to get rid of the bugs without 'em being put back."

She groaned and buried her face in his throat. "I'm not sure whether to punch you or kiss you."

"Find us a co-ed gym and you can do both." He slid his hands around her body and cupped her luscious ass through her cargo pants. God, he'd been right. She was a fucking work of art, two nice handfuls of well-toned muscle, mile long legs, and the kind of curves a man panted after. He hadn't even gotten to taste her dusky nipples yet, had about come the minute he'd yanked open her shirt that morning and gotten an eyeful of her perfect breasts. Speaking of. "You really wanna take a shower?"

"It was just a cover so we could talk."

He grunted. Damn. There went that fantasy. "How about a game of cards?"

"You do owe me a rematch of Go Fish."

A grin popped onto his face. "This time, I'm gonna win."

"In your dreams, Southie." She sighed and rubbed the side of her face over his chest through his turtleneck. "Cuddle with me tonight?"

"You sure?"

"Mmm, yeah. Don't know why you stopped in the first place."

Because she'd gotten pissed at him for wallowing. He bit the thought back and let her go, stepping away from her warmth and light. "Bathroom's yours."

She flashed a grin at him, and he left, closing the door tightly behind him, putting his back to the secret, womanly things she was doing in the bathroom. Probably stripping off her clothes and rubbing scented lotion all over her skin, along the hard muscles of her thighs, up her flat stomach, over the dusky tips of her full breasts.

He threaded his fingers behind his head and stared up at the ceiling, and his thoughts bounced between the bugs planted in their room, the heat pounding through his painfully rigid erection, and her request to cuddle. The mission. He needed to focus on the mission, but even as he reamed himself a new one, he knew it was useless. His focus was unraveling faster than he could reel it back in and there wasn't a fucking thing he could do about it.

THEIR THIRD DAY in Cappadocia was about as fruitless as their first two had been. Jerusha tucked her hand into the crook of Drew's arm and tried to pay attention to the tour guide's droning voice skimming over the region's monastic period as if it were insignificant. She sighed and bit back her irritation. Anybody that could take the fascinating history of the underground city they were exploring and make it sound as interesting as dry toast either had a real talent for understatement or was a complete idiot, maybe both.

She smothered a yawn against Drew's bicep and concentrated on the guide's slurred Turkish. It wasn't her first language or even her dozenth, and she wasn't as sharp in it as she should've been. Maybe if she'd gotten any sleep, it'd be different.

She'd crawled into bed beside Drew at a quarter past eleven, positive she could ignore the attraction spooling between them.

Nope. Her skin had sizzled wherever it touched his and her heart had thudded, and it had taken hours for her to relax. Meanwhile, he'd lain there like a lump on a log and fallen straight into sleep with one arm draped over her waist and his face buried in her hair.

The cad.

At least he'd cuddled with her, just like he'd promised he would. She'd woken up after a scant three hours of sleep, surrounded by him and so comfortable, it had been hard to move, let alone get out of bed. He'd held firm on the no sex rule, too, in spite of a truly magnificent erection, spoiling her morning good.

Drew's bicep flexed under her cheek. "You ok?"

"Fine."

"You get that about the newest city they found a coupla miles from here?"

Crap. No, she hadn't, which is what she got for thinking about Drew instead of listening to the tour guide's spiel. "Sorry, Drew. I'm a little tired."

"You kinda tossed and turned last night." His fingers grazed the line of her jaw, a barely there touch, gone before she could appreciate it. "We'll hit the sack early tonight."

It was a sweet thought, but she doubted it would help, not unless he was willing to renege on the no sex rule. "What's this about a new city?"

"Just found it a coupla summers ago. Hasn't even been fully mapped yet and they've only published a press release on it recently. Guide said something about artifacts or some shit, and something about a team from Boston University." Drew's shoulder lifted, jarring her head where it rested against his arm. "I dunno. Didn't catch everything. Guide has a bad case of mush mouth."

"We'll put it on the list." Along with about two hundred

others in the region. Fortunately, dozens had already been eliminated during the research phase of their job. She sighed and pushed the fatigue away. "You see anything around here? Symbols or carvings or, hell, a big sign reading 'City of the Sisters, This Way'?"

"Saw one that said bad guys, eight o'clock, but that's about it."

She jerked away from him. "Seriously? And you didn't tell me?"

"Figured you saw 'em." His thick, blond eyebrows snapped together and the backs of his fingers stroked over her cheek. "Fuck, Jaybird. You coming down with something? It ain't like you to miss a deet like that."

"Just tired, Drew."

She eased around and glanced behind them. Sure enough, two men dressed in dark winter clothes stood ramrod straight not twenty feet away, one of them blatantly staring at her. She batted her eyelashes and blew him a kiss, and his olive-complected skin flushed red.

She resettled herself against Drew's arm. So what if she was clinging? He was comfortable, and she liked being next to him. He was warm and solid and...stuff. Besides, their public personas were newlyweds. Weren't newlyweds supposed to cling?

"I don't get why the Shadow's using locals to tail us," she said. "I mean, yes, they blend, but they're not exactly professional."

"Seems like they're managing ok, Jaybird. They found us in Konya, followed us here, and we can't seem to shake 'em."

"Yeah, but look. They're just standing there, so obvious even a newb could spot them."

"Maybe they're taking a page from your book and coming out in the open." He tweaked her nose and jerked his chin toward the tour guide. "Looks like he's finished blowing hot air. Wanna corner him and see what he knows about that new underground city?"

"I'd rather roust the stooges," she grumbled. It would probably be more fun than trying to pry information out of a tour guide.

"Later, baby."

His voice had gone husky and his cognac eyes were hot, staring down at her like she was the only thing around him worth looking at. She cleared her throat and eased away, and his expression shuttered. Her heart sank a little lower in her chest. She'd enjoyed that look, enjoyed feeling beautiful, even if it wasn't true. Was there any way she could get him to look at her like that again?

The words were out before she could stop them, and she flinched. Crap. What kind of Daughter blurted out her need like that?

He caught her arm and hauled her against him. "Where do you think you're going?"

"Ah, you know. Tour guide."

"Unh-unh, not until you explain. What kind of look were you talking about?"

She glanced around. Some of the other tourists were staring, none openly hostile, but still. She lowered her voice and tugged her arm where he held her. "Come on, Drew. We're causing a scene."

His hand tightened around her arm. "You tell me about that look and I'll let you go."

"That look," she hissed. "Like I mean something to you outside of this job."

"You ever think maybe you do?"

"But you don't even know me."

"Is that what you think?" He shook his head and let go of her arm, and his expression went so hard and cold, it hurt to see it. "Fuck it. You go talk to the tour guide. I'm feeling a little rowdy."

He pivoted away and stalked toward the two men, and she let him go. He could punch his aggression out on their tails, for all she cared, and good riddance. What did she need a man for anyway? She'd done just fine on her own for decades. So what if she liked being around him? Who cared if he was the first man she'd ever met that wasn't scared of her or intimidated by her, or thought she was so beautiful, he couldn't stop looking at her? She sniffed and scowled at his retreating back. Men were a dime a dozen. As soon as this mission ended, she'd ditch Drew and prove it.

She whirled away from him and tracked down the hapless tour guide, ignoring the screaming voice in her head calling her a friggin' idiot.

THE PLAIN-AS-DAY tails following them blanched in the face of Drew's anger and fled at a fast walk. He pursued, burning through the molten fury rocketing around his gut as he pushed past the few genuine tourists shuffling in and out of the underground city. So he didn't know a thing about Jerusha, did he? Did she think he was just fooling around with her to pass the time? Is that the kind of man Bobby had told her he was, a player, a tinkerer, a fucking asshole that preyed on women, used them up, and hung them out to dry?

Fuck that. He had better ways to spend his time than chasing down a woman. He had a mission to complete, didn't he, a job to do, his professional reputation to uphold? Yeah, he should concentrate on that and not on the taste of Jerusha's skin or the way her scent lingered where she'd rubbed her face all over his arm.

His eyes narrowed on the two dweebs. Mutt and Jeff had apparently wised up and traded rotations with Tom and Jerry. The two new guys both looked like native Turks, one thin, light-skinned, and bushy-headed, the other short, pudgy, and nearly bald under a black-haired comb over.

Drew caught up with them in the parking lot and grabbed the collar of Jerry's coat in one fist, yanking the other man nearly off his feet. In Turkish, he said, "What are you doing staring at my woman?"

Jerry shook his head and his black eyes widened. "I would never stare at a woman who wasn't my wife."

"Hunh. Must've been the other guy then." The guy that had slipped away and was at that moment hoofing it out of the parking lot faster than Drew would be able to catch up. "Look at that. He left you all alone with me."

"Protocol. We're not supposed to be caught together."

"Then you shouldn't have been standing together inside." Drew yanked the guy's collar again, jostling him. "Start talking."

The man lifted his hands in a helpless shrug. "I know nothing."

"Sure you do. You can start with who hired you and end with why you're following us."

The man swallowed hard and brushed his fingers across his comb-over. "*She* knows who hired us."

"Lukas Alexiou," Drew guessed.

Jerry shot a wide-eyed glance at Drew. "Who?"

"Don't play dumb."

"I truly don't know this man."

"Hunh." Drew eased his grip on the man's collar. "You're being awfully helpful."

A small smile tilted the man's wide mouth. "I don't want to be stabbed, and my wife would be very angry if I came home to her with bruises on my face."

Some of Drew's anger melted away. "Is that so."

"Truly." Jerry eased around, hands up, palms out. "We were told to follow only. No hurting, no interfering. Once a day, we report in. As long as we do that, we get paid."

"The other two interfered."

"They saw an opportunity to take the girl. That's all I know."

"Your boss is after Jerusha?"

"Maybe so, maybe not so." Jerry shrugged. "As I said, we

follow, we report in. It's easy money and I have a family to feed."

"Maybe you should find another job," Drew said bluntly. "This one's liable to put bruises on you in places your wife will be really pissed to find."

Humor lit Jerry's dark eyes. "Your Turkish is very good."

"It's rusty." Drew bit back his frustration and tugged his ear. As open as the guy was being, it still felt like he hadn't said much. "Go on, get back to your wife. Next time I see you, though, I'm letting Jerusha handle you."

Jerry paled and sweat popped out on his forehead. "Please don't. We were warned about her."

"You and me both, pal."

Fat lot of good it'd done.

Drew spun away and strode toward the entrance to the underground city. Jerusha was standing to one side, her dark clothing a stark contrast to the off-white limestone rock face behind her. When he drew near, she said, "Find out anything?"

"Yeah." He tugged her out of earshot of the small cluster of tourists standing nearby, debating their next stop. "You know that game at the carnival with the three cups, whatsit?"

"The shell game?"

"Yeah, that, how the guy has a quarter or a ball or whatever inside one of three cups and he slides 'em around, and you're supposed to figure out which cup is hiding the quarter? Only, he drops whatever's in the cup and his hands moving around are just a diversion to keep your eye away from the prize." Drew jerked his chin toward the parking lot, where Jerry was calmly backing a low-end sedan out of the parking lot. "You were right. These guys are as local as they come, not anywhere close to professional. They're just doing a job for some extra cash."

Jerusha's gaze swept toward the parking lot. "You're saying they're just a distraction."

"That's what it feels like." He blew out a sigh and rolled his head, popping his neck. "My gut says we're missing the real tail, that something else is going on and we're not seeing the big picture."

"And that guy had no idea what the picture is?"

"Hell, Jaybird, he doesn't even know who Lukas Alexiou is. He did imply that Mutt and Jeff were trying to kidnap you."

Genuine humor curved her mouth into a smile. "Mutt and Jeff thought they could take down a Daughter?"

"They saw an opportunity. That's what Jerry back there said."

"Jerry?"

"Yeah, you know. *Tom and Jerry*, cat and mouse cartoon?"

"I'm well aware of who Tom and Jerry are, Drew." She stuffed her hands into the pockets of her cargo pants and locked her gaze on the dirt beneath their feet. "I need to do some research. Don't think it's really safe using the Internet connection at the hotel."

"Reckon there's an Internet café around here?"

Her head jerked up. "Are you kidding? Maybe in Istanbul."

"We could find another hotel."

"Then we'd just have to hop every night, and if we did that, they'd stick a GPS tracker on our car and follow us. You went to too much trouble disabling the one that came with the car for us to go through that again." She wrinkled her nose. "Frankly, I'd rather stay put. It's not like it's hard to figure out what we're doing, so they're bound to catch up to us anyway."

"All right, then. We stick with the hotel we have and hope for the best."

Her shoulders hunched around her ears. "You're not going to argue?"

"You're the brains in this outfit, Jaybird. I'm just the hired muscle."

One corner of her mouth turned down like she was gonna argue. A coupla hours ago, he would've hauled her close and kissed her frown away. Now, he figured he was lucky she was still speaking to him. "Let's go find a secure Internet connection."

"Any ideas?"

"One or two." And not a one that was legal. He caught her hand in his and threaded their fingers together. "So, this tour guide. You ever get anything out of him?"

Her frown deepened as she relayed the information she'd wheedled out of the guide. Drew listened with half an ear, his focus more on who was after them and why they wanted to capture Jerusha than on her explanation of what was going on in the world of dirt digging.

Six

A S IT TURNED OUT, there was an Internet café on the Göreme-Uçhisar Road, not far from their hotel. Jerusha set up her laptop next to the desktop computer at her station and groused to herself. That's what she got for assuming. If Drew didn't have sharp eyes, they would've driven right past it, and her none the wiser.

Drew's hand cupped her shoulder and squeezed. "Need to make a call."

She mustered a smile for him. It wasn't his fault she hadn't gotten enough sleep, and she shouldn't have gotten pissed off at him earlier for making her feel beautiful then shutting her out. They were in the middle of a mission. She should've given him the benefit of the doubt, would've if her head was screwed on straight. "I'll be right here."

He slipped away, his booted footsteps quiet on the carpeted floor, his huge body moving efficiently. No wasted actions, no unnecessary movements, just a smooth, even gait and a no-nonsense attitude. She sighed and opened a browser window. Men weren't supposed to be beautiful to watch, were they? And they weren't supposed to distract Daughters from their work, even if they *were* part of that work. Look at what had happened to Dani and Moira. Both of them had let the men they were working with distract them, and the next thing they knew, they lost their immortality and had babies on the brain.

Or, in Moira's case, a baby in the womb.

Jerusha's gaze crept unbidden to Drew, clearly visible through the store's plate glass window. He was just standing there on the sidewalk, back to her, arms crossed over his chest, fingers tucked against his ribs. Wasn't he supposed to be making a phone call?

She shook the thought away and searched for articles on underground cities in Turkey. The search engine returned dozens of hits. Several news articles published in the past few days were near the top of the list. Jerusha clicked through and scanned them, copied the best ones into a research folder on her laptop, and noted the names of those involved in efforts to explore and preserve the as-yet unnamed city.

Twenty minutes into her research, Jerusha glanced up. Drew had disappeared from the sidewalk. She scowled at the screen of her laptop. He was a big boy, a well-trained soldier, and fully capable of taking care of himself. Him moving out of sight was nothing to worry about.

She dashed off an e-mail to her mother and another to Bobby and Hiro, updating them on her and Drew's progress. A third went to Pari, an immortal Daughter Jerusha had worked with several decades ago, asking for a meet.

Jerusha's eyes stole toward the window. No Drew. She pursed her lips and studied the people passing by on the sidewalk outside the Internet café, then huffed out a sigh and tracked down contact info for the people associated with the new underground city. She copied and pasted everything into her research file, typed out a swift e-mail requesting an interview with the man in charge of the work there. Not much hope of him answering back quickly. It was coming up on the weekend. Chances were good he wouldn't be available until the following week.

She checked the window. Drew was watching her through it, phone to ear, the fingers of his free hand stuffed into the front pocket of his jeans. Relief eddied through her. There he was, exactly where he was supposed to be.

She turned back to her work, finished her research in record time, and logged out of her laptop. The door buzzed as it opened, and a moment later, Drew's fingers skimmed down her braid. "Hey, baby. Any luck?"

"Tons." She stuffed her laptop into its case, stood, and settled the strap of her bag on her shoulder. "It looks promising. They've found a ton of artifacts, very nicely preserved, and at least half a dozen tombs are located deep inside the city."

His mouth quirked into a full-blown grin. "You brains, me brawn."

"Yeah, yeah. I need to call Moira real quick, wish her a happy wedding day."

"Thought that was tomorrow."

"It is. She'll be busy tomorrow, though."

Drew placed his broad hand on her lower back and guided her out of the café into the late afternoon chill. "It's Friday."

"Mm-hmm. And?"

"Date night."

She ducked her head, hiding her smile. "We could always play another round of Go Fish."

"If I had a chance in hell of winning, I'd take you up on that. I can't believe you beat me last night three games in a row." He shook his head and eased them through the growing throng of people ambling along the sidewalk. "How about dinner in the hotel's restaurant and an hour of me rubbing you down?"

Her mind leapt to the possibilities, her naked, Drew's hands all over her. Molten heat gathered between her thighs, and she shivered. "You're talking about s-e-x."

"No, I'm talking about helping you relax so you'll get some sleep and stop snapping at me." He unlocked the car and opened her door. "Bobby said you get grumpy when you don't get enough rest."

She slouched into her seat, arms crossed around her bag,

and watched him shut her door, round the hood of the car, and slide in behind the steering wheel. "You talked to my brother about me?"

"I might've mentioned your hair-trigger temper a time or two," he said mildly. "He said if I wanna keep you happy, you need regular meals and a stable bedtime."

A blush flooded her cheeks and she slapped a hand over her eyes. Bobby had made it sound like she was a little kid. When she got back to the States, she was going to kick his ass good, favorite sibling or not.

"Hey, lighten up, Jaybird. He was worried about you, and so am I. We get back to the hotel, you're eating a solid meal and getting a decent night's sleep."

"Maybe I can't sleep because of you."

The words snapped out of her, much harsher than she'd intended. She uncovered her eyes and dared a peek at Drew. His hands were on his thighs, fingers splayed, and he was staring straight out the windshield, expression neutral.

Her fingers curled into fists against her laptop bag. "I'm sorry, Drew. I didn't mean it like that."

"I know, Jaybird." His gruff voice was so soft, she barely heard it above the traffic whizzing by on the nearby road. "Maybe you could take a nice, hot bath after supper. Women like that kinda thing, right?"

"Yeah, Drew. Sure." She buckled her seatbelt and focused her eyes on the dash. "Maybe we could find that co-ed gym first. I'm feeling kinda rusty."

"I thought Daughters didn't get rusty."

"I haven't worked out since we landed in Istanbul."

"There's space in the room, you wanna spar a little."

She took a chance and covered his hand with hers. "I promise not to kick your ass this time."

He snorted out a laugh. "You dream big."

"That's not a dream, sweetie. That's reality." She twined her fingers through his and squeezed. "Come on. I know you're getting hungry."

He started the car, backed out, and drove them to the hotel, and some of Jerusha's shame eased. She'd pushed him right out of his rough Southie humor with her temper, and that wasn't right. She'd do better, though. He deserved better.

She settled into her seat, her hand nestled in his, and set her mind to exploring ways she could make it up to him.

DREW RESETTLED his grip on the tops of Jerusha's feet and focused on her face. When he'd suggested an hour of calisthenics, she'd gone into the bathroom and strolled back out five minutes later dressed in a sports bra, a tiny pair of athletic shorts, and running shoes. The rest of her was beautifully bare, dark skin glistening, lean muscles rippling every time she moved. She might as well have been wearing lingerie for the effect it had on him.

She eased her upper body toward the floor, then curved it into a sit up. "I think that's it."

"Come on, Jaybird. Is that the best you can do?"

"I've already done fifty."

"Yeah, but you're a Daughter."

"What does that have to do with anything?"

"Way I hear it, you're like Wonder Woman or something. Faster than a speeding bullet, able to leap tall buildings in a single bound."

She rolled her eyes and laid down on the towel spread between her and the hotel room's cold, tile floor. "That's Superman, Drew."

"Same thing. You giving up?"

"Why do you keep challenging me? Do you have a death wish or something?"

No, but he did want her to get some sleep. The only two ways he could think of to wear her out were exercise and sex. Since their room was bugged and he sure as hell didn't want to be overheard making love to her, sex was out. "How about pushups, me against you? First one to give out gets laundry duty for a week."

She groaned. "Did Bobby put you up to this? 'Cause if he did, I'm gonna kill him."

He slipped his hands up her feet to her ankles. They were fine-boned and strong, her skin smooth and tempting. "Is that a no? I mean, if you're scared of losing, I'll understand."

"Ok, fine. Let go so I can turn over and play your sadistic little game."

"Baby, you ain't seen nothing yet."

They settled onto the floor beside each other in stiff-armed plank positions, easing down and up in unison, Drew marking off their number. After a while, he fell into an easy, unthinking rhythm, down, up, count, down, up, count, and his mind wandered aimlessly, falling naturally to the woman beside him. Maybe they could watch a movie before they went to bed. Would she let him hold her? Would she ask him to cuddle with her again while she slept? He needed to dig out his sewing kit and reattach the buttons he'd ripped off her pajamas.

God, that had been great. She hadn't complained a bit, either. How'd he get lucky enough to be paired with a woman who didn't mind him ripping off her clothes? Fuck. Couldn't thank Bobby for that. He'd go all protective brother on Drew, and Hiro would have to step in and break up a fight.

Not for the first time. Probably not the last, either.

Drew grinned and ignored the sweat snaking across his skin. He'd come right out and told Bobby he was interested in Jerusha when he'd checked in that afternoon. Bobby hadn't said a word about it. Maybe he figured Jerusha could take care of herself or maybe he didn't give a shit who his sisters dated. As long as it didn't interfere with their work, and it by God wouldn't, what did it matter?

Jerusha grunted and flopped onto the towel on her belly. "Ok, ok, you win. I'll do the blasted laundry."

Drew held his plank and stared at her, astonished. "We're only on eighty-three."

"And you've barely broken a sweat. Meanwhile, I'm getting sore." She shifted onto her side, rotated her right arm back and forth, and grimaced. "Man, I'm out of shape."

Not that he could tell, but if he didn't have to do laundry for a week, who was he to argue? "Turn over on your back."

She narrowed her bright eyes into slits. "Why?"

"I need seventeen more."

"What does that have to do with me lying on my back?"

"Just do it."

She eased slowly onto her back and crossed her hands together over her stomach. "Ok, I'm here."

"Ankles apart."

"This is getting weird, Drew."

"Why? I need an incentive, and you under me sounds like a pretty good motivator."

She plopped her heels onto the floor, a foot apart. "You're such a man."

"It's my best quality." He crab-walked the short distance between them and braced himself above her, hands on the floor beside her shoulders, feet together somewhere south of hers. He dipped down, kissed her throat, and pushed up. "Eighty-four."

"Seriously?"

"Oh, yeah." Dip down, lick her pulse, push up. "Eighty-five."

She shifted on the floor and a slow smile spread across her face. "This has possibilities."

"Mm-hmm." Dip down, nip the skin along her shoulder, push up. "Eighty-six."

"Maybe you could take your shirt off."

"Can't. Have to start all over again." A sweet kiss to her mouth. "Eighty-seven."

Her fingers delved under his shirt and caressed his bare skin above the waistband of his shorts. "How about if I take my top off?"

"Yeah?" He paused above her, considered it, shook his head. "Then I'd be honor-bound to take advantage and we're in a no-sex zone."

"Don't be a hard ass."

"Better me than you." Down, blow softly into her ear, up. "Eighty-eight."

"You're deliberately arousing me."

"No, baby. Wouldn't do that to you." A longer kiss, muscles burning as he held himself above her, their bodies barely touching. "Eighty-nine."

Her fingers dug into his skin. "No, I'm pretty sure that was a hundred."

He laughed, nuzzled her throat. "Ninety."

"You're a friggin' machine, Drew."

"I'm a soldier, Jaybird, used to training hard and long every single day." He peered down at her, meeting her bright-blue gaze. "You want, I'll stop."

She blinked innocently up at him. "But then I'd miss the view. You wouldn't want to deprive me of a great view, would you?"

"Sure would be a shame." And he liked the view he had of her, the feel of her under him, her nails scratching into him. He lowered himself onto her and back up again. "Ninety-one."

"Wait. You didn't do anything."

"I got to feel you. Close your eyes." Her eyelids fluttered shut, and he pressed small kisses to both, then sucked her lower lip into his mouth. "Better?"

"Mmm. You didn't count, though."

"It was ninety-two." Another kiss. "Ninety-three."

"This is really kinda sweet."

"If you say so." Blow softly into her other ear. "Ninety-four."

"Can it be a hundred now?"

"Nope." Suckle the side of her neck, absorb the salty-sweet taste of her skin on his tongue. "Ninety-five."

She gripped the front of his t-shirt and yanked gently. "You're such a tease."

Maybe, but it sure was fun. He nibbled along her jaw. "Ninety-six."

"You have to be getting tired."

Fuck, yeah. His arms were shaky and his abs ached, and he was pretty sure he was gonna fall on her as soon as he hit a hundred, but he didn't want to stop. They'd rushed into everything so fast, he'd barely had a chance to savor her. Was it so wrong of him to want that now?

He finished his last four pushups and eased into the cradle of her body, hips aligned with hers, his forearms braced on the floor beside her head. "Thanks."

"Hey, I got as much out of it as you did." She lifted her knees, ran one leg down his. "We're both covered in sweat. Shower with me?"

"You're sexy as hell, Jaybird, but I ain't ready to squeeze back into that shower stall with you again." They'd barely fit the first time, and fuck if he didn't want to spend a little time with her there, maybe have enough room to kneel in front of her and please her with his mouth or lift her up against the wall and push himself into her, pleasing them both.

"I'll check that the next time I book a hotel for us, see if I can get a bigger bathroom or something."

He drew back and met her gaze. That had sounded an awful lot like she wanted him to hang around a while, or maybe she figured the job would last a lot longer than they'd thought. A thread of something close to disappointment wound into the ache in his stomach. Yeah, that was probably it. She just expected the job to last longer, was all. He levered himself off of her and held his hands out, then pulled her up beside him. "You go first. I need to stretch out a little."

"You sure?"

"Yeah. Go ahead, baby."

"Ok, thanks."

She pressed a fleeting kiss to his mouth and headed into the bathroom, stripping down as she went. Drew threaded his hands together behind his head and watched her, soaking in every detail of her body, the hollow of her spine, the curve of her hip, the contrast of her black braid against her delicious skin. A fucking work of art.

The heat sliding through his blood morphed into a curious tug on his heart. He shook his head and settled into a loose series of gentle stretches, his mind crowded with thoughts of her.

JERUSHA SNUGGLED under the covers with her laptop and opened her research files, one eye on Drew as he wandered around their hotel room. He'd been restless since he'd gotten out of the shower. She nibbled on one corner of her mouth and flipped through open tabs in her notebook software. The bout of exercise he'd coaxed her into had done wonders for her temper and stiff muscles, working out kinks she hadn't even been aware of. Shouldn't it have done the same for him?

He stuffed his dirty clothes into a mesh laundry bag, then shoved hers in on top of his.

"Shouldn't I be doing that?" she asked.

He shrugged and dropped the bag onto the floor beside her suitcase. "Just getting it ready."

"Can I help?"

"I got it, Jaybird."

His voice was muted and slightly gruff, not even close to the snark she was used to getting from him. She sighed and reviewed her notes on the new underground city, trying to fix the details into her mind. One of the largest cities found to date, dozens of tombs discovered, a steady fifty-five degree interior.

Drew opened his suitcase and sorted through his clean clothes, and Jerusha's focus on her work waned. Maybe he needed more to do at night. They were pretty busy during the day, but after supper, there wasn't a lot needing his attention.

One corner of her mouth turned down. When they'd first arrived in Turkey, he'd seemed to enjoy helping her with the research, sitting right beside her every night, wallowing all over her to the point of...

Her thoughts ground to a halt and her heart nosedived into her stomach. She'd needled him about wallowing on her that night he'd walked out on her, and now, he hardly touched her unless she asked. Was that why he kept his distance? Had she touched a nerve, one he didn't want to admit to?

She exed out of the notebook program, closed her laptop, and set it on the mattress beside her. "I wouldn't mind that rubdown."

He pulled on a t-shirt over his underwear and closed his suitcase. "Sure. Let me get some lotion."

"No, don't. Here." She patted the bed beside her. "Let's cuddle while we're at it."

His dark blond eyebrows slipped a fraction lower and his mouth snapped shut. She handed him her laptop and scooted into the middle of the bed. He put her computer away, double-checked the locks on their room's doors, and cut off every light except the lamp beside her side of the bed. He moved his lamp to the far corner of the room, then climbed into bed and settled himself a foot away from her.

She eased closer and skimmed the pads of her fingertips over the stubble covering his jaw, down his throat, across the firm curves of his mouth. "How're your arms?"

"Dandy."

"Not too tired?"

Heat sparked in his eyes. "Not for whatever you've got in mind."

"Who says I've got something in mind?"

"The way you're touching me."

"I like touching you." She liked it so much, it was hard to stop once she started. "Are you growing a beard?"

"Naw, just being lazy." His hand cupped her hip, heavy and

warm. "Used to keep one when I was in Spec Ops. Hides the line of your jaw, makes it easy to change your appearance if shit goes belly up."

"So you kept a razor handy?"

His mouth twitched into a quick grin. "Only if I had to."

She rubbed her fingertips into the prickly hair. "If I asked you to grow a beard so I could see what you'd look like, would you?"

"I'd think awful hard about it."

"I'll grow one for you."

He threw his head back and laughed hard, and she melted into giggles.

"Come on, Drew. Tell me you wouldn't pay to see that."

"God, Jaybird. You're something." He curved his hand around her lower back and pulled her close. "I thought you wanted me to give you a massage."

"I like what we're doing," she said mildly. "Besides, you need one as much as I do."

"I'm good, baby, but thanks."

"So you don't want my hands on you."

"Didn't say that."

He kissed her temple, soft and tender, so much like the sweet caresses he'd given her while he finished his pushups, her heart fluttered in her chest. She'd teased him about arousing her, but the truth was, his touch hadn't been arousing as much as it had been endearing. It had been a long, long time since a man had touched her like that, as if she were more than a bedmate, as if she might hold a piece of him he'd never easily give.

Her fingers strayed to his mouth again, landing on the scar at the corner of his upper lip. It was small, no longer than a quarter inch, and narrow, and her curiosity about it got the better of her. "How'd you get this?"

He folded his arm up under his head and nestled close to her, and when he spoke, his voice dropped to a near whisper. "Street ball. My brother was pitching. Man, he had a fastball like you wouldn't believe. Shot it straight at you so fast, it was scary, but his control was for shit. One day, I didn't duck fast enough, and bam."

She winced. "That had to hurt."

"Like a mother. I was lucky I didn't lose any teeth."

"Bet you learned to duck, though."

"You bet your sweet ass I did."

Rich humor underscored his words. She wound it around herself, tucking it into her heart, and tried to imagine Drew as a scrawny kid playing ball with his brother on the streets of Boston. "Was he older or younger?"

"Older, by three years."

"You hung out a lot?"

"Oh, yeah. He was the best big brother a kid could have. Never complained when Ma made him watch us."

"Us?"

"Me and my kid sister, Trish."

"Right, sorry. He never complained?"

"Not once, but that was Sean. He was a good guy, set on getting scholarships and going to college. Getting us out of Southie, he said."

"But he died instead."

"Yeah. Drive-by shooting a coupla years later, about three months before he was supposed to graduate from high school. We were outside playing ball." He snorted out a soft laugh. "Not much else to do back then."

She knitted her fingers into his t-shirt above his heart. "You were with him?"

"I was with him. God above, I wish I hadn't been." Drew's hand tightened on her skin and his muscles tensed under her hand. "He shoved me onto the sidewalk, took a bullet for me. Fucking bled out right there in front of me, and not a damn thing I could do."

She sucked in a breath. Sweet Mother. What a horrible thing for a young boy to watch. "It wasn't your fault, Drew. You can't believe it was."

"Took a long time for me to realize it, Jaybird. Ma never forgave me, though. Sean was her favorite, her golden boy. Everybody loved him."

Including Drew. His heart still ached for his big brother and the lives they could've lived. She could feel it in his touch, hear it in the hoarse whisper of his voice against her ear.

"After that, the family kinda fell apart. Dad got caught taking bribes. He was a cop. Stupid." Drew's breath sighed across her skin. "He committed suicide the day they took his badge. Trish fell in with the wrong crowd and got messed up in drugs, and Ma was never the same."

"Was that when you went into the Army?"

His sharp laugh held not a trace of humor. "Nope. I went kinda crazy. Got caught trying to jack a federal judge's car."

"Drew."

"I know, Jaybird. Didn't say my dad was the only knucklehead in the family, did I?" He rolled one shoulder and shifted against her. "Anyhow, judge was pissed. Had the cops haul me into his office and gave me the ass chewing of my life. I was sixteen, hot-headed, full of shit, you wanna know the truth, and he whittled all that away, left me not a goddamn piece of myself. And then he gave me a choice. Finish school and enlist, or spend five years doing hard time in juvie."

"You opted for school."

"I wasn't completely stupid, even back then. Not much better now." He wedged a muscled thigh between hers and pulled her leg over his. "Though I must be kinda dense to dump all this on you."

She rubbed her thigh over his. He felt so good under her, his muscles tight, the hair scattered there crisp. Her skin tingled, heating slowly, and a delicious weight settled low in her gut, echoing up, filling her. "I wanted to know. You don't say much about yourself."

"Not much to tell. You, though. I bet you got a ton of

stories, old maid."

She slid her hand under his shirt and across the hard ridges of his abs. "You must've forgotten what happened the last time you called me an old maid."

"Hell, no, Jaybird. I was kinda hoping you'd do it again."

She snickered and tucked her head under his chin, content to just be with him for a while. "You said no sex."

"Didn't I just tell you I'm not the brightest bulb in the socket?"

"I missed that part."

And wouldn't have given it a second thought, anyway. Drew might not be an intellectual, but he was far from dumb. He never would've made it into Special Forces if he were.

"So, old maid. You were born before the Civil War."

"Careful, Drew. Your Yankee's showing."

He propped up on an elbow, his voice low and even. "Seriously, Jaybird. You gotta know I love all things war-related."

"You're such a man."

"I thought we agreed that was my best quality."

Since she liked all his manly parts and ways very much, she couldn't disagree. "I guess you want a first-hand perspective."

"Wouldn't mind it. What was it like?"

"I never saw any of the fighting. Too young. My dad, though, he volunteered when I was, oh, about ten, I think."

"For the South?"

"For the Confederacy. It was our home, Drew," she said gently. "Did you expect us not to defend it?"

"I wasn't criticizing, baby, just curious. What was your dad like?"

"The best man I ever knew, strong and brave and..." The sorrow of losing him welled up, gathering in her throat, as strong as it had been a century and a half ago, on the day her mother received the letter informing them of his death. Jerusha swallowed past it and squeezed her eyes closed, holding her tears at bay. "I loved him so much."

Drew smoothed his hand up and down her back. "Shh, baby. Don't cry."

"Sorry."

"Don't be. I miss my dad, too. He was a crook and a thief, but he was still my dad."

"I know, Drew. I'm sorry."

"Stop with the apologies. Tell me about your dad. He was Cherokee?"

"Nearly full-blooded. Mom was in Tellowee teaching at one of the schools there. Moira was there, too, working on the Archives."

"The Irish hellcat," he muttered.

She laughed. What a way to put it. "I don't know how they met. Mom never told me, but she went into her needing, and he was such a good man, so kind, so thoughtful."

"You loved him."

"More than anything. We spent a lot of time together when I was little, then war broke out and things got kinda tough and he decided to enlist. Broke my grandmother's heart right in two. They'd already been through so much, having to hide when he was a little boy to keep from being marched into Indian Territory, struggling to live while their land was taken and their people scattered."

He raked his fingers gently through her hair, and somehow, his touch soothed some of her sorrow away. She buried her face in his throat, drawing on the warmth and strength and goodness radiating out of him. "The day he left, he told me he'd always live in my heart. I think he knew he'd never come back and he wanted me to know how much he loved me. I watched him walk away with a group of local men headed for war and I never saw him again."

"I wish things had been different."

"At least I had him for a while. A lot of Daughters never know their fathers. Some never even know their father's name, but I knew mine and I'll never forget him, not a single thing about him."

Silence descended around them, a comfortable blanket cocooning their shared secrets. Drew reached across her and flipped off the light, and the room plunged into darkness. They wrapped themselves around each other under the covers, two hearts longing for the families they'd once had, and fell quietly into dreams.

Seven

O N SUNDAY, Drew slipped away from Jerusha and wound through Göreme on foot. He was getting fucking tired of having to watch every word when he and Jerusha were in their hotel room, and he was damn sure ready to have sex with her. No more teasing, no more halfway. He wanted to bury himself in her, watch her bright eyes go wild as he pleased her, and feel her come as she tumbled over the edge with him. Couldn't do that with somebody listening in. Maybe it made him a selfish bastard, but he wasn't sharing her with some stranger on the other end of a bug. She was too good for that, too special.

He stopped in front of a glass-plated storefront displaying a wide range of shoes and casually examined his surroundings. A man half a block down stopped and leaned just as casually against the side of a rock-faced building. Drew snorted and continued down the street. Fucking tail. When was Alexiou going to learn?

Half a mile later, Drew jogged across the road at an intersection and backtracked to the Internet café he and Jerusha had discovered a coupla days ago. He bought a packaged snack, sat down at one of the computers, and logged into his e-mail. His inbox was full of unread messages, mostly junk, newsletters, and notices of replies to forums he kept an eye on. He went through them one by one, shifting some into spam, deleting stuff he didn't need.

His tail slipped inside five minutes in, bought a drink, and settled down at a table on the other side of the room.

Drew shook his head. Subtle these guys were not, and that worried him. After talking with Jerry the other day, his gut kept pinging an alert. Somebody else was watching them, had to be. Not knowing who ate at Drew, and by God, it was time he did something about it.

He stretched his legs out in front of him, knees widespread, and read forum posts. A guy he'd been debating immigration policy with on a gun forum had posted a long-winded diatribe about illegals in the States. Drew tapped out a reply debunking the guy's sadly uninformed opinion, clicked through into another board, and jumped into a heated debate on whether or not iced tea should be pre-sweetened.

That was a no-brainer. Since he'd started living in the South, Drew had developed a taste for tea sweetened when it was piping hot, chilled, and served over chunks of ice with a slice of lemon. Everything else was just a poor substitute. The uncultured slobs that had to sweeten their tea when the water was too cold to dissolve the sugar didn't know how bad they had it. Now that he'd gotten used to the syrupy stuff, he hated traveling outside the South. Nobody else knew how to make iced tea.

When his session was almost up, he yawned and stretched and shut the computer down per the instructions printed in Turkish on a sheet of paper pinned to the wall. He threw his trash away and went into the bathroom. Two stalls on the left, a row of urinals on the right. He pushed the doors open, making sure he was alone, then entered the second stall and locked the door. He leaned down and slid his fingers around the cold bottom of the porcelain tank, and grinned. There was the key, right where it was supposed to be. Now all he had to do was lose his tail.

He managed to shake the man half an hour later. Soon as he did, he hopped a bus headed toward Nevşehir, changed out buses at the first stop, and eventually made it to the Kapadokya

International Airport. It wasn't as crowded as he'd hoped, but anything was better than an empty building. He found an out of the way spot and propped against the wall, and covertly searched the crowds for suspicious activity. When he was sure nobody was watching, he located the maintenance closet, unlocked it with the key left for him in Göreme, and slipped inside, then shut the door firmly behind himself.

The closet was small and packed from top to bottom with haphazardly arranged cleaning supplies. Rows of metal shelving ran around the right and far walls of the room. Brooms, mops and extra mop heads, thick coils of rope, and a length of sloppily wound security tape hung from brackets screwed into the wall on his left. A mop bucket, a waxing machine, and a bulky, outdated vacuum cleaner took up most of the remaining floor space.

The space reeked of ammonia and mildew. Drew covered his nose with his arm and wedged his way through the appliances to the far corner. He crouched and dug under the shelving there, and pulled out a small, black backpack, automatically judging its weight against his supply request.

A man could never be too careful.

He unzipped the backpack and riffled through the contents. A CZ85 pistol, a belt holster, an extra magazine pre-loaded with fifteen rounds of 9mm ammunition, a throwaway cell phone, and, most importantly, a short-range jamming device.

Excellent.

God bless the contacts he'd made during his stint in Spec Ops. When he got home, he'd be sure to thank Bobby for helping set the drop point up, though he'd be careful not to bring up anything having to do with their time in Istanbul, especially around Jerusha. After that one brief conversation, she hadn't pressed him to talk about his time in the Army. It'd come up again, probably sooner rather than later. A woman like that didn't give up her curiosity. She bided her time and struck when a man was least expecting the question, and Drew had no intention of answering her. Some history needed to be left in the past, the off-duty mischief he'd gotten into as a soldier included.

He palmed the CZ85 first. The grip was a nice fit in his hand and just the right weight. He dropped the magazine and checked the rounds, then secured it in the holster he tucked in the waistband of his jeans, snug against his back.

The jammer went in one pocket of his jeans, the cell phone in the other, and the extra magazine in one coat pocket. He left the cash he'd promised as payment in the backpack, then shoved it back into the corner where he'd found it. He made sure everything was exactly the way he'd found it and left as quietly as he'd entered. The key, he kept. Having a nearby drop point might come in handy. Hell, the way things were going, it'd probably be a necessity.

He took the bus back to Göreme in the roundabout way he'd left, hopped off near the Internet café, and walked back to the hotel, half of his mind on the tail he was sure to pick up, the other half meandering through the past few days with Jerusha.

None of the underground cities were open to tourists on the weekend, so they'd done more research, narrowing down their list a little, and spent a lot of time playing cards or exercising or talking about whatever came to mind. It had been fun in a low-key kinda way, and eye-opening, too. She was easy to be with, easy to hold on to at night when the lights were out, easy to care about.

Maybe too easy. He opened the door at the hotel's main entrance and took the stairs to their floor two at a time. If he wasn't careful, he'd fall for her, and that way lay certain heartbreak. Jerusha was immortal, her trust not easily given, and her heart? His shoulders tensed as he jogged up the stairs and into the hallway leading to their room. According to every source he'd been able to dig up, Daughters rarely loved the men in their lives. They used them when they were convenient, ignored them when they weren't, and that was most of the time.

He wasn't fool enough to believe he'd ever be anything special to Jerusha, but he wanted her something fierce. Maybe they could settle into the kind of friendship he'd cultivated with the other Daughters he knew, before he'd understood who and what they were. Friendship, Daughters could do. Love? Almost impossible, far as he could tell.

He scowled at the wall marking the far end of the hall. Not that he was thinking about loving Jerusha. He was just trying to protect himself so it wouldn't hurt when she walked away at the end of their mission, was all. A man had a right to do that, didn't he? And Drew was tired of having his heart stomped on by people who were supposed to care about him.

When he entered their room, Jerusha was propped up on the bed dressed in one of his t-shirts, her laptop open on her shapely thighs.

His heart thumped hard once and flipped over. Yeah. He wasn't thinking about love at all.

She glanced up and smiled. "Hey. I was getting worried."

"No worries, Jaybird." He slipped the magazine out of his coat pocket, tucked it into his suitcase, and stripped his jacket off, then emptied the extra gear he'd picked up on top. "Sorry I took so long, though. Had to lose a shadow."

One corner of her mouth turned down. "I knew I should've gone with you."

"I had it covered."

"I wasn't doubting you."

"I know, Jaybird." He sat down on the edge of the bed next to her and flicked a fingertip over the edge of her laptop. "Having fun?"

She grimaced and closed the lid. "Catching up on back issues of archaeology journals."

"And that's fun?"

"It's boring as the straight and narrow." She patted the bed next to her thigh. "Come unbore me."

He scooted forward and placed a hand against the mattress on either side of her hips. "I've got something for you."

"A present?"

"Mm-hmm." His gaze dropped to her mouth, that sweet, snarky mouth, and heat ripped through him with the force of a Cat-3 hurricane. "If you're ready for it."

She leaned forward and slid her cheek along his. "Just tell me what it is."

He buried his face in her throat, sniffed her skin, breathing in the scent of the soap she used. No perfume for his Jaybird. God, he loved that about her, loved knowing when he put his mouth there, it was *her* he tasted, not some factory produced chemical. "Something to give us some privacy every now and again."

She sucked in a breath and cupped a hand over his thigh. "I'm very ready for that."

"You sure? 'Cause I don't wanna push." He slid her laptop off her lap, then pulled her closer. She felt so good in his arms, fit so well. "Having it don't mean we gotta do anything."

"Come on, Drew. I practically attacked you that first time. Do you really think I don't want to have sex with you?"

"I'm just giving you a choice."

"Ok, fine. Don't expect me to reciprocate."

He grinned against her throat. Yeah, that was just like a Daughter. Hadn't he learned that the hard way? Jerusha on top of him, her hips grinding against his, fast and hard, her head thrown back. Desire speared through him and blood rushed into his dick on a burst of heat. God, he wanted her like that again, wild and beautiful, unrestrained. He reined in his imagination, fat lot of good it'd do. He was already hard as a brick, probably would be for a while.

Jerusha stroked her hand up and down his thigh, edging perilously close to his hard-on. "I thought we could pick another restaurant tonight, try something new. There's somebody I want you to meet."

"Your friend?"

"She's a recluse, doesn't go out in public at all if she can help it. You don't mind going with me, do you?"

"Happy to."

"Speaking of happy." Her hand slid across his body and landed on the fly of his jeans, exactly where he wanted her to touch him. "Let me take care of this."

He nuzzled her skin, licked her pulse. "Later," he promised. After supper, he'd pull out his surprise for her, turn it on, then turn her on. God, he couldn't wait to finally bury himself inside her, couldn't wait to feel her slick heat and make her come so hard, she never wanted it to end.

THEY ENDED UP walking to the restaurant and back to the hotel, then drove to Pari's home in Kayseri. Jerusha tapped her fingernails on her thigh. Her mother was going to have a conniption when she saw the receipts for gas Jerusha had tucked into an envelope in her suitcase. It couldn't be helped. They could opt for independence with a car and pay the exorbitant gas prices or they could place themselves at the mercy of Turkey's public transportation system. It wasn't bad, but it would constrain their freedom of movement and possibly hinder their efforts to work as efficiently as possible.

Drew's thumb rapped out an uneven beat on the steering wheel. Every once in a while, light from a passing street lamp or business flashed off the wedding ring he wore on his left ring finger. He only ever took it off to shower and wash his hands. He even wore it to bed. She hadn't asked why, hadn't been able to formulate a polite way to tell him he didn't have to wear it all the time.

She crossed her legs and toyed with the buttons of her jacket. Was pretending to be married going to his head? Was he confusing their cover with the relationship developing between them? Worse, did he even recognize a difference?

What if that's why he wanted to have sex with her? The butterflies flitting through her abdomen flipped over and sank like rocks in her gut. That was probably it. He just wanted to have sex with her to cement their identities or because he was too immersed in his cover, not because he was attracted to her.

"You ok?" he asked.

"Fine."

"You seem kinda restless tonight."

"I have a lot on my mind."

"Restless and evasive." He patted his right thigh. "Put your hand here and I'll rub it, maybe help you relax some."

"I'm relaxed."

He cut a side-eyed glance at her. "Hell, Jaybird, you're about to rocket out of your seat, you're wound so tight."

She clamped her teeth together. He wasn't irritating her on purpose, and damned if she'd snap at him just because she was worried. "When we get to Pari's, don't say anything unless you're addressed directly."

"What does this have to do with you being restless?"

"Nothing. I just forgot to tell you earlier." When her imagination had leapt to the night ahead instead of focusing on the task at hand. "Pari's old-fashioned and a bit orthodox. She may make a play for you. Try not to let it go to your head."

"My ego ain't that big."

She ignored the sly humor in his voice. It wasn't his ego she was worried about. "Keep your right hand on my left shoulder and stay behind me."

"Now, why the hell would I do that? I ain't never let a woman stand in front of me. Not gonna start now just 'cause you're a Daughter. Shit, Jaybird."

"Just remember that I *am* a Daughter while we're here." She relented and laid her hand on his thigh, and circled her palm over his hard muscles. "It won't be for long. I just need a little help and Pari is nearby."

"You coulda asked me," he groused. "We're partners. You're supposed to tell me stuff so I can help you."

"Like you told me what you were up to this afternoon before you left?"

He tugged his earlobe and a small smile curved his mouth. "If I said you had a good point, would you promise not to skewer me for holding back on you?"

"Drew, sweetie, I'm a woman. I fully intend to skewer you with that the next time I need leverage."

"That's what I like about you, Jaybird. No games, no fuss, just you, undiluted." His eyes cut toward her again. "How do you feel about those clothes?"

"Ah." She glanced down, remembered her jacket was buttoned over the navy blue turtleneck and jeans she wore. "They're clothes, why?"

"I was thinking about ripping them off of you later."

The skin between her thighs tingled and tightened, and her breath whooshed out. Drew so anxious to have her he couldn't wait for her to undress? When was the last time a man had directed that kind of urgent need toward her? Her eyes slid shut. That would be never. Would he really carry his cover that far? Could she honestly believe he wanted her? She could trust him to be straight with her, couldn't she?

She cleared her throat and aimed for casual. "I might let you."

"Think about it real hard, Jaybird. I got all kinds of plans for you. That's just one of 'em."

His voice was soft and throaty, gritty. It scraped over her senses, teasing her with the heavy promise in his words. She clutched his thigh and tried not to dwell on it. Her mind looped out of control anyway, spinning toward the night ahead, consuming every ounce of her reason and then some.

Half an hour later, Drew parked their rental on the sidewalk outside a decrepit apartment building wedged into a disreputable neighborhood along a road so narrow, two cars would have trouble squeezing by one another coming and going. Jerusha got out, tucked her coat around her torso, and hunched her shoulders toward her ears in a futile attempt to protect them from the biting cold. The other car door slammed shut and Drew's footsteps rang softly in the eerie quiet surrounding them. Even in a neighborhood like this, there should be noise. Families eating supper, arguments brewing, radios blaring, something, but it was so still, she could hear her heart thumping inside her chest.

Drew draped an arm around her shoulders and leaned close. "I don't like it."

"Yeah, I know. Sorry. Pari's really old and a little paranoid. Probably nothing to worry about outside that."

He grunted. "If you say so."

"I do. Come on."

She threaded her fingers through his and led him into the building toward the apartment Pari had agreed on as a meeting point. At one time, the building must've been beautiful. Three small bulbs were lit in the glass and metal chandelier dangling from the foyer's ceiling high overhead. Hints of colorful murals peeked through a patina of dirt, barely visible on the cracked plaster walls in the near darkness of the building's interior. The floor was filthy, but underneath the grime, Jerusha could just make out a mosaic pieced together with tiny, painstakingly placed tiles. A wrought iron railing protected the open side of the narrow stairs leading to the upper floors, many of its spokes missing.

They walked in silence up the stairs, picking their way around cracks in the wooden runners. A woman dressed in a loose, linen tunic over black pants was waiting for them on the second floor, her back to the hallway wall. Her dark, kohl-lined eyes flicked from Jerusha to Drew and back again, and Jerusha's instincts jangled. A Daughter, one she didn't know, likely one of Pari's offspring. Jerusha nodded respectfully and continued up the stairs.

Two Daughters were waiting in the third floor hallway, both wearing clothing similar to the Daughter on the floor below. A well-built young man dressed only in a pair of jeans sat on the floor between them, his eyes lowered, one hand wrapped around one of the Daughter's calves.

Here, the décor was normal, modern, clean, and the air was

warm. A thin carpet with an intricate diamond and flower pattern protected the hallway's floor. The walls were solid white, freshly painted, and the arched doors stained nearly black. Fluted glass sconces were set into the walls at regular intervals between the doors, throwing a bright, almost cheerful light across the space.

The unattached Daughter stepped forward and bowed, and her long, dark brown braid swept forward over her shoulder. "Were you followed?"

"No," Jerusha said. "But we're being watched. We don't have much time before our tails grow suspicious and try to find us."

"Of course. Follow me."

The Daughter pivoted on the ball of one bare foot and strode down the hallway, pausing in front of a door halfway down. She knocked, murmured through the crack to whoever was on the other side, then stepped back. "She'll see you now."

Jerusha ducked her head in a polite bow. "Thank you. We won't be long."

The door swung open on a fine-boned woman an inch taller than Jerusha. Wide-set, dark brown eyes peered impassively out of an oval face surrounded by soft, sable curls. Pari's face had always reminded Jerusha of a cameo, serene and classically beautiful, though she wouldn't dare tell Pari that. It never hurt to veer on the side of caution with older Daughters, and there was no telling how Pari might take what Jerusha viewed as a compliment.

She stepped forward, gripped Pari's elbows, and touched her forehead to her friend's. "It's so good to see you, Pari."

Pari cupped Jerusha's elbows. "And you, kaetyrm. You've brought a mate."

Jerusha released Pari and stepped to the side. "This is Drew. He's under my protection."

Pari fixed her expressionless eyes on him. "His features are a bit too rugged, though he's quite lovely otherwise. May I?"

Jerusha stifled a sigh. She'd known Pari was going to ask,

97

hadn't she? And she'd warned Drew. Sort of. "Of course."

Drew shifted into a wide-legged stance with his arms loose at his sides. Pari unceremoniously unzipped his jacket and untucked his shirt, pulling it high. Her fingers skimmed over the bare, sculpted muscles of Drew's abs. "Well-formed. Good in bed?"

Drew's eyebrows shot up. Jerusha met his curious gaze and shook her head slightly. "He is."

"Mmm." Pari's hand slid down and cupped Drew's penis through his jeans. "Half-erect, large enough to please a woman. Has he taken your mark?"

"Not yet."

Pari glanced over her shoulder. "I'm between men at the moment. Perhaps we could negotiate a trade, him for the items you requested."

"He's not worth that much." Drew's eyes narrowed on her, and she smiled pleasantly. No matter what he thought, his ego needed nipping. Not too much, though. She liked his swagger, liked his self-assured confidence, liked the hint of arrogance he slipped into every once in a while. He didn't need to know that, though, did he? "Maybe when I'm finished with him."

Pari's wide, full mouth tilted into a half-smile. "When you've finished with him, he'll be a husk."

"True."

Drew sucked in a strangled breath.

"Tuck in your shirt, sweetie." Jerusha gently tugged Pari away from Drew and temptation. "I don't mean to be rude, Pari, but we're on a tight schedule."

"So I gathered. The Shadow, here?"

"As if you didn't know."

"I'll never tell." Pari glanced over Jerusha's shoulder at Drew and sighed. "Are you certain you don't wish to trade him?"

"Positive."

"Very well. Wait here."

Pari swept off in a graceful swish of linen. As soon as she

was out of sight, a warm length pressed itself against Jerusha's back. A large hand cupped her stomach and pulled her firmly against that length.

"Drew," she murmured. "Be good a little longer."

A rumble of what might've been consent hummed out of his throat. His other hand slid down her arm, and he entwined his fingers with hers. "You sure you want me to be good?"

No, she absolutely wasn't. In fact, she was counting on him being very naughty as soon as they got back to the hotel.

Pari re-entered the room carrying a military green duffel. "Double this for him."

"Nice try." Jerusha accepted the duffel and peeked into it. Two handguns, ammunition, a small case of tracking chips with a receiver, a netbook encased in a hard shell, two lengths of black rope, and climbing gear. Exactly what she'd asked for. "Mom should've already wired the money to you."

"She has." Pari's gaze drifted over Jerusha's shoulder. "Perhaps just a taste."

"Forget it," Jerusha said flatly. With Pari, there was never just one taste. More like a night's worth, two if she hadn't been with a man in a while. "Thanks for getting this together for me."

"Of course. It was a pleasure seeing you again."

"Maybe next time we can stay longer."

"Perhaps by then you'll be finished with this delightful morsel."

Not likely. On the other hand, he might be finished with her.

Jerusha shook the thought off and air-kissed Pari's cheeks. She led Drew through the building past Pari's kin and into the chill night air, and a few minutes later, he eased the car away from the sidewalk into the narrow street.

Eight

B Y THE TIME they made it back to the hotel, Jerusha's nerves were raw and twitchy. Drew hadn't said a word about what had happened at Pari's, not one word asking what was going on or why Jerusha had let the other Daughter touch him. He'd held her hand against his thigh and chatted with her, the small talk she'd come to expect from him. Nothing important, just little things. The latest college basketball standings, an article he'd read concerning tests of a new handgun. Did she want to try the Italian restaurant near the hotel?

He unlocked the hotel door for her, locked it behind them, and pulled her against him, her back to his chest. "I need a shower. Come talk to me?"

"Um."

Wait, no. That wasn't the plan. They were supposed to come back here, turn the jammer on, and have sex. He'd never said anything about a shower. A tiny twinge of disappointment pricked her, deflating the anticipation underlying her tense nerves. That's why he hadn't said anything about their time at Pari's. He'd changed his mind, and wasn't that just like a man?

She swallowed past the lump in her throat and rubbed her palms down her thighs. "Maybe I'll stay out here."

"No." He slid his jacket off and draped it over his suitcase, then sat down on the edge of the bed and unlaced his boots.

"Take off your jacket."

"Drew, really."

He stood abruptly, eyebrows lowered, cognac eyes hot, and stalked toward her. "Take off your jacket," he said, enunciating the words carefully, "or I'll take it off. You know how I wanna take it off, Jaybird?"

"Ah."

"Think hard, baby. Think about what I'm gonna do."

His soft words struck a chord, rousing memory, and her eyes widened. "Oh. Ok. I'll, um. I'll take it off."

She worked the buttons of her jacket free with trembling fingers while Drew stripped off his long-sleeved t-shirt and slid his belt out of his pants. He dropped both on the bed, then closed the distance between them and brushed her fingers aside.

"Nervous?" he asked.

She shook her head, and he grinned.

"Liar," he said softly.

She couldn't argue, not when he was right. She was nervous and she'd lied about it. How could she tell him that, though? She was a Daughter of the People, an immortal warrior hardened against the needs of the heart and the emotions ensnaring mortal women in their insidious claws. Her first time with a new man shouldn't spook her at all, so how could she be so rattled now that she couldn't even undress herself?

His fingers twisted the remaining buttons of her jacket free. She slipped it off, laid it across a chaise, and followed him into the bathroom, one hand over the nerves dancing in her stomach. It was just Drew, adorable, affable, corny Drew. Nothing to be nervous about.

He flipped the shower on full blast, his back to her, his blond head bowed. "You wanna stop, now's the time to tell me."

"I thought you'd changed your mind."

He whirled around, wrapped his hands around her upper arms, and yanked her against his chest. "I'm so fucking hot for you, I can't wait. How's that for changing my mind?"

His mouth came down on hers, fierce and demanding, and he devoured her, as if his hunger for her was so great, he'd starve if he didn't touch her right then. She clutched the smooth skin of his shoulders and gave him what he wanted, gave him everything as desire rose so swiftly in her, her blood boiled. Sweet Mother, this is what she'd wanted, Drew needing her so much, he lost control. She'd wanted to feel, wanted so desperately to ache under his touch, and he made her.

He released her arms and wound her braid around one hand, tugging gently. Her nipples pebbled into tight, sensitive buds under her bra, and she moaned into his mouth.

He broke their kiss and his breath panted in harsh puffs across her mouth. "That's it, baby. That's what I wanna hear."

"Drew, please." She dug her fingernails into his skin and rubbed her hips against him. "Don't stop."

He laughed, low and husky, and walked her slowly backward. "We're just getting started, Jaybird."

Her ass hit the counter, and his left hand fumbled with her jeans, popping open the fastening, shoving them down. His fingers slid into the space between her thighs, unerringly zeroing in on her clit. "Is this what you want, baby? Is this what gets you hot?"

His fingers flicked across the nub of her sex, fast and light, and wet heat flooded into her pussy. She bit her lip and her breaths panted out of her, and she *wanted*. Skin on skin, Drew buried in her so deep, they were one, inseparable, unidentifiable on their own. She cupped the back of his head and urged him into another kiss, deeper, harder, her tongue sliding against his, her teeth nipping his lips, and his fingers slid across her clit and into her pussy, thick and beautiful and deliciously rough.

His hand tightened on her hair. "You're gonna feel so good wrapped around me. I'm gonna make you feel so good."

She already did. Her skin was alive, so sensitive she could feel every thread in her clothes, every molecule of air gliding across her bare thighs, every inch of his fingers twisting inside her. She was full of him and a smoldering, molten heat, ravaged by a need so strong, she could barely breathe around it. If he were inside her, he'd feel that goodness, too. He'd share it with her, echo it back to her, and she would embrace it gladly.

His fingers slipped out of her and he turned her around, pushing her chest toward the countertop. His hand came down hard on her ass, not quite slapping her skin, and the pleasure-pain tingled through her, edging her higher. The zipper of his jeans rasped down, cloth rustled, and then the broad head of his erection nudged at her pussy.

"Look at me," he said, and she lifted her eyes and met his gaze reflected in the mirror. His features were taught, his cognac eyes deliciously savage, and a light sheen of sweat shimmered along his skin. "Brace yourself."

His fingers dug into her skin and his hips surged forward, pushing his erection into her, filling her so tightly, she had no room for anything else. She gasped and closed her eyes, and he pulled out a fraction.

"Sorry, baby," he murmured. "I'll go slower."

She shook her head and tilted her hips back, begging him to take her. She didn't want it slow and easy, not this first time. No, this time, she wanted all of him all at once, if that's the way he needed to give himself.

He rocked into her, his thrusts firm and wonderful. A final push, and he was fully seated, so deep inside her, so good. He rocked again, and she braced a hand on the mirror, holding her body in place for him.

His fingers skidded across her skin and landed on her clit, and his touch wasn't fast and light anymore, it was hard and rough. He pinched and tugged, rocketing her toward oblivion, and when he spoke, his voice was halfway to a growl. "Tell me you're close."

"I am, Drew," she whispered. "Please."

"That's it, baby. Beg me." His hand slipped away from her pussy and gripped the edge of the counter. "Beg me to make you come."

He pushed into her, pumping his hips against hers at a brutal pace, quick and short and hard. The edge of the counter was cold against her thighs, his skin warm behind her as his hips slapped against her ass, and his fingers bruising where he held her hip.

She opened her eyes and watched him as he shoved her toward the edge of passion. His eyes met hers, and in them was a reflection of her own desperate need, of the raging inferno consuming her from the inside out, licking along her skin, tightening her body around him. He leaned over her and quickened his pace, and the utter wanton beauty of him was her undoing. She shattered around him, bursting into a million flickering flames. He gasped her name and came, his release so perfectly hard, it reverberated through her, shooting her into another grinding orgasm.

He collapsed on top of her, pinning her to the counter, and his breaths puffed across her neck. "God, Jaybird."

She huffed out a shaky laugh. "I don't think God had anything to do with that."

"Pretty sure we touched Heaven." He kissed her skin, flicked the tip of his tongue along her earlobe. "It got a little outta hand."

"I liked it."

"Yeah?"

"Oh, yeah." She rested her forehead on her arm and breathed evenly in a futile attempt to control her galloping heart. It was pounding against her sternum so hard, she was sure Drew could feel it. "Why did we wait again?"

"Jammer. Meant to use it tonight, too. Would've if you hadn't threatened to share me."

"What?" She twisted around and met his gaze, so close to hers. "Not one time did I say I was willing to share you."

A slow grin spread across his face. "Uh-huh. So that whole thing about using me up and passing me on to the next Daughter wasn't about sharing me."

Her eyebrows snapped down and she wiggled, trying to escape his embrace. "Not even close."

His eyes slid shut on a low moan. "Oh, yeah. Do that some more."

"I can't believe you thought—"

"Believe it, baby. Thinking about you using me like that got me hot as hell." He kissed her hard and eased out of her. "We're gonna do this again, soon as you're willing."

She sagged against the counter, somehow empty and lost without him inside her. No, that wasn't right. A Daughter was never lost without a man. Jerusha had never needed one outside of family and didn't intend to start now.

Drew's hands cupped her ass and rubbed into her muscles. "That's the finest ass this side of the Mediterranean."

"You said my ass was scrawny."

"I was getting your goat, Jaybird. Mmm, yeah. Let me get rid of this condom and we'll go again."

"You used a condom? I thought you were Catholic."

"Well, yeah, but I ain't stupid."

She sighed into her arms. "Daughter sexuality lesson one. Unless we're in our needing, we can't get pregnant. Lesson two. We're immune to most mortal diseases and we don't carry them, either. Lesson three—"

"Just how many of these lessons are there?"

She ignored the teasing humor in his voice. "We like having sex without barriers."

"Now, that sounds like fun. Gimme a minute and we can go barrierless."

She laughed and pushed up off the counter. "I was hoping you'd say that."

He touched his mouth to hers, sweet and soft, the kiss of a lover entangled from heart to mind and back again, and they undressed each other in the spacious bathroom, knocking down the barriers between them one by one.

DREW TOOK ONE for the team and wedged himself into the tiny shower stall with Jerusha. Fuck all, a man was entitled to savor the first time he had sex with a woman, especially one like her. She'd been so hot, so responsive, it was all he could do to hold back and give her time to recover when what he really wanted to do was be in her again.

He scrubbed a soapy washcloth over her back and frowned. He'd been kinda rough on her, maybe too rough, but she hadn't complained. Any other woman would've, and that's what he loved about his Jaybird. Where other women would squawk about his size and his tendency to go with his gut instinct no matter where it led, she played along, welcoming him, all of him, inside and out.

He'd hurt her, though, and he hadn't meant to, so next time would be gentle, slow, easy. Next time would be about her.

They dried off and tumbled into bed together, curling around each other in the middle of the hotel bed. She slid her fingertips through the hair on his chest and hooked her leg over his hip, drawing him close. "You said you had a surprise for me."

"Mm-hmm."

"You didn't bring it out."

"Waiting for you to recover." He nuzzled her temple, breathing in the crisp, clean scent of her shampoo. "I was too rough before."

She propped herself up on one elbow and peered down at him in the darkened room. "Drew, sweetie, let's be honest here. I like rough and hot and quick. Don't get me wrong, I like slow and easy, too, but with you, rough is good. Great, even. We can do rough anytime you want."

He rolled onto his back, taking her with him. Her weight felt good on top of him, comforting and warm. He tucked a stray strand of hair behind her ear and lingered there, memorizing the swirls and folds and every shiver racing through her because of his touch. "Some women don't like how rough I get. I'm kinda big and I just..." He shifted his upper body on the bed, easing some of his discomfort. "I didn't mean to hurt you."

"Oh, Drew. You're so adorable." She cupped his face and pressed a soft kiss to his mouth. "You didn't hurt me, and if you had, I wouldn't care. It was worth it to be what you needed for a little while."

He opened his mouth on a retort and closed it again. What could he say to that? If he told her he wanted to be what she needed, too, she'd probably go ape shit crazy and walk out on him or something, and no matter what, they had to finish this job. It was too important to her people, too important to BDH, and damned if he'd let her and his team down. So he tucked the need away, hiding it where it wouldn't poke at him all the damn time. Later, he'd drag it out again and find a way to feel her out about it, but now, it was enough to be with her.

She resettled herself on top of him and lowered her mouth to his ear. "I've been meaning to ask you something."

"Anything, baby."

Her soft sigh feathered across his skin. "Why do you wear your wedding ring all the time?"

He tilted his head away from her and met her bright gaze. "Been bothering you, has it?"

Her mouth twisted into a frown. "Sort of."

"What's wrong with me wearing it?"

Her gaze slid away from his and she buried her face in his throat. "I don't know how to ask this."

"Come on, Jaybird. Just spit it out."

"Are you having sex with me because your cover is as my husband?"

The words spilled out of her in a rush, and his gut tightened. Was that really what she thought of him, that he couldn't keep work separate from his personal life, that he would use her just to fulfill an end goal? He wound her long braid around his hand and tugged her head up, so she could see what he was for herself, so she could feel his honesty and never doubt him again. "I've worked with a lot of women in the past, Jaybird. Margaret and

Brigid and others, and sometimes we even went in as married couples. I never had sex with any of them while we were working, not once."

"You wear it all the time," she said softly.

"Yeah, to remind myself of who I am and what we're doing here. That's all, though. I know we're not married and I sure as hell wouldn't have sex with you just because you're convenient and happen to be playing my wife."

Her eyelids fluttered shut. "So wearing that ring doesn't have anything to do with me."

"Maybe a little." He rolled her onto her back and braced himself above her. "I like this thing we've got going, whatever it is. Maybe I'm hoping it'll turn into something real."

A soft smile curved her luscious mouth. "You say the sweetest things."

"Baby, you want sweet, you shoulda picked another man." He rubbed his hips into the cradle of her thighs, and the quiet need banked in his gut roared into vivid, unquenchable thirst. "You gonna pull my trigger now?"

Her eyes flashed open and she laughed. "What is it with you and gun metaphors?"

"Hey, what do you expect? I'm a guy. I like guns." He slid to her side on the bed and traced his fingers over the curve of her breast. "Wanna see what I can do with my trigger finger?"

Her laughter faded into a low, husky moan, and for a long time after, Drew reveled in the pleasure she so readily shared.

Nine

REBECCA CENTERED the single sheet holding James Terhune's translation of the Prophecy of Light on her desk and framed the text with her hands. She'd read it dozens of times over the past few months, and still, its meaning eluded her.

"Daughters and Sons will gather where the bones of the Sisters shall lie," she murmured. The passage seemed to imply that the Sisters had all been buried in one place. If the People could simply discover what that place was, they would be able to take the first step toward bringing the Prophecy to pass, and no Daughter would ever again bear the harsh burden of an endless, empty life.

Rebecca leaned back in her seat and rubbed weary fingers over her forehead. The key had to be in finding Sanctuary. Yes, they had the bones of one Sister at the Archives, but without the other six sets of remains, the Prophecy could never be fulfilled. Surely the other Sisters' skeletons were still together somewhere. Thanks to the hard work of her newest son-in-law, Tom Fairfax, they at least had a place to begin their search. Jerusha would call soon with the news that she and Drew had discovered another clue, and eventually the Prophecy would come to pass, ending the unjust curse weighing upon the People.

Her office phone beeped, signaling a call. Rebecca picked it up automatically. "Hello?"

"Hey, Mom."

Some of Rebecca's worry bled away. "Dani. I didn't expect to hear from you again until this weekend."

"Yeah. I was kinda hoping to stay on the down-low this week."

"What's wrong, darling?"

A soft sigh filtered through the static. "Lukas Alexiou is here. He wants to meet with you."

The blood drained out of Rebecca's head in a swirling eddy and she swayed in her chair.

The Shadow approaches and the Blade must yield.

No. She wasn't ready yet. They were so close to solving the Prophecy. The People needed her now. Her family needed her. Margaret and Jerusha were still immortal, their hearts firmly their own, Moira was pregnant, Bobby was eager to begin a family with the woman he'd loved for so long, and Robert. Rebecca pressed trembling fingers to her lips. How could she leave her beloved husband behind? How could she die now, when she'd had him for such a short time compared to the centuries she'd had to live without him?

"Are you ok, Mom?"

Rebecca cleared her throat and forced her spine straight. She was the Blade, a renowned warrior, a Daughter worthy of the line of Abragni. She would not fail her people now, simply because she wasn't ready to face the end of her long life. "I'm fine, darling. Where is he?"

"In Clayton at a B&B. He has something he wants to trade."

"Did he say what?"

"No. He's being cagey, even for him." A soft, masculine murmur drifted over the line, and Dani snorted. "Dave says Lukas wants to meet you at the IECS. I told him no."

"It would be foolish to allow him a close look at our security," Rebecca agreed. "Is he alone?"

"Ah, well, that's the thing. He's got his nephew with him,

said something about Marco being out of town on business."

Rebecca's eyebrows shot up. "He brought his kin into the heart of the People?"

"Yeah, which just proves my point. The man's mad as the Hatter."

Perhaps and perhaps not. Lukas Alexiou would never have survived his tenure as the Shadow's leader if he were insane. On the other hand, bringing his brother's child into certain danger wasn't the act of a man possessed of all his faculties. "No one else?"

"Not even a driver. He sweet talked Dave into hanging out, and the big lug dragged me along with him."

Rebecca flipped the sleeve of her suit coat back and checked her watch. "I can be there within the half hour."

"We'll be here, talking to the madman."

Rebecca murmured a goodbye and hung up. Her gaze fell on Silverthorn, the first weapon she'd ever earned. Its sharp edges gleamed under the light reflecting off it. The Woman had said Rebecca must yield to the Shadow, and so she would. Her sword would remain locked in its case, awaiting her family's judgment as to its ultimate disposition. She wouldn't face her blood enemy entirely defenseless, though, regardless of the Woman's vision. No Daughter worth her salt walked into her enemy's lair unprepared, and Rebecca had long ago proven her value.

She gathered her purse, tucked a handgun inside, and dismissed her assistant for the day. On the drive into Clayton, Rebecca called Robert and chatted with him, wallowing in the comforting warmth of his presence, however tenuous it might be. If her voice wobbled and her heart throbbed painfully in her chest, surely that didn't make her a coward. A woman could regret not meeting her heart's love earlier, couldn't she? She could regret not having more time with him and still face her demise as a proud warrior.

Three cars were parked in the bed and breakfast's parking

lot, Dani's Jeep, a sedan with Fulton County tags, and a beat up work van. Rebecca parked on the other side of the van, snagged her purse, and got out, locking her car behind her. She picked her way through the graveled parking area and up the rock-lined stairs onto the porch, and entered the sprawling historic house that now served as a temporary residence for area visitors.

Dani was in the foyer gnawing on her lower lip. As soon as Rebecca shut the door behind herself, Dani threw her arms around her and hugged her tight. "Don't worry, Mom. It's gonna be ok, I swear."

"Darling," Rebecca said softly. "I'm fine, truly."

"Don't lie. You know I can feel it."

Rebecca eased out of her daughter's embrace. "Have you had another vision?"

"A couple of nights ago. The Blade, the Shadow." Dani shook her head and twisted her fingers together in front of her waist. "I just realized what it meant, and it was so obvious, too."

"There now, darling. These portents aren't meant to be easily understood. You'll sort it out in time."

"Easy for you to say," Dani muttered. "His Madness has commandeered the sitting room. Come on. I'll show you."

Their footsteps cracked against the hardwood floor, echoing through the barren hallway. The sitting room was located behind the door on the left past the stairs to the second floor. It was a cozy room, small and sparsely furnished. French doors were centered in the far wall and bracketed by tall windows covered in sheer drapes. The remaining walls were painted a soothing off-white tinged with a hint of pink and decorated with tasteful landscapes framed in dark wood. A settee and two matching chairs covered in a subtly textured scarlet upholstery were arranged on top of a square area rug around a Queen Anne style coffee table. A silver tray holding a porcelain tea set rested on top of the coffee table.

The tasteful décor barely registered. Rebecca's gaze focused on the man sitting on the settee dressed in a sharply tailored, charcoal gray suit next to a tow-headed boy of perhaps six who appeared to be deeply engrossed in a coloring book. So this was Lukas Alexiou, the man that had, at the tender age of thirteen, wrested control of the Shadow from his father and led it into the twenty-first century. He glanced up and stood, his pale features impassive under stylishly cut midnight hair. He smoothed a hand over the boy's head, though his piercing blue eyes were fixed on Rebecca.

"Director Upton," he said, his voice a cultured blend of Yankee and the Mediterranean. "Thank you for agreeing to meet with me on such short notice."

Rebecca stepped into the room and settled on a chair across from him as Dani joined David against the wall by the door. "Dani tells me you've come here to negotiate a trade of some sort."

"In a manner of speaking." He sat and hooked an ankle over one knee, holding it there with one elegant hand. "Certain artifacts went missing from a recent dig at Sandby borg in Sweden."

Rebecca's interest piqued in spite of the dread clawing at her gut. "You have these in your possession?"

One corner of Lukas' mouth twitched upward. "Only a fool would admit to owning such highly sought after artifacts, let alone to bringing them into the presence of a woman with your reputation."

"And you're no fool."

"In spite of what your daughter believes, no, Director, I am not."

"Hey, now," Dani said, and David shushed her with a well-placed elbow in her ribs.

Rebecca folded her hands in her lap and regarded her enemy steadily. "You have them within easy reach."

"Easy enough."

"And you wish to trade them for something you believe we have."

Lukas' smile widened and his eyes lit with emotion for the first time since Rebecca had entered the room. "I wish to trade one favor for another. Tell me, Director. What would you give to have the artifacts turned over into your safe keeping?"

"I would have to know they were actually in your possession first," she said carefully.

"Assume they are."

"Then I would be willing to listen."

"No more than that?"

Rebecca pressed her lips together into a hard line. "What do you want?"

"A visit with an old friend."

Humor rose, pushing aside the last of her worry, steadying her nerves. "The Shadow has no friends in Tellowee."

"Are you certain, Director? This friend is old. Her life stretches beyond your memory into the People's shrouded, sacred past."

"We have many such Daughters, Mr. Alexiou."

"Not like this one." The smile slipped from his face and his knuckles whitened. "This one has slumbered for so long, she no longer recognizes the world around her."

"The Oracle," Rebecca breathed.

"Precisely."

"How do you know about her?"

"I have my ways, as you have yours." He placed both feet firmly on the floor and rested his hands on his thighs. "It is imperative that I speak with her as soon as possible, for everyone's sake."

Rebecca studied her enemy, considering the ramifications of his knowledge. A few months ago, the Woman with No Face had told her a member of the People was helping the Shadow. That leak had never been plugged, in spite of her and Bobby's best efforts to the contrary, and now, that lack was coming home to roost. "Why should I let you see her?"

"As I said, it's for everyone's sake."

"Not good enough."

"All right, then." He sighed and his eyes dropped to his knees, hiding their bright spark. "I can speak to her, and she will listen. Would you not like to communicate with her, perhaps learn of her past, and yours?"

"How can I trust you with her? How can you possibly believe I would let you anywhere near...?" Rebecca inhaled a sharp breath and clamped her jaws together. "You wish to trade the stolen Sandby borg artifacts for a visit with the Oracle."

"I do."

"I need time to consider your offer."

"Of course." He stood and regarded her, an odd expression on his coldly handsome face. "Your pictures do you no justice, Director. It was a pleasure meeting one of the People's most dedicated warriors."

She nodded and stood, facing him squarely, as the proud warrior she was. "I'll have Dani relay a message when I've made my decision."

"Thank you."

She pivoted and walked away, her shoulders tense, waiting for him to strike and destroy her, as the Woman's vision had foretold.

His cultured voice cut through the air between them. "Director? Call her Nala. Perhaps that name will gain the reaction you seek."

Rebecca paused in the doorway and stared into the hallway beyond. *Nala.* He knew the Oracle's name. How could that be, when none within the People remembered her as anything but the woman they'd found in a grotto millennia before?

"I'll contact you soon," she said, and left while she still could.

JERUSHA AND DREW eliminated city after city over the next week. Some had no known tombs. Others were in such poor condition, they couldn't be entered. Jerusha carefully noted their findings in each case and sent daily reports to her mother and brother using a well-devised code. It wasn't unbreakable, nothing was, but it would be hard to decipher. Anything putting a kink in Lukas Alexiou's nose was worth the extra effort.

And she enjoyed that on a near daily basis. Their local tails were still hanging around making perfect nuisances of themselves. They hadn't tried to corner her again, more's the pity. She would've enjoyed taking them down a notch or three. Plus, Drew seemed to enjoy watching her work, and anything that pleased the big guy was bound to end up with him pleasing her.

She hid a smile against his arm and tuned out their current tour guide's monologue on the various ways the underground cities had been used. They'd heard that spiel dozens of times already, enough that she felt no guilt in ignoring it.

Besides, Drew smelled really good. She sniffed his jacket again, inhaling the sharp, clean scent of detergent mingling with the subtle masculine spice of his deodorant. They'd gone back to doing their laundry separately as soon as her week on duty had passed. Maybe she'd challenge him to pushups later and see if she could outpace him so he'd have to do her laundry for a week.

He shifted his stance and tucked his hands against his ribs. If the past week had been productive work-wise, it had been downright eye-opening on the relationship front. They'd fallen into the easiest sort of friendship, teasing each other mercilessly, hanging out during their downtime, playing game after game of Go Fish while talking about nothing and everything.

And after, Drew turned his little surprise on and they made love for hours at a time, sometimes rough and tumble, at others so gentle, her heart ached. He held nothing back, giving so freely of himself in that raw, honest way of his, she could do nothing less than reciprocate. He was the first man she'd ever done that with and the first one she'd ever wanted for more than a weekend.

She enjoyed being with him, and he seemed to enjoy having

her around. Only a fool would waste the opportunity she'd been handed to be with him.

She tucked her fingers into the slight space between his hand and his ribs and stroked her thumb across his knuckles. The longer they were around each other, the more she wanted him around. What would he say if she asked him to stick with her after they found the City of the Sisters? Would he want to be with her longer or would he walk away when the job was done?

He leaned close and whispered, "Cut it out, Jaybird. You're turning me on."

"I'm not doing anything," she whispered back.

"Your hands are on me. You think I need more?"

Humor wound its way into her voice. "You're so easy."

"You have no idea," he muttered. "Cut it out so I can concentrate."

She stilled her thumb and glanced at the tour guide. He looked exactly like the last three, gaunt and ashen and a little unkempt, as if he spent too much time underground and not enough time taking care of himself. "You should've memorized this by now."

"Sometimes they go off script." He wiggled his fingers against hers. "Come closer. I miss holding you."

"We just got out of bed four hours ago."

"And? I like holding you."

And she loved holding him, loved finding comfort in his embrace. He was solid and strong and snarky, even in the middle of sex so consuming, the feelings he aroused in her lingered for hours afterward. If she could give even a tiny amount of that back to him, maybe it would be enough to lure him to London.

Or maybe she could pass her work off there to another Daughter and move back to Tellowee. There was no danger of her falling into mortality. Of course not. Drew was, well, Drew, big and adorable and so sexy she was having a hard time keeping her hands off of him, but she wouldn't lose her heart to him. That was pure impossibility.

117

But they could be friends, couldn't they? Maybe even friends with benefits, as long as the passion lasted. She wouldn't regret that part of their relationship fading if they could hold on to the friendship.

They visited one more city that day, hiking in along a poorly marked trail. The entrance was boarded up and surrounded by warning signs, and Jerusha resigned herself to visiting it after the more accessible ones were eliminated, climbing gear in tow. Drew had been itching to break in to something. Looked like this one would give him his thrills.

That night, she sprawled crosswise on the hotel bed while inputting their findings into her database. Drew was doing pushups on the floor beside the bed, pumping smoothly through them like he did nearly every day. She shook her head and typed in a description of the last city they'd visited. He put her to shame where exercise was concerned, but she sure did enjoy watching his workout.

She saved her database and exed out of it into her e-mail. The top message was a reply from one of the people associated with the newly discovered underground city she'd been trying to get a look-see at. She scanned through the e-mail, read it again more carefully. Temel Baştürk, an archaeologist with the Nevşehir Cultural Museum, was willing to meet with her the following Monday during the museum's regular business hours. He made no promises on granting an actual tour of the new city, but the invitation was a good start.

"Are you at a hundred yet?" she asked.

Drew grunted. "Ninety-three."

She propped up on an elbow and studied his sweat-soaked skin. Bless him, he'd left his shirt off. Every muscle in his arms stood out in sharp relief as he pushed up and eased down. A slow, burning heat pooled within her, low in her gut, and her nipples hardened into blissfully tight peaks. Would she ever tire of watching him? Would she ever want to?

He shoved himself off the floor and padded toward the bed.

"You rang?"

"I have something to show you."

He lowered himself onto the bed beside her and read the e-mail. "Seems promising."

"Yeah. I thought maybe we could take care of that soon."

"Mmm. I've got something you can take care of."

He rolled on top of her, pinning her to the bed, and she shrieked and smacked his chest. "You're soaking wet, Drew."

"Got something needs doing." He nuzzled her throat and rubbed his erection against her core through the layers of their clothing. "You interested?"

"Is that thing like that all the time?"

"I told you to quit touching me."

She huffed out a laugh. "I've been over here minding my own business, and you were working out. There was no touching involved."

"I was remembering you touching me earlier." He sucked her earlobe into his mouth and nibbled gently. "Slow and easy, skin on skin. Do that to me again, baby."

The husky plea shivered through her, and she melted under him. "Just this once," she whispered.

"One time'll never be enough, Jaybird, not ever."

He captured her mouth in a sweet, tender kiss, and she touched him exactly the way he wanted her to, for as long as he needed.

Ten

JERUSHA DRAGGED Drew to the Nevşehir Cultural Museum as soon as it opened on Monday. The stone masonry complex sprawled across a city block and stood three stories tall. Drew rubbed his earlobe and studied the imposing exterior. He liked museums as much as the next guy, but maybe when they got back to the States, they could take in a basketball game or hockey or something. All this history shit was overloading his brain.

Jerusha's nails bit into the inside of his arm through his jacket and shirt. He tugged her fingers loose and hooked them around his bicep where they'd do less damage. "You ok, baby?"

Her hand tightened on his arm. "I'm fine."

"You've been a little jittery since we got the invite here."

"Yeah, sorry. It's just..." She blew out a breath. "I feel like we're finally making some progress."

"Your mouth to God's ear," he muttered.

"Getting tired of me already?"

"Not you." He was a long way from getting tired of her or wanting her out of his life. Maybe in a decade or two, she'd wear him out, and Pari could laugh her ass off and say *I told you so.* "Next time we do this, though, I wanna dig in the dirt or something."

"Digging in the dirt's not all that exciting either." Her hand fell away from his arm. She opened the door and stepped over the threshold, Drew close behind. "I was thinking. When we're finished here, maybe you could visit me in London."

"Why do women always bring up important relationship shit when a man can't talk it out?"

She flashed her carefree grin at him. "It's a thing."

A harried looking man in his early thirties strode toward them. His thin face was pulled into a scowl behind a full, blue-black beard and his white button-down shirt and dark slacks were slightly wrinkled. His rush through the museum came to an abrupt stop half a dozen feet away from Drew and Jerusha.

"Please tell me one of you is Dr. Jeri Willingham," the man said in Turkish.

Jerusha raised a hand. "I'm Dr. Willingham. You must be Temel Baştürk."

"Dr. Baştürk, newly minted. My apologies, but would you mind coming back another day? We had a break-in last night."

"I'm sorry to hear that. Is everyone ok?"

"Yes. Nothing was even taken. In fact, we have no idea why anyone would go to such lengths except to make a mess. Several rooms were left in a state, including my office."

"We're really only here to gain access to the underground city you're excavating."

Temel studied her, his dark eyes solemn. "I thought you might be interested in the artifacts."

"We are," Jerusha assured him. "I'd like to see the site first, and while I appreciate the problems you're having, my leave from work is running out. It will be months before I can visit again."

"I can't go, but there's a security guard on site. I can have him walk you through."

"Thank you. Could we come back in a day or so and study the artifacts you've already removed?"

"Dr. Willingham, please—"

"Surely you can spare an hour of your time, Dr. Baştürk."

Temel's gaze drifted to Drew. "Your wife is quite persistent."

Drew shrugged. "That's one way of putting it. She'll drag me back here every day until you give in and show her the artifacts."

"That would be a tragedy," Temel said. "Come back tomorrow afternoon. Perhaps by then I'll have my office set to rights."

Jerusha nodded once. "Thank you, Dr. Baştürk. I deeply appreciate your patience."

"You can thank me with a generous donation to the museum. Come. You'll need directions."

They followed the archaeologist through the museum to his office, and Drew whistled. Somebody had done a good number on it, yanking books off shelves, emptying the contents of drawers and file folders onto the floor. Place looked like a tornado had whirled through it. It'd take the doc more than a day to sort everything out.

Dr. Baştürk jotted down directions and phoned ahead to the security guard, then shooed them out of his office. Forty-five minutes later, Drew parked the rental in a dirt parking lot outside the unnamed underground city. A single car was already there. The beat up sedan was backed in, front end to the road, and held a lone occupant. The man got out and strolled toward them, hitching the pants of his uniform up under his paunch as he went.

Drew and Jerusha got out and met the guard halfway.

"We're the Willinghams," Jerusha said.

The guard nodded. "Ahmed. Dr. Baştürk asked me to show you around."

"Thank you, Ahmed. Could we start with the tombs?"

"If you wish. Follow me, please."

Ahmed trod heavily out of the parking lot onto a narrow path worn into the snow-dusted, beige earth. Jerusha took off after him, and Drew followed her, half his mind on the possibility of visiting her in London, the other half on the twitch of her firm ass under her pants. Fucking beautiful. When they got back to the hotel, maybe he'd coax her into letting him take her against the bathroom counter again.

The path wound around outcroppings and enormous fairy chimneys, and petered out at the mouth of a low-roofed cave. Ahmed dug a tiny flashlight out of his jacket pocket. "This is the only way in for now. The other entrances were sealed off long ago."

"A protection against attack or discovery?" Jerusha asked.

Ahmed shrugged. "Dr. Baştürk would know."

He ducked inside the cave, Jerusha hot on his heels.

Drew stifled a sigh and wedged his burly frame through the entrance. The tight space didn't bother him, but he was by God getting tired of being too big for his surroundings. He followed the bouncing beam of light ahead of him, nearly bent double at the waist. At least Jerusha didn't think he was too big. Fact was, she seemed to like his size, and for her being all Daughterly tough and shit, she enjoyed letting him manhandle her.

His mind shot to the night before and the way he'd manhandled her onto her knees and taken her from behind. She'd arched her back and tilted her hips into his thrusts, wild and unrestrained, and begged him to let her come, and he had. Eventually. He shook his head and focused on the narrow path. God, he had it bad. Having sex with her was supposed to help his concentration, not absorb all his attention.

Though he didn't mind having her running around in his head at all hours, naked or not.

The cave's ceiling sloped gradually upward, ending in a carved arch barely visible under the erratic swings of the guard's flashlight. Something clicked, then dim light flooded the area. Drew stepped into a cavern and snapped his jaws shut. The thing was huge, half a football field deep at least and maybe twice that in height in places. The floor descended in large, flat steps toward a central circular depression. Giant columns ran from the floor to the curved ceiling and glowed green near their tops. Doorways were carved into the opposite wall between darkened tunnel entrances and were stacked one on top of another, like doors into an apartment building. The guide that had spilled the beans about this place had said something about the city going on for miles. If it did, it must've held thousands of people in its heyday.

"Holy shit, Jaybird," he said. "This is even bigger than Derinkuyu."

She swiveled toward him and scowled. "Potty mouth."

He hunched his shoulders around his ears. Jesus, she was strict.

She whirled away and, in Turkish, said, "Which way are the tombs, Ahmed?"

"There are several sets, but this way leads to the most interesting one." He swept his hand toward a tunnel on the right. "We need lamps, though. There's no lighting back there yet."

Ahmed retrieved three, battery operated camp lanterns from a box tucked against one wall and led them into the tunnel he'd pointed out. It twisted and turned, branching into other tunnels, widening into caverns, then narrowed again into a single path. Drew created a mental map in his head in case he and Jaybird needed to come back. Maybe they wouldn't have to, but it never hurt to be prepared.

The tunnel dead-ended in a small, circular grotto. The guard held his lamp high, throwing light across a single, raised rectangular stone. A chill skittered down Drew's spine. The thing reminded him of an altar used for human sacrifices.

Seven holes had been carved into the walls, spaced at regular intervals around the grotto. Jerusha knelt in front of one and held her lantern close to the wall. Her fingers brushed over the rock under the opening. "Blessed Ki."

Drew walked over and crouched beside her, his lantern held high. "What is it, baby?"

"The Eye of Marnan. Look." She pointed to a symbol scratched into the wall, a stylized eye roughly the size of her palm. "We found it, Drew. We really found it."

"Not to be a downer, Jaybird, but how can you be sure? I mean, it's just an eye."

She shook her head sharply and her silky hair shimmied around her face. "It's not just an eye, Drew. Don't you see? This is the symbol of one of the Sisters."

Her voice was soft, reverent, and a slow smile spread across her beautiful mouth. Drew smoothed a hand over her back, then pushed himself upright. "Reckon I'll check the others."

"Me, too." She snagged his free hand and pulled herself into a stand. "Ahmed, did Dr. Baştürk's team find anything in these niches?"

Ahmed shrugged. "Two sets of bones, I think. You should ask him."

"I will," Jerusha murmured. She wandered around the perimeter of the room, stopping in front of each niche. The next one had an ex underneath. "Two spears, crossed. The symbol of Bagda."

The third was marked by two circles, one set inside the other. The inner circle was bisected by a plus sign. "Eleni," Jerusha said.

Drew cocked his head. "You sure that's not a pizza?"

She laughed and moved to the next niche. Underneath it was a simple triangle, point up. "Ganenda."

The fifth niche had a circle with four lines radiating away from it, north, east, south, and west. "Lilleni," Jerusha explained. "Twin to Eleni."

The next to last one was a plain circle. "Kiya. We think this is supposed to be an ouroboros, though it has to predate the Greek symbol by millennia."

Ouroboros, a snake endlessly eating its tale. "Infinity," Drew said.

Jerusha glanced at him, eyebrows arched. "You know your symbols."

"I ain't as dumb as I look."

She stood on tiptoes and bussed his cheek. "I don't think

125

you're dumb at all, sweetie."

Yeah, right. That's why sometimes she forgot and treated him the same as her kid brother. He shook it off. Her treating him like a man every night more than made up for that. "What's the last one?"

She knelt on the floor in front of the last niche and touched her forehead to the symbol carved into the rock beneath it. "A crescent moon, the symbol of Abragni, youngest of the Seven. My ancestress."

Drew laid a hand on the crown of her head. "I'm sorry, baby."

"There's nothing to be sorry about." She laughed weakly and curled her free hand over the ledge of the niche. "This is where she was after she died. We know so little about her life. So much of it's been lost, but this is something we know now. She was here, Drew. Her bones were here."

Ahmed cleared his throat. "It's interesting, yes?"

"Very." Jerusha sighed gustily and stood, a smile on her face in spite of the tears brimming in her eyes. "We can go now."

Drew rubbed his hands up and down her arms. "You sure, baby?"

"Positive. This is what we were searching for, Drew. This is the City of the Sisters."

"Good. We can go home now."

She laughed and dried her tears. "No, sweetie. We still have a lot to do here."

"Well, damn," he said softly. "And here I was hoping to take you to a basketball game back home."

"I'll take a rain check, definitely." Her hand crept into his, small and chilled and just a little shaky. "This calls for a celebration."

He grinned. "Oh, yeah, Jaybird. It absolutely does."

The guard led them safely out into the chilly January morning. Drew didn't mind the cold. Jerusha's joy warmed him for a long time after and then some.

THEY WERE QUIET during the drive back to the hotel. On the walk to their room, Drew cupped Jerusha's nape and strummed his thumb up and down her skin, slow and easy. The excited nerves pinging through her calmed a little, quieting under his caress. How could his touch arouse her to such tremendous heights during sex and soothe her back to normal, too?

As soon as they entered their room, she stripped off her jacket and gloves and headed toward the bathroom. Inside, she flipped the shower on full blast. Drew shut the door behind himself, leaned against it, and grinned.

"Oh, cut it out," she said, laughing. "Honestly, is sex all you think about?"

"Nope. I think about lots of stuff, like how beautiful your eyes are and how soft your skin is and how much I wanna kiss you."

She shook her head and boosted herself onto the counter. "That's sex, Drew."

"That's me enjoying you," he countered. "If sex is out, I guess you wanna talk about our lack of shadows."

The rest of her nerves evaporated. Bobby had been right. Drew was good. She should've trusted her brother's judgment more from the get-go instead of holding herself back. Bobby would never give her less than his best. Next time she'd remember that, though Drew was shaping up to be an outstanding partner in every way imaginable, on the clock and off. Why would she want another partner when she had him?

She opened her arms and beckoned him into the cradle of her body. If they had to talk business, at least they could be comfortable. "When did you notice?"

He settled between her thighs and gripped her waist. "Not long after we left this morning."

"And you're just now telling me, why?"

"Figured you didn't need me to point out the obvious, Jaybird, what with you being a smart cookie and all."

She brushed her cheek against the stubble of his beard.

What was it with him and intelligence lately? "Any thoughts on why they might have abandoned us?"

"Dunno. Maybe it has something to do with the B and E at the museum."

"Nothing was taken."

"That Doc Baştürk knew, what? About half an hour after he got there, the day after it happened?" Drew snorted. "Come on, Jaybird. Give the man a break."

"I'm not that hard on men," she muttered.

"That ain't what Pari said." He jerked her hips forward on the counter, fitting them firmly against his own. "About this invite to London. You got room for me to stay a while? 'Cause I got vacation time coming."

She grinned against his throat and snuggled into him. "There's no basketball in London, not the kind you're after, anyway."

"So we'll do something else. Just not ruins and shit. I'm getting my fill here."

"You're so adorable."

His hand snaked up her back and toyed with the ends of her hair. "Yeah? How 'bout you prove that."

"Gladly," she murmured, and spent the whole afternoon doing just that.

The next afternoon, Jerusha talked Drew into revisiting Nevşehir Cultural Museum. They checked in at the kiosk just inside the entrance and relayed a message to Dr. Baştürk that they were there. He hustled out not long after, appearing every bit as hassled and harried as he had the day before.

"Dr. Willingham, Mr. Willingham. I was expecting you this morning."

Jerusha slid a sly glance at Drew. That morning, they'd been otherwise occupied in a very pleasant manner. "We were trying to give you time to get your office sorted out."

"My office needs more help than I can give it. Ahmed told me you found what you were looking for in our newest site."

"We did." Jerusha stuffed her hands into the pockets of her jacket. Excitement still hummed through her, lifting her into an edgy nervousness. Where was Drew's rough touch when she needed it? "He said your team discovered remains in the tomb he showed us yesterday."

"Two sets of skeletal remains, both fully intact and in excellent shape."

"Anything else?"

"Just the bones, though I wouldn't have minded an explanation of the symbols carved into the walls there." Temel's thick, dark eyebrows shot toward his hairline. "Ahmed said you seemed very familiar with them. I'd love to hear what you know."

"I can put you in contact with someone who can explain them better than I can." And probably with more grace than Jerusha would be able to muster right then. "Were the remains found inside the niches?"

"Surprisingly, yes. Ah." Temel glanced behind him. "That's in my office, somewhere. I just had my hands on it."

Jerusha's heart flipped over and boomed in her chest. "Your team recorded which set of bones were found in which niche?"

"Naturally. Follow me and I'll show you."

Temel wended his way through exhibits and visitors, and stopped at a plain, metal door painted a grungy off-white. He unlocked it and held it open, waved Jerusha and Drew inside, then led them through the winding hallway to his office.

Jerusha halted in the doorway and stared at the chaos. Drew's burly warmth pressed against her back, and she relaxed into him. "You've barely made a dent."

Temel scooted around his desk and sifted through folders. "Unfortunately, I have other obligations. Getting a new security system installed for the museum, for one, and this work is quite tedious. I'm trying to sort everything exactly right as I go. It's a much harder process than I anticipated."

"It looks like you still have a long way to go."

"I'll get there, eventually." He held a slender manila folder up. "This is it, though it's not all our work. I haven't found some of the photographs we took in that particular tomb."

"Told you so," Drew murmured.

Jerusha elbowed his stomach lightly. "Photographs can be retaken, Dr. Baştürk. Knowing which set of bones belonged in which niche is irreplaceable knowledge."

"There, we agree. Here." He flipped the folder open and zigzagged a fingertip across its contents. "We found one set of bones in the first niche on the left, the one marked by an eye."

Marnan. Jerusha pressed her lips together, stifling her need to give voice to the name. "And the other?"

"In the niche marked by the pizza pie symbol."

Drew snickered, and Jerusha elbowed him again. Eleni would likely haunt them forever if she could hear Drew and Temel's comparison of her symbol to modern-day junk food. "Would it be possible for me to examine the remains?"

"The first set, yes. We have those on site."

"Not the second set?"

"No. We worked with Boston University during the initial season. An overenthusiastic doctoral candidate shipped the second set of remains there." Temel shrugged and closed the folder. "We're trying to get them back for comparative purposes, but my colleagues in Boston are reluctant to part with them and the other artifacts they have until they've been fully examined."

That wouldn't be a problem for her and Drew. Between the two of them, they had the skills necessary to retrieve Eleni's remains and return them to their rightful place among the People, and they were going to do exactly that as soon as they finished in Turkey.

Temel led them into the rooms serving as storage for the museum's artifacts, pulled Marnan's remains, and scrounged gloves for Jerusha. She examined every single bone of the complete skeleton. "These are in truly remarkable condition."

"The controlled temperature inside the city probably played a role in that, but only a part." Temel shrugged. "We found other remains in tombs scattered throughout the city, and none were as beautifully preserved as the two discovered in that particular tomb."

Jerusha rotated the skull between her hands. Had the curse that had unnaturally prolonged the Sisters' lives also filtered into their bones or had the Lady Ki had a hand in their preservation? "Have you tried to do a DNA test on her?"

Temel glanced between Jerusha and Drew. "I never mentioned her sex."

"It's a hunch. The width of the pelvis, the height, the delicate bone structure." Jerusha met Temel's suspicious gaze evenly. "I've examined skeletal remains before."

His shoulders slumped. "Of course. My apologies, Dr. Willingham. My nerves are edgy after the break-in."

"No apologies are necessary. Having someone toss my office would rattle me, too." She replaced the skull in its cushioned container and stripped off her gloves. "Thank you for allowing me to view these. You've been very gracious during a rather trying time."

"I appreciate your opinion, trying time or no. Perhaps I'll have my office organized soon and can make copies of the photographs we took. You'll leave your contact information?"

"Of course," Jerusha murmured. She and Temel chatted a while longer, then Jerusha tucked her hand into Drew's and they left.

Outside, the crisp air stung her cheeks. Snow flurried down, falling lightly onto the sidewalk, and she glanced at the leaden sky. "Did you get everything we needed?"

"I got it, Jaybird. When do you wanna do it?"

"Soon." She threaded her hand through the crook of Drew's elbow and rested her head on his arm. "I'm afraid someone else will beat us to it if we don't go in now."

"We need time to prepare."

"I know. Tomorrow night?"

"Not ideal, but doable. Let's get out of the cold."

She allowed him to tug her down the street and into their rental, and studied him as he started it and eased into traffic. Yes, Drew was turning into a splendid partner, and she saw no reason at all why she should have to give him up when they finished this job.

Eleven

A PLAN WHIRRED through Drew's mind. He'd been waiting for a little action, and now, his wish was coming true. Breaking into Nevşehir Cultural Museum and retrieving the Sister's bones would be a piece of cake compared to some of the hijinks he'd pulled during his stint with the Delta Force.

A twinge in his gut reminded him to detail it out anyhow, take it slow, work out the kinks. Jerusha might not be too worried about their shadows disappearing, but something about it bothered Drew. He just hadn't figured out the whats and whys yet. Having to complete weeks worth of planning in a single day didn't help.

First thing after they got back to the hotel room, he scoured it for bugs, dumped them in the sink, and ran water over them. Jaybird leaned a shoulder against the doorframe, her bright gaze steady. "You sure that's a good idea?"

"Yup. We need privacy so we can work out what we're gonna do. Long as one of us stays put, the bugs won't be replaced."

One corner of her mouth tilted up and her half-smile hit him with the force of a Mack truck on the front end of a tornado. Damn, she was beautiful, and she was his.

"You're manly, adorable, and you have a plan. How did I get so lucky?"

He dried his hands off and smirked. "You ain't seen nothing yet, Jaybird."

Drew built a fire in the room's fireplace and they settled in front of it, shoulder to shoulder on a low-backed chaise as he outlined a rough plan, refining it with her input. They scoured the Internet for more detailed blueprints of the museum's interior, plotted escape routes using Google Earth, and worked out the dozens of details that went into planning a robbery.

Did he like doing it on such short notice? Fuck, no. Spur of the moment was fine. When you were loose and ready for anything, your body reacted before your mind could think. Ninety-nine percent of the time, that worked out great.

This halfway shit really worried him, though. They didn't have time for detailed surveillance, didn't have time to think it through, and they'd scrounged up just enough info to be dangerous. Getting comfortable in the job was just as deadly as going in blind. He had a shit ton enough experience to know a half thought out plan was way less than ideal.

One of them stayed in the hotel room at all times, guarding against another intrusion while the other hunted down the items they needed to pull off their caper. Drew spent that night surveilling the museum from nearby buildings, marking off the guards' schedules, making notes on their faces and postures.

None of the guards he observed carried guns. That didn't mean they lacked access to weapons. It was something he and Jerusha were gonna have to watch for as they worked. Hopefully, this would be a simple in-and-out. Slide in through the back door, retrieve the bones out of storage, exit the way they'd come, and nobody the wiser.

The closer the time drew to their go, the harder the alarm bells rang in his gut. He was missing something. Damn it, what was he missing? A first floor B and E should be easy. No stairs, the back door led straight to the storage room. They had to bypass the security office, true, but that was no big. He went over the plans again and again in his mind, picked them apart, examined every detail, put everything back together again, but no matter how many times he studied them, he couldn't figure out where the weakness in their plan was.

THE NEXT NIGHT, Jerusha got an early supper for them from the hotel's restaurant. They ate it in their room and went over the plan one more time. Drive into Nevşehir, park three blocks away from the museum, walk in, get the bones, walk out.

Be home in time to make love to his woman well before the sun came up.

He repeated that in his mind as Jerusha picked the lock on the museum's back door. A wickedly cold wind whipped through the alley, cutting straight to bone, and he shivered. Next time they picked a gig, it had damn well better be in a warm place, maybe somewhere tropical, like Fiji. The People had to have stuff they needed doing in Fiji, didn't they?

He readjusted the strap of the supply duffel slung over his shoulder. "Hurry up, Jaybird. It's colder than a witch's tit out here."

She paused and glared at him. "A witch's tit? Really?"

"It was the coldest thing I could think of," he muttered. He rubbed his thumb over the underside of his left ring finger through his glove and cursed under his breath. Jerusha had made him leave his wedding ring in the hotel, right next to hers. His hand felt oddly empty without it. "How much more time do you need, woman? We've already been out here a full minute."

"Wimp." She twisted her mouth into a frown and jiggled the tools in her hands. "It's been more like ten seconds. Plus, the damn thing's rusty."

"Hey, if you can't do it, just admit it and I'll do it for you."

"The day a Daughter needs a man's help is the day..." The lock clicked open and she flashed a grin at him. "Oh, ye of little faith."

"I got faith."

135

"Uh-huh. Right."

"I do," he said, but she'd already yanked her toboggan down over her ears and squeezed inside. He hitched the duffel higher and followed her in, and they stole quietly through the museum. They'd opted to break in half an hour before midnight, during the solitary guard's last round. The next guard would arrive soon, but they had plenty of time before that happened.

Drew slid around a corner and manned lookout while Jerusha picked the lock on the storage room. So far, so good. The guard was right on schedule, making rounds somewhere on the other side of the building. Drew scanned the hallway they'd just exited and forced his heartbeat to calm. Plenty o' time. Nothing to worry about. No problemo...

"Psst."

He jerked around, and Jerusha frowned at him. "You're jumpy tonight."

"Well, shit, Jaybird. It ain't every day a man breaks into a fucking museum."

"Potty mouth," she whispered, and he rolled his eyes.

Good thing the security cameras didn't have sound, not that it mattered. They hadn't even tried to avoid them. Dr. Baştürk knew their faces, he knew their builds, and he knew their interest in the Sister's bones. It'd take him about a minute to put two and two together and come up with twenty-two. Before Drew and Jerusha could check out of the hotel and head for Dodge, the police would have BOLOs out on them. Entering the country under assumed names wouldn't keep anybody from recognizing a face plastered all over the evening news, but there, he and Jerusha were already covered, had been before they'd touched down in Istanbul. They had an alternate exit plan that didn't depend on having to go through security checkpoints to leave the country. It wasn't the easiest way to travel, true, but it'd do the trick.

Jerusha waved him into the storage room, and he shut the door behind himself. She unloaded the packing foam they'd stuffed into one of their supply duffels while he retrieved the Sister's remains. Together, they carefully wrapped each bone in a layer of foam and taped it together with precut packing tape. The skull got special treatment, a wad of foam Jerusha tore off and stuffed inside the head, followed by a layer of foam taped around it.

The little bones were the trickiest. Jerusha dumped those into plastic baggies, then wrapped the lot.

"Won't they break or crack or something?" Drew asked.

"Probably not. They're not really that fragile, for all their age." She tucked the last bone into the duffel, zipped it shut, and hefted it over her shoulder. "Ready?"

"God, yes." He inhaled a sharp breath, let it out slowly. "Be careful."

She stood on her tiptoes and bussed his mouth. "Always, sweetie."

She opened the door a scant inch and scanned the hallway, then slipped into it. Drew clutched the doorknob and breathed through the nerves wriggling around in his gut. Jesus H. Christ, he needed to get ahold of himself. He'd never been this jumpy on a mission, never, not even the first time he'd gotten caught in heavy fire during guard duty in Afghanistan. And shit, he'd been as green as a standing pine tree back then, eighteen years old, barely two months into his first rotation. He hadn't panicked, hadn't even blinked an eye. He'd just reacted, exactly the way he'd been trained to, and his world had narrowed to two realities.

He wanted to live and he wanted to live as a free man. Powerful motivation when you were on the wrong end of a terrorist's gun.

When he entered the hallway, Jerusha had her back to the opposite wall and was peeking around the corner. She faced him and put one finger over her lips, cautioning him to silence. He eased toward her and settled against the wall by her side, then caught what she had, the brush of footsteps along thin carpeting, a little loud and chaotic for one person.

137

The guard was coming back, probably headed for the security office in the adjoining, perpendicular hallway. Drew flicked his sleeve back and checked the time. Ten minutes early. Fuck. Good thing they'd planned for exactly that scenario. All they had to do was wait until the guard entered the room, sneak past the opening of that hallway, and break into one of the office's that had an outside window before the guard reviewed the security footage and figured out there were intruders inside the building.

Thank fuck the museum hadn't had time to implement stricter security protocols.

Down the other hallway, a deep, male voice said, in Turkish, "You can show us the package?"

"Yes, yes," another man said. "I promised you, didn't I?"

"And the woman the day guard told me about. She hasn't been back?"

Drew froze. Oh, fuck. Jerusha grabbed his forearm and slowly shook her head, her expression so tight, he thought it might shatter.

"We haven't seen her," the second man said. "Was it truly necessary to bring so many people?"

"The woman is dangerous."

"Bah. She's a woman, soft, pretty, delicate. How dangerous could she be?"

"If given the chance, she could wipe out a small army on her own. I don't plan on giving her that chance."

"You are a cynical man," the second man said. "Not a good way to live."

"We aren't paying you to judge, only to deliver the bones."

"Fine, fine. This way."

Jerusha banged the back of her head softly against the concrete block wall, and Drew raced through their options. Escape Plan B was out. It required crossing right in front of the approaching men's line of sight. Escape Plan C required getting into the second story and climbing out a window or, worse, going off the roof. They had the supplies packed in the duffel he carried, their emergency contingency bag. Unfortunately, getting into the second story meant reentering the storage room and climbing into the cramped dumb waiter running between the basement and the top floor, and the footsteps were getting awfully fucking loud.

Jerusha slid her duffel off her shoulder, drawing his gaze, and dug her gun out of the holster pinning it to her lower back. He bit back a sigh, eased his duffel to the floor, and pulled out his gun. Man, he hated Escape Plan: Situation FUBAR.

She tugged on his arm. *It's going to be ok,* she mouthed. *Trust me.*

He nodded once. Yeah, he trusted her. It was the bozos walking down the hallway that had him worried.

Jerusha dropped to her knees and fired around the corner, aiming high. Male voices erupted into alarmed curses and half a dozen or more bodies scrambled for cover. Drew faced the wall, one leg behind her, the other by her side and glanced around the corner. New hole in the ceiling, check. Guard peeking out from behind the security office's door, check. Fucking hired thugs ducking into doorways and drawing weapons, check and check.

Drew rested his forehead on the cool wall. "Next time, we're gonna go to Fiji," he whispered. "Pretty sure everybody there's too drunk on piña coladas to carry a gun."

Jerusha grinned up at him and rubbed her hand over his calf through his pants. "Fiji can be our next stop, sweetie. You're not the only one with vacation time coming."

"Hell, Jaybird, if you'd told me that, I woulda already made the reservations."

"Daughter," the first man they'd heard speak said in precisely spoken English. "Surrender quietly and I promise, no harm will come to you or your man."

Jerusha rolled her eyes. "A, I'm alone, and B, do you really expect a Daughter to just surrender?"

"We know you're travelling with a companion."

139

She laughed. "I'm a Daughter. Men come and go. Sometimes, I don't even bother learning their names."

Drew frowned down at her. Was that true? Had she really been with men she didn't even know? Were men that disposable to her?

She shook her head at him and squeezed his calf. *Stop*, she mouthed, and he shrugged off the worry. When they got out of this, they were gonna have a long talk about men and women and respect, even if he had to sit on top of her to get her to listen.

"We want the bones, Daughter, and you're standing in our way. We will go through you if we have to."

"You can try."

"Don't be ridiculous—"

Jerusha stuck her hand around the corner and fired, *bam, bam, bam.* A hail of answering gunfire rang through the hallway.

Drew crouched low to the ground, his body between her and any ricocheting bullets. "What the hell, Jaybird?"

"He's stalling," she said flatly. "Ten to one, more men are on the way."

Of course, they were. If his brains were screwed on straight, he would've caught that, too, but no. They'd been too busy screaming at him that something was wrong. Like, say, somebody else trying to steal their booty.

The gunfire paused. He and Jerusha returned fire, emptying their magazines, then ducked behind the corner as the men down the hallway opened fire again.

Drew dropped his gun's magazine out, inserted a fresh one, and chambered a round. "I hope you know what you're doing."

"Relax, sweetie. I've got a plan."

She dug her fingers into the front of his shirt and jerked him into a hard, quick, smoking hot kiss. When she let go, he slumped against the wall. "Your plan is to kiss me senseless in the middle of a gunfight?"

"My plan is to provide enough cover to distract them until you can get out with the bones."

The gunfire aimed at them paused. Drew peeked around the corner and fired half his rounds into doorways where he knew men crouched. Somebody grunted and another shrieked, and Drew leaned into the wall, satisfied he'd made an impression. "I'm not letting you do that. We go in as a team, we get out as a team. That was the plan."

"Don't be such a man."

"Hard not to be when I am one. Besides, I thought you liked my manliness."

She sprawled out on her stomach between his legs and fired around the corner. "Nine times out of ten, I adore your manliness. Right now, I need you to do what I tell you to."

"I ain't leaving you behind."

She wiggled onto her back and gazed up at him, and his heart flipped over and settled into a new beat. His Jaybird, feisty, spitfire Jaybird. No way was he leaving her alone. She'd never make it out in one piece. Besides, they had a vacation in Fiji to plan.

"Drew, sweetie, listen to me. I can take down every man out there with my bare hands. You, on the other hand, have the height and strength to execute an alternate escape."

She held her hands up, and he pulled her into a stand, huddling with her as bullets flew down the hallway and embedded themselves into the concrete wall mere feet away from where they stood, spraying debris into their bodies.

She snagged his nape and tugged him down to her mouth, and whispered, "Get outside. Work your way around the building. If they get the better of me, chances are good they'll knock me out, tie me up, and leave me here for the police to find. You can get me out of jail, Drew, but if you don't go now, neither one of us will make it out of here alive."

He tightened his grip on her waist. "Don't ask me to abandon you."

"You're not, I swear. Get what you need out of the supply duffel, then go." She cupped his jaw and rubbed her palm over his scraggly beard. "Please, sweetie. I need you to trust me."

"I don't like it."

"You know this is our best option."

He touched his forehead to hers and gripped her nape. "Swear you'll be ok."

"I will." She kissed him gently through a slight pause as guns were reloaded and fired, and he opened for her, deepening the kiss, taking what they both needed to tide them over until they each made it safely out. She eased back slowly, softening her caresses, and dropped onto her heels. "They must have somebody feeding them ammo."

"Yeah. You sure about this, Jaybird?"

"Positive. Now, go."

"You better come after me."

"I will."

Her mouth quirked into her carefree grin. She whirled away from him, peeked around the corner, and fired a single shot. A man screamed, hoarse and hollow, and something heavy thudded to the floor.

Drew shook his head and dug through the supply duffel, reloaded his gun with the extra ammo they'd brought along, and set it on the ground at her feet. She'd need it more than he would, and he needed to travel light. He snagged a length of rope and the duffel holding the bones, cupped a hand over her foot as a *see you soon*, and launched himself toward the storage room door.

She'd better make it out the other side of this alive. If she didn't, he was by God gonna kill her.

Twelve

J ERUSHA CALMLY FIRED one bullet at a time into the hallway, choosing her targets carefully. The men trying to steal the bones were careless, wasteful. For the love of all that was holy, they were facing a single woman with a dwindling supply of ammo. A couple of guys firing at her until her bullets ran out, then a bout of hand to hand, and they'd have her, but no. Did nobody use their common sense anymore?

The door to the storage room snicked shut and she breathed out her relief. Drew was safe now, out of harm's way. If a stray bullet ricocheted into her, big deal. She'd heal without even a scar to show for it, but if one hit him, it might seriously injure him, and then where would she be? Stuck in the middle of a gunfight with her man bleeding out and her unable to help him.

No thanks. She didn't love him, might not ever, but she cared for him much more deeply than she should. Somewhere between the day they'd started planning their trip to Turkey and the moment their best escape routes out of the museum were cut off, he'd wiggled his way into her heart. As she'd lain on the floor staring up at him, bullets pinging into the walls around them, something else had hit her, the bone deep certainty that Drew would never let her down. In that moment, a calm had settled over her, harkening a rare, clarified knowledge.

She could put her life in his hands, and he'd always be there to catch her.

She'd never trusted a man so fully, not her beloved father, not her favorite kid brother, not anybody. Ki willing, she'd make it through this and could trust Drew for a long time yet to come.

In Fiji, where nobody even thought the words *snow* or *cold* or *Shadow*. He should've mentioned that idea first instead of the basketball game.

She emptied her last bullet into the wall two inches above an unknown man's head, then crouched low to the ground, her back to the wall. Had Drew made it out yet? Was he waiting for her outside, raring to bust in and rescue her?

She huffed out a laugh and scrubbed a gritty palm across her forehead. Her family would never let her live that one down, but at least she'd have Drew. He was safe. He had to be.

In the hallway, the gunfire sputtered to a halt. Jerusha pushed her way up the wall. "Ready to surrender?" she yelled.

The group spokesman laughed. "He told me you'd be arrogant."

He, who? The guy's boss, maybe Alexiou? And why wasn't *he*, whoever he was, there? She checked her magazine, just to be sure, and heaved out a sigh. Nope, not a single bullet left. "You should've listened."

"I should've," the man agreed. "Come out now. As long as you don't fight, we won't hurt you."

"The last time a man said that to me, I wound up locked in the hold of a frigate bound for Katmandu."

"Seriously?"

"I wouldn't lie." Unless she needed to. She hadn't reached that point yet. "Why do you want the bones?"

"Why do you?"

"Duh, that's kinda obvious."

"And our reasons are just as clear. Kick your weapons out."

Footsteps pattered over the carpet. Jerusha snuck a look around the corner and slung her empty gun straight at the approaching man. It thunked into his skull and he dropped to the floor, clutching his forehead.

Somebody sighed and the man she'd been talking to said, "Why did you do that? I told you if you stopped fighting, you'd be safe."

She snorted. "Yeah, like I'm gonna believe that."

"We were given strict orders. Bring you in alive and unspoiled."

"So you can torture and kill me? Sorry, but I'll have to pass."

"You're coming with us one way or the other."

"I choose *other.*"

She tossed Drew's empty gun into the hallway and leapt after it at full speed, automatically assessing the obstacles in her path. The guy she'd clocked in the forehead had passed out. Three more men ducked into doorways and blood trails on the institutional gray carpet marked the paths of two others, likely where they'd retreated to tend their wounds. One man stepped into her path, his bulldog mug set in determined lines.

She jerked to a stop half a dozen feet away from him. Oh, crap. The bodyguard from the Konya Archaeological Museum, the one accompanying the Greek tourist she'd suspected was a member of the Shadow.

He lifted a gun and aimed it at her heart. "No more fighting, Daughter. Hand over the bones and come quietly."

She held her hands out to her sides. "The bones are long gone. You'll never get your hands on them."

His gentle smile softened the rugged planes of his face. "We'll find your companion and retrieve the bones, though I fear he may not survive the process."

Her heart shrank into a tiny knot in her chest. She schooled her face into an expressionless mask and hardened herself. Nobody threatened her man and got away with it. Nobody.

She ducked to the side and catapulted toward the man, coming up under his arm. Her shoulder dug into his solar plexus, and he grunted and staggered back. She wrapped her arms around his waist and lunged, and they thudded onto the hard floor, grappling for control of the gun. Had to get it, had to make it out, had to save Drew.

The man heaved his hips up and rolled, taking her with him. She shoved her foot into the ground, continuing their roll, and came out on top, one hand on the wrist of his gun hand, the other drawn back for a strike.

The cold metal of a gun's barrel pressed into her temple and she froze.

"Surrender," a hard voice said, and she laughed.

"Fuck off," she said, and dropped onto her back on top of the legs of the man beneath her. She curled her legs up, kneed the hand of the man holding the gun on her, and somersaulted into a handstand, then onto her feet. The man cursed and swung the gun toward her, and she kicked out, hitting him in the chest.

The bulldog-faced man popped onto his feet, aimed slightly to the side, and fired. "The next one is in your thigh, Daughter."

"You have to pin me down—"

Something jabbed into her back and thousands of volts of electricity jolted into her body. Everything froze, her heart, her breath, the men in front of her, and her mind spasmed in a kaleidoscope of colors. The electricity ceased coursing into her and she sagged to the ground. The bulldog-faced man walked over to her, threaded his fingers into her hair, and yanked her head up. His balled-up fist loomed into view and connected with her jaw, popping her head into the floor.

Drew, she thought, and blacked out.

DREW SHUT the storage room door behind himself and jogged toward the interior wall where the dumb waiter was supposed to be, behind a row of four-drawer filing cabinets.

Hell with that.

He stashed the bones out of the way, gripped the back of a filing cabinet, and heaved it onto its front edge, then let go. It

146

crashed into the floor, clanging loudly. The frame cracked and bent, and he snorted. That's what they got for sticking the damn thing in front of the dumb waiter.

A second filing cabinet went the same way. Drew stepped over its remains and tapped a knuckle against the dumb waiter's wooden doors. Hollow, no handles. Probably hadn't been used since the electric elevator was installed God only knew when. He tapped again, located a halfway flimsy spot, and pushed hard. The wood fractured under his hand, and he yanked it back on a frustrated curse. Damn it. Now he had splinters.

He snarled at the door leading into the hallway. When they got out of this, Jerusha owed him big time. First, they got shot at, then he got splinters in his hand. What could possibly go wrong next?

He wiggled the rest of the ruined doors off, wrapped his uninjured hand around the ropes hanging in the center of the shaft, and tugged hard. Something high overhead snapped and the ropes slackened. Drew jumped back just as a heavy, metal pulley whizzed past the open doorway. Half a second later, it clanked against the bottom of the shaft. He stuck his head inside and squinted into the darkened space where the rope had disappeared, then glanced up. No dumb waiter, no rope, no handholds that he could see.

He backed out of the shaft and leaned his forearms against the jagged opening. Well, fuck. He'd had to ask what could go wrong, hadn't he.

He mulled it over for a minute. There was no way around it. He'd have to inch his way up by pressing his body against the sides of the shaft. Not too hard going down. A really stupid idea going up.

Why had he taken this job again? Right. Bobby had asked him to. Drew rolled his shoulders and stretched. At least he'd gotten Jerusha as part and parcel. She sure as hell made a lot of crap worthwhile.

And maybe she'd kiss his booboos when they got back to

the hotel later. Kissing was good, right? Especially when it led to him and her getting naked and sweaty.

He stuffed the rope into the duffel, readjusted its straps, and hooked his arms through them, settling the duffel securely against his stomach. The gunfire in the hallway dwindled to the occasional, random pop. He glanced at the door. She'd be ok. She was a Daughter, strong, agile, fast as lightning. If she wasn't outside half an hour after he got there, he'd come in for her, just like they'd planned. It would work out. Everything was going to work out fine.

He shoved down the uneasiness poking at his gut and heaved himself feet first into the shaft. It was narrow, not much wider than his shoulders and almost as shallow. He braced his feet against the far wall and, in slow, careful increments, maneuvered himself crosswise in the shaft with the dumb waiter's ruined opening on his left, next to his dominant hand.

Just in case the doors one floor up were sealed shut, because that's the way his luck was running.

He pushed his back and one foot into the wall, resettled the opposite foot six inches higher, and scooted up. The rough, plaster wall scrubbed into his skin through his knit turtleneck, and Drew ground his teeth together. Yup, that was gonna hurt later. Couldn't be helped, so he blocked it out of his mind, resettled his weight, and shoved himself half a foot higher.

One down, nine or twenty more to go, depending on how far apart the floors were. He'd never quite worked that out in his head when they were studying the blueprints. Though, come to think on it, those blueprints had been part of an article on the building's history. He hadn't expected them to be accurate to the nail, but he'd sure as hell expected them to mark out where the fucking floors stopped and started.

He focused on climbing the shaft, ignoring the burn in his muscles, the scrapes on his back, and the uncomfortable press of the duffel into awkward and unusual places. The mission was paramount. Getting the bones out was priority one, Jerusha priority two, himself behind both. Bobby and Hiro were counting on him. *Jerusha* was counting on him. By God, he wouldn't let her down.

Light's reach slowly diminished as he traveled upward and the sounds of gunfire stopped all together. Every few feet, he slid his left hand along the wall, searching for the door, and marked his progress by the half steps he was taking up the sides of the shaft. Eight feet, ten, thirteen. No doors. Fuck.

He sucked in a breath. Sweat gathered in sticky pools under his arms and seeped into the cuts in his back, stinging like a mother. He forced his trembling muscles to steady and gradually inched his way upward. Fifteen feet, nineteen, twenty-four.

His palm hit wood.

He leaned the back of his head against the wall. Thank fuck. Now all he had to do was get the doors open.

He fumbled along the wood, searching for a crack or a handle, and found not a goddamned thing. He cursed roundly under his breath and slammed the side of his fist into the wood, as close to the center as he could get. It crumpled under the blow and a thin stream of light shattered the shaft's darkness.

He hit it again and again and again, tore pieces away when he could, and eventually opened up a space big enough to fit through. He glanced into the room and grunted. Looked like an office, kinda cushy, too, and empty in spite of all the noise he'd made. He maneuvered himself around, eased out head first, and dropped onto the floor in front of the obsolete dumb waiter.

He slid the duffel off and rolled onto his side, staring into the opening, then laughed. A huge, framed landscape with a hole punched into the middle of it was hanging crookedly over the place he'd just crawled out of. Fuck all, he'd punched through an inch of plywood and tough canvas, and hadn't even heard the damn frame rattle against the wall.

He forced his aching muscles to move and staggered toward the room's lone window. It was modern and slid easily open. He stuck his head out and sagged against the frame. He was on the fucking third floor. Jesus H. Christ, no wonder it'd taken him so long to get out of the dumb waiter's shaft.

Whatever. He had enough rope to make it to within ten feet of the ground, as long as he could find a stable tie off, and he could drop from the bottom of the rope, no problem.

Being tall was downright handy sometimes.

He pushed the heavy, mahogany desk to the window, retrieved the rope, and secured it to one of the desk's legs. He tugged hard, judged it good enough. Somebody sure was gonna be surprised when they came to work in the morning.

He slung the rope out the window, secured the duffel to his back, and eased into the night, his hands wrapped around the rope, his feet braced against the museum's rock siding. Fucking cold. Fiji was looking better all the time. Him and Jaybird on the beach, her in a bikini, the ocean beating against the sand. Yeah, that'd do it. He walked his way down the building, spooling the daydream out, shutting out the icy air, the ache in his back, the splinters in his hand.

Halfway down, his foot slipped, upsetting his balance, and his body slammed into the side of the building. Pain ricocheted through muscle into bone and he clamped down on a grunt. Fuck all. Next time, Jerusha could be the second story man and he could fight it out with the bad guys.

He reestablished his balance and climbed down to the end of the rope, dropped to the ground, and crouched in the shadows clinging to the building. Nothing moved, not people, not animals. He oriented himself and crept around the side of the building toward the main entrance. Nothing.

He frowned as he repositioned the duffel's straps across one shoulder. The other guys hadn't come through the back. The alleyway behind the museum was too narrow for cars, had been created long before those were a glimmer in anybody's imagination, but the men weren't out front, either. There were side entrances, sure, but the most convenient way to move into and out of the museum was through the main entrance.

A car's engine cut through the night's icy stillness. Drew reacted, racing across the street and into the shadows of the buildings beyond, in an area sheltered from the worst of the slight wind. A minute later, two police cars eased to a stop in front of the museum and a handful of police officers piled out.

He grunted. Must be a slow crime night.

Drew studied the scene and waited, his thumb flicking along the empty space where his wedding ring should've been. The cops were gonna haul Jerusha out any minute now. As soon as they did, he could go back to the hotel, pack their belongings, and relocate somewhere close by until he could figure out how to rescue her. Turkey had a fairly even-tempered justice system, had since the shift to a secular government in the early 1920s. No more chopping hands off for theft or any of that bullshit. Accused criminals went through a process similar to modern Western judicial systems. If all else failed and he couldn't break her out, the IECS could hire an attorney to get her out of whatever charges the police threw at her.

Half an hour passed and the sweat threatened to freeze on his skin. He flexed his fingers, stretched his blood into circulation in his numb limbs, and waited. Eventually, a police officer exited the building and cordoned off the area. An ambulance pulled up to the curb, its attendants raced into the museum with their equipment, and not long after, they wheeled somebody out, one of the bozos by the looks of him. The security guard Drew had glimpsed stumbled after them, guided by a police officer, one hand holding what looked like an ice pack to his head.

The uneasiness in Drew's gut roared to life. He'd been in the shaft too long. He'd missed too much. Damn it. Where the fuck was Jerusha?

He broke into the building across the street from the museum, scrounged a clean shirt and a blanket, and found a good watch post in an empty apartment on the second floor. As the night rolled on and people came and went through the museum's main entrance, the uneasiness morphed into panic and the panic into cold fear.

Jerusha never came out. Nobody even close to her size and build exited the museum.

Another ambulance pulled up and carted an injured man off, and the other packed up and left. Civilian vehicles screeched to a stop next to the curb. Men and women in rumpled clothing got out and entered the museum. Temel Baştürk, probably the museum's directors and other muckity mucks, and still no Jerusha.

Drew tucked his fingers between his arms and his ribs, his mind a chaotic jumble. Where was she? What had happened to her after he'd left? Goddamn it, he should've known better, should never have left her there alone, immortal Daughter or not. Even she had her vulnerabilities. Even she could be stopped by a bullet. Is that what had happened? Had somebody shot her, killed her even?

No, they would've brought her body out by now.

He huddled under the blanket and replayed the night in his mind. Breaking in, packing up the bones, getting caught by those bozos in the hallway. Jerusha's kiss, her daredevil smile, and his slow climb up the shaft.

His mind fixed on that point. Why hadn't those men come after him? Had they figured he had the bones and decided to take Jerusha and exchange one for the other at some later time? Why hadn't they followed the logical path of the shaft and waited for him in the upper stories?

Hell, he didn't even know who *they* were. Maybe the Shadow, maybe black market dealers of some kind. Not much of a difference between the two in his mind.

He chewed on the whole mess until the first light of dawn peeked over the horizon. Dr. Baştürk and the others exited accompanied by the police, the building was securely locked, and Jerusha was nowhere to be seen.

Drew doubled over around the queasy churn in his stomach. The hotel was out. Dr. Baştürk had probably already identified him and Jerusha from the security feed. The car was three blocks away. By the time he got to it, somebody would've reported it and the police would be all over it.

He clenched his hands into fists against his thighs. Where was she? Where was his Jaybird? How in hell was he gonna track her when he didn't even know who'd taken her? He'd promised her he would. Goddamn it, he'd promised her he'd come back for her, and look at him, a ragged mess with no clue on how to find her, let alone help her.

A face popped into his head and he eased slowly upright. *He* didn't know where to start looking, but he knew somebody who did. All he had to do was get there without arousing anybody's suspicions and that was no big. He'd done that kinda thing a thousand times before, him and Bobby and Hiro and the rest of their team, and for Jerusha, he could do it a thousand times more. He threw the blanket off, heaved the bones over his shoulder, and quietly exited his hidey hole.

Time to get his Jaybird back. When he found her, somebody was gonna pay.

Thirteen

SOMETHING WAS touching her face. Jerusha held death still and opened her senses to her surroundings. Water splashing into itself. The rustle of fabric. The creak of a chair, and that something touched her again, wetting her face in gentle swipes over a bruising ache in her jaw.

Drew?

She sniffed delicately. A damp mustiness, the faint hint of an unfamiliar cologne, the lingering scent of dry cleaning fluid. Not Drew, but who?

A smooth palm cupped her uninjured cheek. "I know you're awake."

The rich, deep voice was cultured, its English heavily flavored by the rhythm of the Mediterranean. Jerusha lifted her eyelids slowly, squinted against the light piercing straight into her brain, and studied the man holding her. He was coldly handsome, his features chiseled and refined. His eyes glittered like dark diamonds on either side of a hawkish nose. A stylishly cut suit hung in perfect lines over his medium build and his midnight hair curled in waves against his high forehead.

Memory stirred, and with it, an unwelcome connection. That nose, that voice. Sweet Goddess, this was the businessman from the Konya Archaeological Museum, bulldog-face's companion. What was he doing here?

"Do you know why I enjoy being with Daughters?" he

154

asked.

She shook her head slowly.

"They're straight-forward, open, generally honest." His thin lips curled into a smile. "Admirable qualities in a woman."

Her muscles tightened and encountered resistance, and she tested it. She was sitting upright in a hard chair, and something was binding her to it, at her wrists, her ankles. No gag, not a bad thing. She just wasn't sure she wanted to talk.

The man dipped a washcloth into a basin of water sitting at the edge of her vision and squeezed the excess moisture out. "It's been a long time since I've had the pleasure of a Daughter's company."

"Why are you holding me?"

He ran the cloth gently over her jaw. "You intrigue me."

Great. Just what she needed, for a man who was probably a member of the Shadow to find her interesting.

"And you remind me of someone, a Daughter I knew long ago." He dropped the washcloth into the water and cupped his hands around her face. His palms were smooth and cool and incredibly tender. "She took something from me, something I value highly. I want it back."

Jerusha held herself absolutely motionless within his touch. "I don't know what that is."

"Don't you?" He released her and stepped back. "Perhaps it's time I acquired a new lover. Daughters make excellent sexual companions, and you, I've heard, are wild in bed. My men enjoyed listening to you and your man."

She sucked in a breath. Oh, crap. She and Drew must not've found all the friggin' bugs in their hotel room. No wonder their tails had done a Houdini. No need to follow somebody when you knew everything they were doing.

"You're not my type," she said.

He smiled, cold, calculating. "I will be, once Marco is finished with you."

"Marco?"

The man's smile widened. "Alexiou, my nephew. Surely you've heard of the brother of the infamous leader of the Shadow."

Every cell in Jerusha's body ground to a screeching halt, freezing her from the inside out. "Who are you?"

"Pinico Alexiou, youngest brother of the previous Shadow, at your service." He bent toward her and smoothed a hand over her hair. "I look forward to getting to know you better, after Marco breaks you."

He brushed his mouth over hers, his lips soft and supple, and a fear she'd never known scrambled through her. She was being held by Pinico and Marco Alexiou, two of the most dangerous men she'd ever heard of. Why had they taken her? She was just a foot soldier, a nobody. She didn't know anything, didn't even know where Drew had disappeared to with Marnan's remains. What good could she possibly be to them?

A door creaked open and a shoe scuffed along the floor. Pinico released her and stepped back, and a younger man moved into her line of sight. He was just as handsome as Pinico, just as cold, just as frightening. Marco Alexiou, had to be. The family resemblance was too strong for him to be anybody else.

"You started without me," Marco said in a strong Yankee twang.

"We'd barely begun." Pinico clapped a hand to Marco's shoulder. "Try not to get carried away this time. I'd like her as unspoiled as possible when you're finished."

Marco nodded solemnly. "I'll try."

"Good. Enjoy yourself." Pinico slid a finger down Jerusha's cheek. "Eat when Marco offers you food, Jerusha, darling. You must keep your strength up."

"How do you know my name?"

"Facial recognition software. Amazing what modern technology and decades of surveillance photos can accomplish."

Pinico turned on his heel and stalked out of the room, and Marco moved into the center of her vision, blocking her view of the door.

She met his gaze evenly. "Torturing me won't get you anywhere."

"Who said anything about torture?" He shifted his stance and straddled her knees, one foot on either side of her legs. "I hate the People. They've taken so much from us."

He said it calmly, without rancor, and she matched his tone. "Ditto on the Shadow."

"An odd thing for us to have in common, our mutual hatred of each other." He skimmed his fingertips over her cheekbone. "You have the most beautiful eyes. What color would you call that shade of blue?"

"I honestly have no idea." She yanked her arms up, straining against the duct tape binding her to the chair. "Let me go and I'll find a color chart."

"Nice try, but no. I like you right where you are." His fingers drifted down her cheek and tucked into the top of her turtleneck. "Knit fabric. Couldn't you have worn cotton?"

"Knit shifts with your movements. Cotton binds."

"True." He sighed and fished a pocketknife out of the front pocket of his slacks. He flipped it open, jerked the hem of her turtleneck out of the waistband of her cargo pants, and held the fabric away from her stomach. "Hold still. Wouldn't want to hurt you."

She sucked her stomach muscles in, well away from his hand. He dug the tip of the knife into the hem and worked the blade into the hole and up the center of her shirt, ripping it in two.

He paused near the top. "Head back. Steady now."

She tilted her chin up. Torture she'd survive. Taking a knife to the throat wasn't a pretty way to die, and she wasn't ready to meet the Great Lady yet. She had to see Drew again. He'd promised to take her to Fiji. At the very least, he owed her a basketball game.

The fabric ripped, jerking against her skin, and the tip of the knife flicked into her skin. Marco clucked his tongue. "Sorry. The knife slipped."

The cut didn't sting, but that wasn't the point. "Right. It slipped."

"Really." He set the knife on the tiny table holding the basin of water and folded the pieces of her shirt away from her torso. "Black lace. A beautiful complement for your skin. What's your favorite color?"

"Black," she said flatly. "Do you have a thing for colors?"

"I thought you might appreciate fresh underwear in a few days, after you've settled in." He brushed the backs of his fingers across the top of her breast, above her bra. "Soft skin."

"I moisturize regularly." She wiggled to the side, away from his touch. "Get on with it, will you? I've got a vacation to plan."

"What's the hurry? Your man has no idea where you are, the People will think you've abandoned your mission, especially if we can track down your companion before he contacts them. We have plenty of time to get to know each other."

She pursed her lips. "I'd rather go to Fiji."

"We can, once we're finished here." An unnatural light burned in his deep blue eyes as he leaned toward her. "I'm going to enjoy breaking you."

His mouth latched on to her throat and he *mmmd*. His hand crept around her neck and wound around her hair, holding her still, and she stared up at the ceiling, memorizing its features as Marco pressed hot, open-mouthed kisses across her throat. Unevenly spread plaster, cracks near the doorway, water stain overhead. An old building. Maybe the basement?

Marco eased back. "Relax. I'm not going to hurt you, not so soon into our pleasure."

"Pretty sure rape hurts," she retorted.

"I have no intention of raping you, Jerusha. Pinico wants that part of you, and I've promised it to him, so relax. Enjoy yourself. Think about your man if it helps." He shifted her head to the side and whispered into her ear. "I'll be thinking about my wife. She can't find this kind of pleasure anymore, thanks to a Daughter."

His free hand fumbled with the fastening of his slacks and he pulled his dick out.

She trained her gaze on his face. "Not impressed."

"You will be."

He ducked toward her and bit into the flesh at the base of her neck, sucking hard. His fist tightened around her hair and his other hand slapped over his dick in a steady rhythm.

Jerusha focused on the ceiling and disconnected herself from what he was doing, shutting down her emotions. No fear, no anxiety. He wasn't hurting her. It was disgusting, yes, but it didn't hurt, and as long as he didn't go any further, she'd be fine. Drew was going to come for her, if she didn't get herself out of this mess first, and soon, this would all be a memory.

In Fiji, where it was warm and mojitos were plentiful.

Marco pressed his forehead into her shoulder and groaned, and hot streams of ejaculate splattered onto her bare stomach. "Oh, God. Oh, God, that's good."

She rolled her eyes. What was it about men and their dicks? "Glad I could help."

A laugh shuddered out of him. "I'll bring you some water. For drinking, not for bathing. You'll wear my cum until you give in and accept your situation."

Well, she'd had worse things on her skin and lived to tell the tale, though Drew would probably be pissed when he figured out what had happened.

Mmm. Drew pissed at Marco when Shadow Junior was within easy reach? Oh, yeah, she wanted to see that. Maybe she'd pop some popcorn. A good show was always better with a snack.

Marco kissed her throat and eased upright, then zipped his pants closed. "I have a little business to attend to, but I'll be back in a couple of hours with some water and we can do this again."

"Thanks for the warning. I'll be sure to escape before then."

"There's no escape, Jerusha. Resign yourself to that."

He walked away, and she tuned him out, settling herself into a nice fantasy involving Drew, suntan lotion, and an empty beach.

DREW JACKED a beat up truck and zigzagged out of Nevşehir toward Kayseri. He'd panicked. What kind of trained operator panicked under pressure? It'd never happened to him before, not once, and the only reason he could think of for it to happen now was Jerusha.

He stared out the windshield at the road whizzing by under his ride's tires and rubbed a palm over the ache in his chest. Helluva thing for a man to discover, that he loved somebody about two shakes after she was kidnapped. At least, he was pretty sure it was love. He'd never fallen into it before, hadn't even come close, so maybe he was wrong. Maybe it was heartburn or something and his little head was just out of control, messing with his emotions.

He slowed the car and signaled for a right turn. Half hard all the time? Yup. Dreamed about her constantly? Also a yup. Couldn't wait to see her again? Oh, fuck, yeah.

He rotated the steering wheel, easing his stolen truck onto an empty street. So maybe it was his dick talking or maybe it was really love. Didn't matter. She'd put her life in his hands, trusted him at long last, the way a woman was supposed to trust the man in her life. Besides, she owed him a trip to London, and hell if he'd let her forget it.

He ditched the truck blocks from Pari's and walked in, duffel slung over his shoulder, his hands deep in his pants pockets, his back one huge, dull throb. The sun's thin, early morning rays barely warmed the air above freezing and the chill bit into his skin, numbing him to the core. He swept his gaze over the landscape, searching for a hint of Pari's people, and caught the twitch of a curtain on the upper floor of what appeared to be an abandoned building.

Good. Somebody would tell her he was coming. Hopefully,

that would cut down on the hassle.

A woman was waiting for him at the front entrance to Pari's building, one shoulder against the scuffed siding, her coat open, a hand on the gun strapped to her hip. She nodded toward the door, and he entered, her close behind.

He hesitated at the base of the stairs. Two fucking flights. What was it with him and third floors lately? The woman nudged his back, and he took the hint, forcing his exhausted legs up the stairs at an even pace.

On the third floor, the woman grabbed his elbow and guided him down the empty hallway toward Pari's door. She knocked, then entered, and tugged him inside behind her.

Pari was sitting on a low chaise, ankles crossed, her long, dark curls loose around her shoulders. She wore a peach baby doll under a knee-length kimono style robe and her narrow feet were bare. "Drew. What an unexpected pleasure."

He grunted. "You know why I'm here."

"I'm afraid not, though I'm happy for the company." She patted the chaise beside her. "Sit, please, and tell me all about your escape from your lovely captor. Did she let you go willingly or did you have to fight your way out?"

"Jerusha is my partner," he said flatly, "and if it's all the same to you, I'll stand."

"Don't be silly. You're swaying on your feet."

Fucking bullshit small talk. How did Jaybird stand it? "I need help."

"Naturally."

"Jerusha's been kidnapped. I don't know where she is and I need help finding her."

Pari stood slowly and crossed to him. "What's in the bag?"

He pressed his lips into a thin line. "The remains of a Sister."

Her dark eyes widened and her hand drifted to the straps slung over his left shoulder, touching them lightly. "Truly?"

"I'm not trading them for your help."

"That isn't the price you'll pay for my assistance."

"Name it."

She smiled. "Not yet. First, explain to me how Jerusha managed to get herself kidnapped and what you know of those who took her."

He rubbed the heels of his palms into gritty eyes, but he told her, every single piece he didn't consider confidential. Not their bigger mission, no, just the part about attempting to steal the bones and Jerusha sending him and them out of the museum while she held off half a dozen bozos.

When he wound down, Pari stroked her fingers over his beard. "You're exhausted."

"It's been a long night."

"I'm sure." She glanced at the woman who'd escorted him up. "Chana, please draw a bath for Drew and fetch a meal for him."

"His back needs tending," Chana said.

"Find what you need."

Chana slipped away, and Pari turned back to him. "My youngest daughter, Chana. She'll be in charge of your care while you're here. Please don't attempt to escape her. She's a good tracker."

Drew scowled at her. "I'm not a fucking prisoner."

"No, Drew, you aren't, but you are my responsibility until we locate Jerusha and return you to her." Pari's sensuous lips curved into a warm smile. "She's a dear friend. I'd hate to drive a wedge into our friendship, should something happen to you."

"I can take care of myself."

"Of that I have no doubt. Still, a Daughter has her duties and you are now mine."

He rolled his shoulders. Fucking Daughter attitudes. Was that the way Jerusha saw him, as a goddamn duty she had to fulfill? He added that to the list of things he intended to set her straight on, first thing after he got her back. "You'll help me find her?"

"Of course. As I said, she's a dear friend. Naturally, I'll need payment for supplies and the use of my kin."

"Naturally," he said drily. "How much?"

She laughed, a gentle tinkle of sound. "I don't want money, Drew. I want you."

"Fuck that, Pari. I'm not for sale."

"Not even in exchange for the life of your woman?" She pivoted away from him, her stride graceful and sure, and reclined against the arm of the chaise. "Are you not willing to trade something of equal value to her?"

A slow burn boiled into his blood. "Quit fucking around. The longer we wait to go after her, the colder the trail gets. I bet you know how that works, what with all your centuries of living."

"Millennia," she murmured. "You'll remain with her as long as she wants you, after which you'll have sixty days to settle your affairs and present yourself to me, forever after to be mine. Those are my terms. Take them or leave them."

He dropped his gaze to the area rug covering the floor. Its design was intricate, abstract, and it was probably older than him by decades, maybe more.

How long would Jerusha want him?

His heart pinged and he sucked in a breath. She didn't seem in too big of a hurry to get rid of him, seemed pretty damn happy to spend time with him, as a matter of fact, but that couldn't last forever. An immortal Daughter had to get bored of men eventually, and he was going to age, nothing he could do about it. His body would wear out, and not long after, she'd have no more use for him. He'd be an empty husk, used up, a dry shell of a man, but if that's all he could have with her, so be it.

Tears stung his sinuses. Would he even have a full decade with her before she walked away?

He swallowed down the sorrow clogging his throat. "Is there a time limit on how long she keeps me?"

"Until she's finished with you. Oh, Drew."

She sighed, and he lifted his gaze and met hers evenly

through blurred vision. Fuck it. He didn't care if this woman saw him cry. He really just did not give a good goddamn what he had to do, as long as the end result was Jerusha getting safely home.

"You love her," Pari said.

"That's none of your business."

"It's certainly pertinent to our arrangement."

He dug his fingertips into his palms, ignoring the sting of nails biting into too cold flesh. "Do we have a deal or not?"

"We have a deal," she said softly. "Your life for hers. I regret that you've already given her your heart, but perhaps by then it won't matter."

"It doesn't matter now," he said, and she shook her head.

"She'll hurt you, Drew. She won't mean to, but she will. I'd rather you not carry that burden."

The door creaked open and Chana said, "Bath's ready."

"Go with Chana. Cleanse yourself, fill your belly, rest while you can. I'll send someone to your hotel to retrieve your and Jerusha's belongings, and my kin will begin the search for your heart's love."

He nodded and stumbled out of the room behind Chana, so numb, he couldn't muster the strength to argue.

Fourteen

J ERUSHA WORKED her limbs against the tape holding her to the chair. By her count, she'd been in it at least twenty-four hours, probably closer to thirty-six. There were no windows in the room, though it was well lit, but the rhythms of life wherever she was gave the time away. Regular meals, guards changing shift outside the lone entrance, most of the lights flipped off for a block of hours, presumably so she could sleep.

A thoughtful gesture, if a useless one. She'd dozed fitfully during the dark hours, but she could do that with the lights on. In between, she'd observed her surroundings, searching for weaknesses and a way out.

The door swished open and a woman entered bearing a tray of food, her hair and neck hidden under a lavender hijab. The same woman had brought food and water to Jerusha the day before and fed it to her in careful bites between Marco's frequent visits. Jerusha hadn't bothered to poke at the other woman. Chances were good the Alexious were paying her generously. That kind of money nearly always ensured loyalty.

But she had to call her something, so Jerusha had settled on Daisy, simply because it was the name of the first female cartoon character that had popped into her mind.

Drew was such a bad influence.

She bowed her head, hiding a smile, and peeked through

her lashes at the world beyond the slowly closing door. One guard, male, broad shouldered and lean, a Mini-Uzi slung over his shoulder. As if she couldn't figure out a way around that.

Daisy set the tray on a table and carried the basin on the adjoining one into the barebones bathroom tacked onto one side of the room. Without fail, the woman brought in fresh water before a meal and cleaned Jerusha's face and hands, and without fail, she left the icky mess of Marco's semen coating Jerusha's torso and pants.

Six times yesterday, not counting the first, twice already that day. Her shoulders ached under the marks he'd bitten into her skin, not to the point of true harm, but enough to irritate her. She was beginning to see why Marco had chosen this particular brand of torture. Having his bodily fluids sticking to her in a grimy mess was demeaning, sure, but it didn't hurt her. Eventually it might wear her down, if she was there long enough, and Marco was sure to move on to something that really did hurt. Fortunately for her, she had a former Delta Force Operator in her corner, and if all else failed, she'd rescue herself.

Because she was a Daughter and Daughters didn't need men to get them out of sticky situations.

Either option was going to take time, though. Two more days minimum before Drew would strike, and that only if he'd managed to follow her abductors. It could be several days, maybe as long as two weeks, before he came for her or she managed to break out on her own. She just had to hold on until then.

She swallowed the broth Daisy spooned into her mouth and ignored her full bladder. A handful of men would come in with handcuffs after the meal and let her use the bathroom. She'd bloodied one's nose the previous night while trying to escape, and earned a glare from the man and a chiding cluck from Marco.

At least he hadn't tried to wiggle a promise out of her not to try again.

The door opened and the devil himself stepped inside.

Jerusha deliberately flattened her gaze. "Oh, it's you."

"Happy to see me?"

"Sure, that's exactly what I'm feeling."

Marco's smile was boyish and almost sweet. "It's too bad you'll lose your spirit over the next few weeks. I'm beginning to enjoy it."

Daisy gathered the remains of Jerusha's meal together, bowed toward Marco, and scurried out the door.

He stalked toward her, his dick already tenting his slacks, and Jerusha withdrew into a basketball game, Georgia Tech versus Duke. Tech scored, the crowd went wild, and Drew slid his hand into hers, his laughter full of that rough Southie charm she adored.

REBECCA'S HEELS clicked sharply against the bed and breakfast's hardwood floor. Ten days had passed since Lukas Alexiou had requested an interview with her, ten days since he'd offered to exchange artifacts for a visit with the Oracle. Once Rebecca's shock had worn off, leaving him alone to stew had seemed the best option. Now, though, she couldn't afford to wait any longer. She needed his help, needed to know if he and his kin had kidnapped Jerusha.

She paused outside the sitting room doors and pressed a trembling hand over the sick worry in her gut. Having a child captured by the Shadow Enemy was every Daughter's worst nightmare. That it had occurred while Jerusha was on a vital mission was doubly upsetting. Drew was working on retrieving her, but if Rebecca could pry information out of the tight-lipped Shadow as an added condition of his meeting the Oracle, perhaps it would hurry Jerusha's rescue along. For her children, she'd gladly bargain with the devil.

Rebecca straightened her shoulders, wiped the worry off her expression, and entered the room.

Lukas was sitting on the settee next to his nephew, reading a book to the young boy. He glanced up and smiled. "Director. What a pleasant surprise."

"I'm afraid the feeling isn't mutual, Mr. Alexiou." She nodded toward his kin. "You may wish to send him out of the room."

Lukas marked their place in the book and handed it to his nephew. "Go to your room, Steven. I'll be along shortly."

Steven grinned and scampered off the settee and across the room. He paused in front of her and tilted his head way back. "You're not as big as Dani."

Rebecca sighed. Of all things for a child to notice, why did it have to be her own lack of height? "No, darling, I'm not."

"She promised not to eat me." Steven's mouth twisted into a frown. "You're not gonna eat me, are you?"

"Whyever would I want to?"

He shrugged and fingered one corner of the book he held. "Mama said Daughters eat little boys, eat 'em right to the bone."

Lukas stood up and buttoned his suit jacket over his lean stomach. "The director will not harm you, Steven. Run along now."

The little boy heaved a heartfelt sigh and trudged out of the room, and Rebecca arched one eyebrow at his uncle.

"My apologies, Director. His mother was seriously injured by a Daughter not long after his birth. She insists on filling his head with nonsense." He gestured toward the chair opposite him. "Please, have a seat. Have you had a chance to consider my offer?"

"I have." Rebecca cleared her throat, then perched on the edge of the chair's cushion. "That isn't why I'm here."

He unbuttoned his jacket, settled onto the settee, and crossed an ankle over one knee. "Oh?"

She tamped down her irritation. After all this time, she should be used to the games people played, but oh, how she hated enmeshing herself in the political when her child's life was at risk.

And so, this time she would not.

"My daughter, Jerusha, was kidnapped yesterday during a mission in Turkey."

One corner of Lukas' mouth turned down. "I'm sorry to hear that, Director. Have you had a ransom demand or—?"

She slashed one hand through the air. "Please don't insult me, Mr. Alexiou. We both know your people have her."

"My people."

"Of course. Who else would want the items she was after?"

"And what was she after?"

She pressed her lips into a hard line. "As if you don't know."

"Humor me, please."

"The bones of a Sister."

Lukas' carefully controlled expression erupted into laughter and he leaned forward. "You've truly found a Sister's remains? Outstanding."

She clamped her jaws together. That wasn't the reaction she'd expected, and it wasn't one she was prepared to deal with. The Shadow, happy over the People's success? It was unheard of.

His laughter faded. "But of course, she had them in her possession when she was kidnapped."

"Fortunately, no. Her partner managed to smuggle them away. He's searching for her as we speak."

Lukas folded his hands over his ankle and tapped a thumb against the leg of his slacks. "And you believe I had something to do with this?"

"You or your people."

"Not on my direction," he said flatly. "I have a strict rule against harming Daughters and I severely punish anyone who disobeys me."

Her mind flashed back to something Dani had told her, about the man that had killed Linda Terhune the day Lukas Alexiou had ordered the kidnapping of her daughter, Amelia.

That man had wound up dead in a slum in New York. According to Dani, his death had been a direct result of Alexiou's orders.

"You've kidnapped one of ours in the past," she said.

"And will not hesitate to do so again, should the need be great." He inhaled sharply through his nose. "Still, I had no hand in your daughter's situation. If you truly believe someone within my organization has kidnapped her, I will gladly assist your efforts to retrieve her."

Rebecca sat back in the chair. Just like that, after millennia of enmity, this man was willing to help her? "Why should I trust you?"

"Because you have something I need."

"The Oracle."

He inclined his head. "Precisely. The best interests of both our peoples are served by such a meeting. I will do whatever I have to in order to facilitate it."

Relief sighed out of her and she nearly slumped. Only her innate pride kept her spine rigidly straight. "Will you help us find my daughter?"

"I will. Excuse me, please."

He retrieved his cell phone and dialed a number. A moment later, he said, "Mr. Winstead, I have need of your assistance. No, it's Marco. He's in Turkey on business. It's come to my attention a Daughter has been kidnapped there and I have reason to believe he's involved." Lukas' eyes shot to Rebecca. "Of course. You know what to do."

He dropped the phone onto the coffee table. "You already have people working on it."

"She's my daughter."

"And her mission is paramount. Every second counts now, Director. Time is running out and we have much work to do."

"I haven't made a decision regarding your request."

His mouth quirked into a half smile. "Yes, you have, but no matter. Mr. Winstead will know something within a day or so. If needs must, I shall travel to Turkey myself and aid in the search."

"Because you'll do anything to see the Oracle."

"That's part of it, Director, but not all. Your daughter's mission is critical." His hands gripped his thighs tightly. "She must succeed. I will do everything in my power to aid her success, including hunting down my own brother."

Rebecca sat back in her chair. For some odd reason, she believed him, and that disturbed her on a level so deep, she refused to examine it closely, for fear of what she might find.

THE COMPUTER SCREEN blurred for the nth time. Drew rubbed his fingers wearily over his eyes. They burned and ached, a lot like the rest of him, and had since he'd lost Jerusha. Three days. Three goddamn days since the morning he'd staggered into Pari's apartment searching for help, and they were still miles away from finding his Jaybird.

One of Pari's endless stream of kin had hacked into the security cameras scattered around Nevşehir and tracked the vehicle carrying Jerusha to the outskirts of the city, into the unmonitored farmland beyond.

Drew had watched the museum's flickering outside security feed over and over again. Two men had carried Jerusha out of the building. Her head had lolled and her body had hung limply between the men. Every time he saw the way they'd beaten her down, his stomach twisted into a greasy knot in his gut.

A heavy hand fell on his shoulder. Drew jerked out of a half doze and twisted around. Saul, one of the few men in Pari's compound, was standing behind him, his flinty gaze locked on the computer screen Drew had been studying. As soon as Drew had met the former Turkish Maroon Beret, he'd recruited him to help find Jerusha and hadn't regretted it a single minute since. Saul was tough, a creative thinker, and he knew exactly what it was like to live under a Daughter's oppressive thumb.

"How is the work?" Saul said in deliberate, accented English.

"You know, I don't mind Turkish if English is a pain."

"I need to practice." Saul pointed at the computer. "You have something?"

"Naw. Just going over the same ground." Ground he'd covered a million times already, searching for something, anything, that would lead him to his blue-eyed lover. "Any word on the car tags?"

"It takes time, Andrew."

Drew scowled. Why the hell did Saul insist on calling him by his full first name when he refused to share his own surname? Nobody Drew had met at Pari's seemed to have one, but maybe that was just a thing here. "It's been three days."

Saul's hard gaze shifted to Drew. "In the United States, everything is online, yes? Here is not the same. Some small areas are still..." Saul's mouth pressed into a thin line among the angular planes of his lean face. "Converting to computers and the Internet."

"Yeah, well."

Drew scrubbed his hands over his face. God, he needed sleep. He just couldn't. Every time he drifted off, Jerusha's face popped into his head and whatever dreams he'd been having morphed into nightmares. Her blood spilling in crimson dots across an interrogation room's floor, her body bruised and mutilated, her spirit crushed. He woke up sweating with his fingers ripping into the sheets and his heart galloping in his chest.

His mind fixed inevitably on one uncontested fact. He hadn't saved her, not in his dreams, not in reality. She'd trusted him to save her, and he hadn't been able to. He hadn't made it out of the museum quick enough, hadn't managed to find a single, solid lead, and he missed her. God, he missed her so much, holding her, breathing her in, sharing her laughter.

And the blood, so much blood spattered across the floor, Jerusha's bright blue eyes forever sightless...

Saul shook Drew's shoulder, jarring him awake, and Drew slumped into his seat.

"Sorry, man. I guess I dozed off."

"Go to bed, Andrew. Chana will give you a sleeping aid."

Drew sighed. He hated taking meds, fucking hated it, but if he didn't get some sleep soon, his brain would turn into mush. He'd be useless to Jerusha, useless to the team Pari had assembled for him, useless to himself. "Yeah, guess I'll do that. G'night."

"Sleep well," Saul said.

Drew waved a tired hand at him and fumbled his way through the compound in search of Chana, his mind weaving through the scant information they'd gathered on the men that had taken his Jaybird.

Fifteen

A NIGGLE OF AN IDEA nudged Drew toward wakefulness. He grunted and tightened his arm around Jerusha's waist. What a nightmare. Losing her to unknown abductors, the frantic wait for her to come out of the museum, begging Pari for help. Just a dream. Thank God.

He buried his face in her hair, breathing her in, and frowned. Was she using another shampoo? He didn't remember her getting a new brand, but what did he know. He was just a guy. One brand was as good as another.

He slid his hand up and cupped her breast through her t-shirt, kneading it with his palm. Yeah, that was it. She was nice and full and...

Not the right shape. He jerked his hand away from whoever he was holding. That wasn't Jerusha. Holy shit. Who was he in bed with?

He struggled through layers of blankets and, bizarrely, an arm slung around his waist from behind, and sat up. He groped his way across whoever the fuck was in his bed and flipped on the lamp sitting on his nightstand, flooding the bed with dim light, and froze. Chana lay partially under him. Pari's security tech, a Daughter he barely knew, was on the other side of the bed. Both were sleeping peacefully.

And he didn't remember getting into bed with either one of

them, wouldn't have done so even if they'd offered. Fuck's sake, he was with Jerusha and he cared about her too much to sleep around.

His breath churned in his lungs and he scrambled out of bed, searching for clothes. Ohgodohgodohgod, Jerusha was gonna kill him. He'd been trying to earn her trust, trying to prove she could believe in him, and what had he done the minute she turned her back? He'd cheated on her, that was what, and he didn't even remember it, couldn't remember a fucking thing after walking out on Saul, so tired he could barely see straight.

He stuffed his legs into the first pair of pants he found and yanked them on over his underwear. Fuckfuckfuck. What the hell had Chana given him last night?

She groaned and stirred, then flipped over onto her back and glared at him through narrowed eyes. "What's wrong?"

"What's wrong?" He huffed out a thready laugh and braced his palms on his widespread knees. "You wake up in my bed and wanna know what's wrong?"

Her bow mouth tilted into a frown. "Mother asked me to watch over you during the night. We were worried you'd react poorly to the medicine we gave you."

"We didn't, er..." He bowed his head and steadied his breathing. "No sex?"

"Of course, not. Mother insisted we respect your bond with Jerusha."

Drew staggered to the bed and sank onto its edge. "Oh, thank God."

"Are you ok?"

"Peachy." He hadn't cheated on Jaybird. That was the important thing to remember here. If he could hammer that point home to her, surely she'd forgive him for waking up with two other women in his bed. "I'm gonna go find Saul. You guys just, ah, just stay there."

"Ok," Chana said slowly. "If you don't mind our using your bed."

175

"Go right ahead."

But he'd damn sure change the sheets before he slept in it again.

He padded barefoot out of the bedroom Pari had assigned him and ducked into the kitchen. The apartment building they were in might look like a dump on the outside, but it had a helluva nice interior, especially on the upper floors, and the kitchen was no exception. Gleaming stainless steel fixtures nestled between solid wood counters stained a rich honey color. Two round four-seater tables were set opposite the appliances, there mostly for the convenience of people drifting in and out of Pari's compound between mealtimes.

For the place to look deserted, a shit ton of people came and went.

He grabbed a bowl of a weird granola cereal and settled onto a rail-backed chair next to a curtained window, eating on automatic. Snow drifted down outside in soft flurries, coating the ground several stories below with a fresh layer of white. Maybe somebody had figured out whose name those car tags were registered under. Maybe they'd have an address soon and could hash out a rescue plan, and Jerusha could come home where she belonged.

The niggle that had awakened Drew nudged him again and he sat straight up in his chair. Son of a bitch. He'd had the answer all along, would've retrieved it sooner if sleep deprivation and worry hadn't driven him half out of his head.

He plopped his nearly full bowl down by the sink and jogged toward the tech room. Saul was sitting inside scanning what looked like security footage from a street cam.

Drew flipped a folding metal chair around and straddled it, then jerked his chin at the array of screens hung along the wall. "You got security feed from the museum's interior?"

Saul swiveled toward Drew. "You've seen it."

"Dude. I'm so out of it, I don't remember going to bed with two women and neither of 'em mine. Run it by me again, wouldja?"

Saul's fingers rapped over a keyboard and one of the screens lit up. "There."

"Just the part where they're dragging her out of that hall."

The feed flickered and skipped ahead, and Drew jabbed a finger at the screen. "Right there. Can you isolate that guy?"

Saul tapped away and the image blew up, slightly pixelated but clear enough to make out the face. Drew banged his forehead lightly against the top of the chair. Fuck all. That man had helped carry Jerusha out of the building. The image must've embedded itself into Drew's mind and nagged at him until he was alert enough to do something about it.

He sat up and rolled his shoulders, shrugging off his fuck up. "That guy was in the Konya Archaeological Museum the day me and Jaybird visited. He was with a businessman, some muckity muck Jaybird said might be Greek. Probably with the Shadow Enemy, too."

"How long ago?"

"Two and a half, maybe three weeks."

"If the museum has a security camera, the feed has probably already been overwritten."

"Shit." Drew scrubbed a hand over his head. "Any ideas?"

"We have dossiers on many members of the Shadow. It would take time to search them all."

"Figures."

Saul crossed his arms over his chest and slouched into his chair. "You mentioned a break-in at the Nevşehir Cultural Museum prior to your arrival."

"Yeah, coulda been the same crowd. What're the chances they cased the museum before the break-in?"

"High. Even an amateur familiarizes himself with his target."

"We got that feed?"

"I need an hour. Favi's assistance would be appreciated, if you could find her."

Drew searched his mind and came up blank. "Which one is

Favi again?"

Saul slid an amused glance toward Drew. "The woman that usually helps you here."

"Ah, right." The other woman he'd woken up with. At least he knew her name now. "Be right back."

Drew jogged back down the hallway and entered his room. Chana and Favi had curled around each other in the middle of his bed and were fast asleep. Man, he hated having to wake them up, but if Favi could help get Jerusha home faster, oh, well. He stopped six feet away from the bed.

Because sometimes, Daughters woke up mean and it was better to be a long way outta their reach when they did. He hadn't had personal experience with that, but he'd heard the rumors and he'd met enough Daughters to believe it.

He talked Favi and Chana awake, ignored Favi's grumpy request to *stop calling me a guy*, and hustled her back to the tech room. Chana walked in behind him, yawning, and handed him a shirt, and he shrugged it on, eyes glued to where Favi and Saul worked.

It took hours. Drew didn't understand half of what was going on and he didn't care. He settled his still-healing back against a wall, tucked his fingers against his ribs, and waited. As the day passed, something light grew inside him. Hope, maybe. Excitement definitely. They were on the right track. God willing, they'd uncover something soon that would lead them to Jerusha.

A FEW DAYS LATER, Drew crouched behind the high wall surrounding Pinico Alexiou's estate and gritted his teeth against the cold. After he'd put two and two together, they'd been able to connect the man that had kidnapped Jerusha to the elder Alexiou. They'd been in the process of searching for his local holdings when Rebecca had called with the news that Pinico owned a farm outside Nevşehir. She had blueprints and the most likely locations Jerusha would be held in, and that was fine and dandy with Drew.

What disturbed him was how she'd figured all that out. Seemed like playing with fire to rely on intel gathered from Pinico's nephew, the leader of the Shadow, the People's mortal enemy, but they'd verified the info and vetted it thoroughly, and damned if it hadn't been on target.

Drew shrugged it off and waited for the go. How they'd gotten the intel didn't matter. That it got them to Jerusha days faster than they would've been able to get in on their own was the important thing.

Chana's soft voice issued the go through his headset. Drew nodded at Saul, and over the wall they went, two shadows used to blending into the night. Not long now and they'd have Jerusha, and when they did, it'd be a long time before Drew let her go again.

THE SUN shone down on Jerusha's skin. She smiled and turned her face into the warmth. Fiji had been such a good idea. Thank Ki she'd taken Drew up on the invitation. They'd had so much fun together, strolling hand in hand along the endless, white sand, dipping their toes into the bright blue water.

Making love for hours on end, no worries, no responsibilities, just him and her, skin on skin.

The weight of his absence smothered her. She missed him so much, missed hearing his rough voice, missed snuggling against his hard chest, talking for hours.

No, wait. That wasn't right. How could she miss him when he was here with her in Fiji? She turned in slow circles, searching the empty landscape. He was right there, had been just a minute ago. Where had he disappeared to this time? Honestly, he was like a ghost, slipping away from her when she least expected it.

"Drew," she called. "Drew!"

Gunfire erupted somewhere nearby and she whirled around, her heart in her throat, then sagged onto the sand.

Nobody was there. It must've been her imagination. Now, if she could just find Drew, everything would be perfect. They could take in a movie, maybe play Go Fish. She was ahead, twelve games to eight. She grinned and traced his name in the sand, adding a little heart at the end. Maybe she'd let him win again, just to watch him smile.

A door creaked open, startling her, and footsteps scrambled over concrete behind her.

Panic ripped through her and she launched herself off the sand into a full-blown run. No, she had to get away, had to find Drew. He'd promised to come back for her, he'd *promised*, and Drew never, ever broke his promises.

A gentle hand cupped her shoulder, and she shrugged it off. That's always how it started, with soft hands and a boyish smile. Then came the kisses and the bites, and lately, his skin on hers. She shuddered. Nasty little man. He should really keep his cum to himself.

"Jerusha, baby."

Her stride faltered and she eased to a stop. "Drew?"

"I'm here, Jaybird. I've got you."

She glanced left and right. The beach was empty, miles and miles of it, not a soul in sight. "Drew?"

A hand tapped her cheek. "Come on, baby. Open your eyes."

A familiar female voice swore, low and long. "I would hate to be the man that did that to her."

"Don't worry," Drew said, his voice flat. "Somebody's gonna pay. If she don't do it, I sure as fuck will."

Jerusha smiled, tried to. An ache on her lip stopped the gesture halfway through, and the pain roused her out of her dream. She groped around her body and her hands landed on a muscled forearm. Her eyes popped open. The most beautiful sight in the world swam into focus two feet away from her. "Drew? Is it really you?"

"Yeah, baby." His expression was stone hard and cold

under a neatly trimmed beard, and his cognac eyes glittered. "We're gonna get you out of here, ok? Just hang tight while we find a blanket."

"I've been hanging. Fiji's really nice this time of year."

"I know, baby. I swear we'll get there soon."

"No, I mean..." She frowned. Hadn't he just been there with her? Or was that another dream she'd lost herself in while Marco did his thing all over her skin?

Another spate of gunfire, more footsteps, and the woman who'd spoken stepped into view, blanket in hand.

"Chana," Jerusha said. "What are you doing here?"

"Rescuing you." Chana unfolded the coarse blanket and draped it over Jerusha. "Explanations can wait. We need to leave now."

Drew nodded sharply. "Clear a path."

Chana pivoted and raced away. Drew tucked the blanket around Jerusha and lifted her high against his chest. She rested her head on his firm shoulder and closed her eyes. She was safe now. Drew had found her, and she could relax for a little while.

She dozed off and on, only peripherally aware of her surroundings and the pain throbbing through her body at odd moments. Gunfire, screams and shouted orders, the bitter cold of winter air, then Drew easing her into a really warm space. The scrub of tires on pavement and another burst of iciness.

"Almost there, baby," Drew said gently. "Goddamn stairs. How come Pari doesn't fix the fucking elevator?"

"Potty mouth," Jerusha murmured, and Drew's chest expanded into her cheek on an inhale.

"Half out of it and she's chastising me," he said.

Chana laughed. "She's a Daughter."

"Yeah, yeah. Just go run a hot bath for her. She ain't sleeping with filth all over her."

"Semen," Jerusha said. "It's Marco's semen."

"I'm gonna kill that mother fucker."

Ha. Hadn't she told Marco that Drew would get pissed

about that? And Shadow Junior hadn't listened. Serve him right if Drew tracked him down and beat the shit out of him. Popcorn. She'd promised herself popcorn for that show, and by golly, she'd earned the treat.

The sway of Drew walking halted near a stream of rushing water and the blanket fell away. "I'm gonna sit you down in the water. You're beat up pretty bad, so it might sting a little."

"Need to be clean."

"Yeah, I know. I'm sorry, baby. I'm sorry."

She curled her fingers into his shirt. "Don't be, Drew. You got me out. I knew you would."

"Not quick enough."

"You were right on time." She yawned, winced at the pain throbbing through her. "Damn curse is kicking in. Wash me, will you? I'll probably fall asleep halfway through."

"Don't worry, baby. I've got you."

A smile blossomed in her heart. "I know, sweetie," she said, and passed out.

Sixteen

JERUSHA WOKE gradually. A rough palm circled over the back of her hand. She blinked her way into full awareness and smiled at Drew. He was sitting in a chair beside her, holding her hand between his, staring at it like it might disappear if he let go.

She yawned and stretched the aches and pings out of her sore muscles. "Hey, sweetie."

He glanced up, and some of her happiness evaporated. His eyes were bloodshot and worry lines had dug their way into the skin around his mouth and eyes. "Morning, Jerusha."

Her heart stuttered in her chest. *Jerusha.* He hadn't called her that in weeks. "Time is it?"

"Nine forty-five a.m., not twenty-four hours since we got you." He cleared his throat and fixed his gaze on her hand again. "They had you for a solid week."

"I figured. Hard to tell time in that place, but I figured it'd take a while for you to find me."

"I shoulda had you sooner, would've if I hadn't panicked." He bowed over her hand and pressed it to his forehead. "God. It took me too long to get out of the museum, took me too fucking long to connect everything together. We had to get Alexiou's help to get you out. Your mom was not happy about that, either."

Queasiness eked into Jerusha's stomach. She curled around

183

it, facing Drew, and brushed her hand over the crown of his head. His hair was getting a touch too long. She'd have to cut it for him soon.

"Which Alexiou?" she asked.

"Lukas, the Shadow leader guy."

"He knew about this?"

"Not the impression I got, but I could be wrong." He kissed her fingertips, her palm, her wrist. "You hungry? I can scrounge something, bring it back for you."

"I'm starving. Please tell me you have something here besides lamb."

"What's wrong with lamb?"

"It's about all they fed me. Lamb stew, lamb kebobs, lamb with half a dozen different kinds of bread."

"They fed you?"

"Three regulars a day." And most of it had been more than edible, surprisingly enough. Her hand slipped off his head and landed on the bed, and she sighed. "Why aren't you up here holding me?"

"You're not up to that."

"I promise you I am." She patted the bed once, about all she had the strength for. "Come on, Drew. I missed you."

He shook his head and released her hand. "Back in a jiffy."

The stutter in her heart jittered into a tremor. What was wrong? Was he simply being overcautious or was it something more? Had Marco's treatment of her somehow changed Drew's mind about their relationship?

No, it couldn't be that. He'd rescued her, hadn't he? Carried her here, wherever *here* was, called her *baby* and *Jaybird*, the way he was supposed to. He'd cared for her, cared about her enough to do for her. Those weren't the actions of a man no longer interested in a woman.

But still, he seemed awfully subdued for her rough and ready Southie. And she really needed him to hold her, really needed him to ground her in reality for a good, long while so she didn't get lost in her head again.

He walked in carrying a glass of water and a plate heaped high with food, then settled into the chair beside the bed.

Jerusha scooted around, propped a pillow against the wrought iron headboard, and sat up. "About this moratorium on cuddling. I thought we'd settled that a couple of weeks ago."

Drew's hand tightened on the plate. "You want me to feed you or can you handle it?"

"It's a sandwich, Drew. I think I've got it."

He handed her the plate, set the water on the nightstand, and leaned back in the chair, fingers tucked against his ribs. "Roast beef, mayo, lettuce, tomato. Hope you like it."

"I'm sure it's fine." She inhaled a careful breath. No sharp pains along her ribs. Excellent. Now if she could just figure out what was wrong with Drew, everything would be hunky dory. "Are you upset at me?"

His eyes widened. "No."

She bit off a chunk of the sandwich, chewed slowly, swallowed. Mmm. Drew was a damn fine sandwich maker. "Am I damaged goods? You know, now that Marco's ejaculated all over me?"

Drew glanced sharply away. "Don't matter what that bastard did to you."

"So you still want to fuck me."

He flinched. "Jesus, Jerusha."

"I think it needs to be said. Are you willing to fuck me now that he's done what he did?"

He stood up abruptly and the chair fell over, banging onto the floor. His hands bunched into massive fists held rigidly at his sides and he glared at her. "Don't say that. Don't ever say that again. I don't care what that bastard did to you. I don't fucking care, but I'm not gonna hurt you like that. Don't ask me to, Jaybird, not after he—"

"Raped me? Is that what you think happened?"

Drew blanched and sagged to his knees beside the bed.

"You don't gotta say it."

"You don't need to think it, either. Marco didn't rape me, Drew. All he did was bite me, paw my breasts a couple of times, and ejaculate all over me. Cringe worthy, sure. Not enough to permanently damage me."

"You're bruised from head to toe."

"I tried to escape pretty much every day."

"They *hurt* you. They fucking beat you."

"Yeah? You should see the half dozen guys I took down."

He jerked his head up. "This isn't a goddamn joke, Jerusha. They took you. I didn't know where you were and I couldn't get to you, and while I was trying to figure it out, you got hurt."

"And it's your fault, is that it?" She sighed and leaned the back of her head against the headboard. "I live with the knowledge that every time I go out, I might get captured, and believe me, what Marco did was mild compared to what his predecessors have done."

"I could've gotten there—"

"Fuck it, Drew." The last of her energy seeped out of her and she closed her eyes. "I trusted you to find me as soon as you could, and you did."

"You trusted me?"

"Of course, I did."

"To come get you."

She opened one eye and stared at him. "That's what we're talking about, so yeah."

His lips twitched into a slow smile. "Am I a man or your kid brother?"

She wrinkled her nose. "Ew. I don't sleep with my brother, not even just to sleep. He snores and hogs the covers, and he's a real pain in the ass sometimes. Don't know how Indi puts up with him."

"But you trust me."

"I think we just covered that ground."

"Yeah, we did." He pushed himself off the floor and sat

down beside her at the headboard, his long legs stretched out next to hers. "You sure you're ok?"

"I might need three or four showers a day for a while, but yeah. I'm ok, thanks to you."

"No thanks to me." The backs of his fingers brushed across her thigh. "Thank fuck he didn't rape you."

A few more weeks and Marco might've, but Drew really didn't need to hear that. She rested her cheek against his shoulder. That was more like it, safe, solid, wild as a buck Drew. Her man, right next to her, where he belonged. "So you were just upset because you thought I'd really been hurt."

"That was a lot of it, yeah. Not all, but enough." He jiggled his leg into hers. "Eat up. We got another set of bones to find."

"Work, work, work," she said, and he grinned.

"Nose to the grindstone, baby."

So she ate and she rested, and she didn't let Drew out of her sight for any longer than she had to while she healed. They had a week to make up for, a week Marco and Pinico had stolen from them. Jerusha refused to let anything come between her and Drew again.

THAT NIGHT, Drew held Jerusha as she slept. She'd insisted on him coming to bed with her, and he hadn't had the heart to refuse, good intentions to the contrary. He'd meant to slip out of bed as soon as she fell asleep, meant to retrieve a sleeping bag and a pillow and sleep on the floor beside the bed. Instead, here he was hours later, still beside her.

She'd clung to him since they'd gotten her out of the Alexious' clutches, and it killed him to see her like that. No matter what she said, she'd been hurt in there, maybe down so deep she didn't even realize it. He'd get her the help she needed to heal, though. He'd find a way to prop her strength up until she could stand on her own again, lend her as much of his as she needed, for as long as she needed it.

Her fingertips twitched against his chest and she groaned. He smoothed a hand over her back in slow circles, soothing her, and his heart cracked and throbbed. For days, he'd been so consumed with the need to find her, he hadn't given a single thought to his conversation with Pari. He loved Jerusha, loved her more than he'd ever dreamed of loving another person, and wasn't that just his luck? After years of searching for the one woman he could spend the rest of his life with, the one that snared his heart was the one woman who'd never give hers away.

He shrugged it off. Whatever. At least he'd have her for a while, maybe a few years, if he was lucky. He closed his eyes and imagined what that would be like, waking up to her every day, sharing his life with her, maybe having kids.

His hand slipped to her hip and he resettled his head on the pillow. Yeah, kids. He'd never wanted 'em before, would probably be a shit lousy dad, but Jaybird would make up for it. She'd be a great mom, patient and kind, always laughing. Their kids would have her eyes and his height. He could take 'em out, teach 'em to throw a ball, and she'd always be there for them. She'd never tell them she loved one more than the other even if she did. It wasn't her way and thank God for it.

She stiffened against him, and he popped abruptly out of longing into cold, hard reality.

"Drew?"

"I'm here, baby."

Her breath puffed against his chest, fast and hard. "Where are we?"

"Pari's."

She sagged against him and rubbed her forehead across his sternum. "Ok, that's good."

"You ok?"

"Yeah, I'm... I'm fine."

He squeezed her hip gently. "You don't sound fine. What's wrong?"

"Nothing. It's just... I thought we were in Fiji again, playing cards on the beach."

"What is it with you and Fiji?"

"When Marco visited me." She swallowed and her voice thinned to a bare thread. "When he was there, I'd kind of think about you instead."

"Nothing wrong with that."

"No, I mean I'd lose myself in you. We went to a basketball game, Tech versus Duke."

"Tech better have won that one," he growled, and she huffed out a short laugh.

"We played cards. Go Fish. You tried to talk me into strip poker, but I wouldn't let you."

He tugged her closer and tucked her head under his chin. "There you go, being all strict again."

"I know. I should've given in, shouldn't I?" She sniffled and drew in a ragged breath. "I missed you so much, missed everything about you, so I wrapped your memory around me and I stayed there as much as I could, remembering the way you smell, the way you laugh, this glint you get in your eyes when we make love. It saved me, Drew. It kept me sane while I waited. You kept me whole."

A sob escaped her chest, and something inside Drew twisted. "Let it out, baby. Cry if you need to."

"I don't want to cry. He's not worth it, Drew. Nothing he did hurt me bad enough to deserve tears."

"That don't mean they're not there. I know you're tough, Jaybird. I know how hard it is to show it when something's stabbed right through you, but you don't gotta hold it in. Get it outta your system, and once you do, don't ever look back at what that asshole did to you."

"Oh, Drew. Sweet, beautiful Drew." She sniffed and wrapped herself around him. "Don't let go. Please don't ever let me go."

"Not ever," he murmured.

Her sobs cut through him, right into his core. They were

quiet, like she was ashamed somebody might hear, but they were there. She cried for a long time, and he held her, whispering to her, doing what he could to comfort her. When she wound down, he cleaned her face and got her some water, and after, he nestled her against his chest and rocked her back to sleep, surrounding her with love the only way he knew how.

Seventeen

THE ORACLE'S temporary home was an innocuous bump in Tellowee's landscape. Rebecca sat in her car, waiting for Lukas Alexiou's arrival. That he'd helped her find Jerusha had no bearing on Rebecca's decision to allow him entrance into the Oracle's presence. The simple fact of the matter was that the Oracle refused to speak to anyone and they needed to know who she was. Even the remote possibility that Lukas could communicate with her outweighed the risk of allowing him near the ancient Daughter.

An engine hummed through the morning air. Rebecca got out of her car and smoothed a hand over her outfit, a black turtleneck tucked into thin, loose slacks. She'd opted for comfort over fashion, a necessity should Lukas betray her trust and threaten the Oracle.

Dani's Jeep eased to a stop behind Rebecca's car. The passenger's side door opened and Dani slid out. "Hey, Mom. Sorry we're late. Steven needed a snack."

"You're not that late, darling."

David got out of the driver's side, helped a grinning Steven out of the back, and carried him over. "He wants you, Dani."

"Flirt," Dani said, and Steven launched himself at her, latching on to her with a happy laugh.

David helped Lukas out and removed the other man's

blindfold. Like Rebecca, the Shadow had dressed down, or had dressed in what she assumed was casual clothing for him. He wore a simple collared shirt tucked into khakis under his wool jacket, and was no less powerful for the lack of a tailored suit and matching tie.

He shifted his briefcase from one hand to the other as his gaze zeroed in on Rebecca. "Thank you for allowing me to visit her."

Rebecca's smile held no humor, only the cold cunning others feared. "I needn't tell you what will happen should you choose to break my trust."

"I have no doubt whatsoever that I won't live outside the moment."

"Then we understand one another. Do you have the artifacts?"

Lukas lifted his briefcase. "When I've seen her, I'll turn them over to you."

"Fair enough. This way."

She pivoted toward the house and strode up the narrow dirt path to its entrance. The door opened long before she got there. Luna stepped into and blocked the entryway, her mocha face expressionless. "Director."

"Handmaiden. Is she ready?"

Luna nodded and stepped back, and Rebecca led the small party into the Oracle's quarters. They wound their way through the home under the weighty stares of a handful of Handmaidens, all alert for the slightest hint of betrayal on the Shadow's part.

Rebecca paused outside the Oracle's bedroom. "Are you ready?"

Lukas' gaze fell on the door. "I confess to being a tad nervous. Do you think less of me for it, Director?"

She didn't, though she refused to admit it. It was nice to know the famed Shadow had a shred of humanity left within him, after everything he was rumored to have done. She opened the door and gestured him inside, but he was frozen where he stood, his expression soft, his free hand loose at his side.

"Nala," he said softly.

The Oracle pushed herself out of the rocking chair she'd been sitting in and took two halting steps toward him. "Gulnar?"

"Lukas," he said, and burst into a spattering of an oddly familiar language Rebecca couldn't quite place. The Oracle replied, her voice firm, and the two carried on a brief conversation under Rebecca's watchful gaze.

She'd wanted to know how the Oracle would react to the name Nala. Now she knew.

Lukas handed the briefcase to Rebecca. "I need to greet her properly. You may not wish to witness this."

Rebecca turned Lukas' briefcase over to Luna. "I stay."

He nodded, stepped inside the room, and shrugged his coat off, then laid it on the floor inside the door. His fingers twisted the buttons of his shirt apart one by one and he tugged it out of his pants.

"What are you doing?" Rebecca asked.

"Greeting her properly. A woman of her age is accustomed to men exhibiting certain behavior. Submission, for one." He pulled his undershirt off, folded it, and dropped it on top of the growing pile of clothes beside him. "I tried to warn you."

She glanced away from the chiseled planes of his lean chest. "Not very hard."

He slipped his shoes and socks off, then unfastened his pants. Nala said something, and he smiled. "She wants to know why you're blushing, if you've never watched a man undress before."

Rebecca narrowed her eyes at him. "I never blush."

He shrugged and pushed his pants down to his ankles, stepped out of them, and folded them on top of his other clothes. "She asked. I translated. Is that not why you brought me here?"

It was part of the reason, which he very well knew, damn the man. "Could you kindly not remove your underwear?"

"I had no intention of removing them in your presence,

Director. You may not blush, but I do." He removed his wristwatch and dropped it onto the floor. "Steven, please come greet Nala with me."

Dani set the boy on his feet inside the door. "I'm just gonna go wash my eyes out with acid now."

Lukas shot a sour glance at her. "My body is not that repulsive, Ms. Nehring."

"Think that if you gotta," she said, and whipped out of the room at a fast walk. David rolled his eyes and followed her down the hallway, and Rebecca shut the door on the Handmaidens crowding into the space he'd vacated.

Lukas crouched on the floor next to Steven and rubbed his elegant hands over the boy's shoulders. "She won't harm you. She may try to harm me, however. If she does, run to the director. She'll protect you."

Steven nodded, and Lukas' gaze slid to Rebecca's. "You will protect him."

It wasn't a question, and though his arrogance ruffled her feathers, she let it pass. "No harm will come to your heir in this house."

"Thank you." He sucked in a breath, let it out slowly. "Wish me luck."

He dropped to his hands and knees and crawled slowly toward the Oracle, Steven at his side, and Rebecca stifled a gasp. He wore an *aenkanien*, a wife's mark, tattooed into his left shoulder blade. It was of an elegantly formed flower, inked along the natural curve of the bone under his skin, its petals drooping toward finely depicted roots. On his right shoulder blade, where his children's marks would go if he were of the People, two trees grew side by side, one white, the other black, their trunks intertwined as their branches reached toward the sky.

How odd, that the leader of their enemy would follow the customs of the People.

"You're married?" she asked.

He paused, head bowed. "I belong to someone, yes."

"Who?"

"You already know the answer to that, Director."

He resumed his crawl and halted with the crown of his head nearly touching the Oracle's knees. "Nala," he said, and whatever conversation followed, Rebecca understood not a word. Nala slid her fingers through Steven's hair and murmured something, and the little boy grinned up at her, blinking his eyes in a flirtatious wink. Lukas slid his arm around his nephew's waist, kissed him on the forehead, and spoke in a low voice to the boy.

Steven nodded and bounded toward Rebecca, holding his arms up to her. She swung him onto her hip, cradling him protectively.

Lukas turned his face partially toward her. "Please take him to Ms. Nehring. Nala wishes to be with me."

"By *be with*, you mean—"

"Please, Director. Not in front of Steven." He shifted onto his knees and lifted Nala's shirt, baring her stomach. "This may be beyond even your tolerance for blushing."

Nala lifted her gaze from Lukas kneeling in front of her and stared at Rebecca, her expression so dispassionate, a chill shivered down Rebecca's spine. Lukas Alexiou belonged to this woman, a woman that had been asleep for centuries prior to his birth? How was that even possible? How had he known she'd awakened and why had he waited until now to solidify the claim?

Rebecca opened the door and stepped into the hallway. Her last glimpse of the reunited couple was of Lukas kissing his way across Nala's skin, his hands trembling on her hips, and of Nala stroking his hair gently, a tender smile softening her expression.

JERUSHA KNOCKED on Pari's door. In the past three days, her bruises and wounds had mostly healed and the ick factor of having Marco's body fluids dried into her flesh had lessened, helped along by a hot shower whenever her skin crawled. She was slipping less and less into fantasy, thanks to Drew's nearly continual presence. Bless him, he'd tolerated her weakness better than she had and hadn't even blinked when she'd blubbered all over him.

News of the theft had spread rapidly across the region, along with clear pictures of her and Drew's faces. The outrage that followed was predictable, if a little wearing, sparking a renewed cry for repatriation of Turkish artifacts currently held in foreign museums.

Jerusha didn't care one way or the other. The Sister's remains belonged with the People, not locked in a stuffy storage room in a museum halfway around the world. That she would have a hand in returning them to their rightful place was a matter of pride. Having to burn an identity and start all over again building a new one was of little consequence. She'd wanted time with Drew, hadn't she? And now she had the perfect excuse to linger in Tellowee, not far from where he lived.

Pari opened the door and smiled. "Come in, Jerusha."

"Thanks." Jerusha stepped inside and air kissed Pari's cheeks. "I just came to tell you goodbye and to thank you for helping Drew retrieve me."

"I will be handsomely rewarded." Pari glided into her living room, trailing a faint hint of exotic perfume, and sank gracefully onto a beautifully upholstered chaise. She waved one hand toward the tea set placed on the low table in front of it. "Tea?"

"Yes, please." Jerusha perched on a nearby matching chair and studied Pari as she poured tea, humor rising in spite of the direness of her previous situation. "How much did Mom pay you?"

Pari handed Jerusha a delicate cup resting on an equally fragile saucer, then lifted her own. "Not your mother, darling. Drew."

Jerusha laughed. "Oh, get real, Pari. Drew doesn't have that kind of money."

"I didn't ask for money."

Jerusha's breath froze in her lungs. "What have you done?"

"I bargained for what I wanted. He agreed to my terms."

Jerusha thunked the saucer and cup onto the table, rattling them against one another. "What terms?"

Pari sipped her tea. Her dark, tilted eyes glimmered over the cup's rim. "Him in exchange for you. When you're finished with him, naturally."

"Naturally," Jerusha said faintly and placed a hand over the irregular hum of her heart. "He offered himself willingly?"

"Quite. In fact, he seemed determined to throw his life in front of yours, whatever the cost to him. I do believe he's in love with you."

"He can't..." Jerusha slumped into the chair and stared at the ceiling. Drew loved her? No. That couldn't be right. Cared about her, sure. Of course, he did, but love? No way. "How long do I have left with him?"

"As long as you want him."

"And if I want him forever?"

"We've been friends for a very long time, Jerusha, and in all that time, I've never known you to want a man long enough to risk your heart." China rattled onto wood and silk rubbed against itself. "Whether your interest lasts a week or a decade, we both know you'll eventually tire of him, and when you do, he will present himself to me, forever after to serve my needs."

Jerusha forced herself upright and gripped her thighs with rigid fingers. "What if we have children?"

"I would never deprive a child of her father's care. On this you have my word."

Jerusha nodded. "Ok. I guess that's ok."

"Darling Jerusha, you know I shall care for him. He'll never want for anything while he's here, never need anything I cannot provide."

Yes, he would, Jerusha's heart shouted. He'd need her. She was his Jaybird, wasn't she? Could he really live without her? Had making that bargain been so easy for him? And he'd done it so readily. How hard had Pari had to argue to get what she wanted? A minute, an hour, a single day?

Had everything between them been a lie? The sweetly stupid nickname, the beautiful sex, the light in his eyes when he held her. Had any of it been real?

"Come, now," Pari said. "Tell me all about your plans to reclaim the second set of bones. I'm dying to hear your adventures. I so rarely have my own anymore."

Jerusha picked up her tea and sipped it between a halting explanation of her and Drew's sketchy plans to travel to Boston and recover Eleni's bones, but her mind wasn't on her conversation with Pari. It was on her heart, quietly shattering into a million irreparable pieces inside her chest.

DREW REPACKED the Sister's bones one by one. There hadn't been time to check them before, but now that he and Jerusha were close to going home, he wanted to make sure he hadn't damaged them during that crazy climb out of the museum.

Jerusha should've been there to help. She was the expert at this, but their stay in Turkey was coming to an end and she'd wanted to spend a little time with Pari before they left. He didn't begrudge it. A woman needed friends same as a man, though maybe Jerusha hanging out with this particular friend wasn't such a hot idea right now, what with him having sold himself into slavery to said friend.

Pray God Jerusha never found out about that. She didn't need to know, and he had absolutely no intention of telling her. What happened to him when she was done with him, well, that was his business, wasn't it.

He zipped the duffel closed and set it with their other luggage on one side of the room he and Jerusha had shared, then sank onto the edge of the bed. Already, he dreaded the time when he'd have to come back to Turkey, probably never to leave again. There were worse things than being a sex slave to a beautiful, eternally youthful Daughter, though for the life of him, he couldn't think of a single one.

Fact was, he couldn't think of anything around the wad of hurt in his gut except Jerusha, but that was a given. She'd drifted into his heart about ten seconds after their second meet, give or take a week, and seemed to've settled in there for the long haul.

And that was ok. He'd work it out somehow, and she'd never have to know he'd traded himself so she could live.

The door opened and in she walked, her skin so pale, it was brittle.

He held out a hand for her. "Hey, baby. What's wrong?"

Her sure stride faltered inches away from his fingertips. "You've been asking me that a lot lately. I think maybe it's time I asked you the same thing."

He let his hand drop and scrubbed his damp palms down his thighs. "What do you mean?"

"When were you going to tell me, Drew? About Pari, about making a deal with her. How could you?" Her voice broke and her hands clenched into shaky fists at her sides. "How could you do that to me?"

The blood rushed out of his head and every cell in his body went numb. "Jaybird, listen to me. I can explain."

"Explain what? That you threw me over the minute my back was turned?"

"It wasn't like that."

"Then how was it? How could you possibly think I would approve of you promising yourself to another woman when you were supposed to be with me?" Her lips trembled, then firmed into a hard slash across her face. "I thought you cared about me."

"I do care about you, Jaybird."

"Don't lie to me, Drew. Not now." She backed away from him, slowly shaking her head. "I can't believe I trusted you. I can't believe I was so wrong about you."

"You weren't," he said softly, and gathered his courage to tell her what was in his heart. "You're right about one thing, though."

Her shoulders slumped. "I am?"

"Yeah. Thing is, I don't care about you, or not just care, anyhow. I love you, so much. I'm full of you all the time, every day, when I'm awake, in my dreams, inside and out."

The hurt drained out of her expression. "You love me."

"Kinda crazy, huh? I mean, not the loving part. Of course, you're totally loveable and..." He cringed. Everything was coming out all wrong. She probably thought he was an idiot or something, and wouldn't that be about par for the course? "I mean, it's kinda crazy, me finding a way to love somebody, really love them."

"You love me? Sheesh." She staggered to the bed and dropped down beside him. "I was working my way up to a good mad, and now you've completely ruined it."

"Bobby does that to me all the time. Fucking hate it." He eased an arm around her shoulders and hugged her close. "When we got trapped and you asked me to leave, didn't I promise I'd come back for you?"

She turned her cheek into his chest and nodded.

"I don't make promises often, Jaybird, but when I do, I by God do everything I can to keep them." He exhaled a harsh breath. "I had to climb up the dumb waiter shaft."

"Escape Plan C," she murmured.

"Yeah, only the pulley broke and, well, it wasn't pretty. By the time I got out, you were gone. I waited for hours, Jaybird, and you never came out, and the longer I sat there, the more I panicked."

"You, Mr. Nerves of Steel Martin, panicked?"

"I did. First time for everything, right? That was when it hit me that maybe I was panicking because it was you." He barked out a short laugh. "Sure as hell, I never panicked when I had to dig Bobby's ass outta the fire."

She placed her hand on his thigh and squeezed. "And we're grateful for every single time."

"He saved me a lot, too." Him and Hiro both, in more ways

than anybody knew. "Long story short, the only thing I could think of was to ask Pari for help, and you know what she wanted. My life for yours. I was glad to do it, Jaybird. Do it again if I had to."

"I didn't want you to sacrifice yourself, Drew. That was never supposed to happen. You were supposed to get out and be safe."

"And I was, but you weren't, and there's the rub." He kissed the top of her head, grazed his cheek over her silky hair. "Look, I know you're gonna leave me someday, but don't let it be about this. I did what I had to do. Don't hold it against me."

"She's already crowing about getting you."

"Let her. Possession is nine-tenths of the law and she ain't got me yet. Speaking of." He leaned back, dug around in the front pocket of his jeans, and pulled out their wedding rings. "I can't believe you made me take mine off before we went into the museum. Good thing, though. No telling what would've happened to yours."

Jerusha rubbed her fingertips over the rings. "I thought they were gone for good."

"Chana got them when she packed up our things at the hotel. I've been saving putting them back on for a special occasion."

"Like when you needed to bribe me out of my mad."

He laughed. "Yeah, something like that. Here."

He slid hers on her finger, then slipped his on. The simple weight of the gold band was somehow right, like a part of him had been missing and the ring fit the absent piece exactly. "I know we're just playing our roles here, Jaybird, but I want you to remember something every time you look at that ring."

"That you're crazy as a loon?"

"That you can always count on me."

"I think I already knew that."

"Believe it," he whispered, and kissed her soft and easy, soothing away the hurt he'd unknowingly cut into her heart.

Eighteen

THEY SNUCK OUT of Turkey in the dead of the night. Chana and a small team escorted Jerusha and Drew as far as the coast to a yacht Pari had granted them access to.

For a price.

From there, they sailed to Italy, then boarded the IECS' private jet. Airport security was a breeze to bypass, thanks to the IDs Saul had made for them, thankfully included in the same package as the yacht.

During the long flight to the regional airport in Gainesville, Georgia, Jerusha and Drew talked, played cards, took a long nap. He was affectionate, kind, but he refused to make love with her. That barrier would have to come down. She just wasn't sure how to breach it yet.

Rebecca had a car waiting for them when they arrived around midnight. Jerusha directed the driver to Drew's house halfway between Gainesville and BDH Security's offices in Gwinnett County. Marnan's remains had waited who knew how long to be rediscovered. One more night wouldn't matter either way.

Drew unlocked the front door using the spare key he kept tucked into a hidey hole. Jerusha dumped her luggage onto the floor near the entrance and wandered through the house, stretching out the kinks of travel as she walked.

"Shower?" Drew asked.

"I would love one." She paused in front of a window overlooking the backyard and squinted into the night. "I think your bird feeders are empty."

"That's what I get for paying a teenager to keep an eye on them."

"Want me to fill them?"

"Naw. I'll do it in the morning. Birds won't be back before then anyhow."

His footsteps were quiet along the carpet, his arms relaxed as he wound them around her waist. He nuzzled her cheek and *mmmd*, and she leaned into his strength.

"You don't seem like a bird watcher," she said.

"Never was one until I moved here. I rented this really shitty apartment in Gainesville for a while." He laughed softly. "Landlord hated me."

"Let me guess. You cheated at Go Fish with him."

"I'm not the cheater here," he muttered. "Anyhow, first morning I was there, this pair of blue jays landed on the balcony, squawking like nobody's business. Woke me up, and let me tell you, I was pissed."

"I can't imagine."

"You wanna know about the bird feeders or not, wise ass?"

She bit her lower lip, hiding a smile. "Sorry."

He shook his head. "Thing about blue jays is, they're mean and ornery and make a shit ton of noise, but they're beautiful, too. Their wings are this rich shade of blue. Prettiest color I ever saw, and they reminded me of something."

"Did you ever figure out what?"

"Took me a while, but yeah, I did, the day you walked back into my life." He tugged her around and hooked his hands on her waist. "You never wondered why I call you Jaybird?"

Her heart did a funny little flip. She slid her hands along his chest, absorbing some of his heat. "I just thought you were trying to get my goat."

"Yeah, I guess it started out like that. Didn't end that way, though."

"So you think I'm mean and ornery and my eyes are pretty. Hunh. I can see why you love me."

He laughed and bumped his hips into hers. "Baby, I love you 'cause there ain't nobody like you. We fit so good together."

His gaze fell to her mouth and lingered, and her breath caught in her throat. This was it. He'd kiss her and take her into the bedroom, and they'd make love the way they used to, and everything would be ok. Her time under Marco's less than tender care wouldn't come between them anymore. Surely Drew could see she was putting that behind her. Surely he could see how much she needed his touch.

His expression shuttered and he eased away from her. "Bathroom's yours."

She rocked back onto her heels. "You don't want to share a shower with me?"

"I'll catch one later." He bussed her forehead and let her go. "Think I'll check my e-mail while you're cleaning up."

He snagged their luggage and toted it into his bedroom, and she stared after him, completely flummoxed. Ok, then. She'd shower now and he could take one later, but after that, he wouldn't have anywhere left to run. The house was only so big, after all, and they were sharing a bed.

She narrowed her eyes on the entrance to his bedroom. And a Daughter only allowed her man so much leeway. If he didn't want to have sex with her, he could explain why, and he'd be explaining it as soon as she could pin him down.

DREW CROOKED a hand behind his head and stared up at the ceiling. Another night alone with the woman he loved, just him and her and a king-sized bed. Oh, yeah, and the memory of what that rat bastard Marco Alexiou had done to her. Layers of dried ejaculate coating her skin. Bite marks all over her body, some nearly healed, others so fresh, the skin around them was still red when they'd rescued her.

She'd tried to hide it from him, but he knew exactly how many times she'd attempted to scrub the man's filth off her skin, long after it was gone. Some things didn't heal so well. Some things couldn't be erased just because she wanted them to be.

The toilet flushed, water ran in the sink, then out she walked, every beautiful inch of her, wearing one of his t-shirts and cotton underpants. He fixed his eyes on the ceiling and ignored his dick stirring inside his underwear. Yup, him and her and a bed for a whole night. What could possibly go wrong?

She switched the lights off and climbed in beside him. "Cuddle with me?"

"Yeah, sure, baby."

He held out an arm, tucked her against his side. She skimmed a hand along his waist, hooked a leg over his, and rested her head on his chest, and he sighed. Yeah, that was where she belonged, right next to his heart.

"Are you ever going to make love to me again?" she asked.

He wheezed out a laugh. "God, Jaybird. Where'd that come from?"

"You haven't, not since you saved me."

"You're still healing," he said gently, and sure as hell, she didn't need his cum in her, not until she got a grip on everything.

"I'll heal faster if you touch me."

"I touch you all the time."

"Not like I need you to." Her hand skidded over his abs and rested on his erection. "What happened the last time you tried to put me off?"

His stomach muscles clenched together and heat rocketed through his blood. The last time he'd tried to slow her down had been the first time they'd played together, and she hadn't taken no for an answer. "Come on, Jaybird. Stuff happens when a man does that."

"Stuff happens."

"Yeah, you know. Bad stuff and...stuff."

"You mean you'll ejaculate," she said flatly. "Like Marco did."

He winced. Yeah, this conversation was going swell. Why had he wondered what could go wrong? "Let's give it a little more time, ok?"

"Let's not."

She squeezed his dick, and his hips shot into her hand. Oh, God, that was good, so good. "That's not fair, baby."

"Who said anything about being fair? I want you, Drew, and I want to move past this. The only way to do that is to have sex."

"No, we can give it time and—"

She licked his nipple and her hand stroked his erection through his underwear. Need erupted within him and he hissed in a breath.

"Please, Jaybird. You know I can't resist, and I don't wanna hurt you."

"You're not going to hurt me, Drew. You've never hurt me, not intentionally, and you won't now."

He wound his free hand around the sheet and forced his hips into the mattress, away from her hand. "You don't know that. Maybe seeing it will mess you up even more."

"It's a risk I'm willing to take." She scooted up on the bed and touched her mouth lightly to his. "Give me something good, Drew, a new memory to replace the bad. I want everything to be right between us, not just the way we feel about each other, but everything. I want to enjoy all of you without him getting in the way."

"I want that, too, baby."

"Then let me pleasure you. Please, Drew. Don't hold back on me now."

He closed his eyes and tried to think around his pounding heartbeat and the roar of her under his skin. "Promise me you'll stop the minute it starts bothering you."

"I swear."

Her hand delved under his underwear and her fingers encircled him, stroking from base to tip, hard and eager and demanding.

His balls tightened and the muscles around his dick tingled and burned. "Oh, fuck, Jaybird. Slow down a little."

"Maybe next time." She nibbled her way across his jaw and whispered, "I want you in my mouth. Can I suck you off?"

Her words burned through him as surely as if she'd actually put her mouth on him, shoving him brutally close to the edge of release. "Holy shit, gonna come."

He jerked the covers down and shoved his hips into the circle of her fist, and pleasure thrummed through him, bursting out in hot streams of cum over her hand. It went on and on, echoing through his blood with every pump of her fist over his cock, and finally ebbed into a quiet, contented hum.

She released him and kissed him gently. "Back in a minute."

"Yeah, huh, 'k."

She laughed and scooted off the bed, and he lay there like a lump of Drew shaped goo. God, what she did to him, and so easy, too, like she knew exactly where she had him.

Right in the palm of her delicate, little hand.

Water splashed on in the bathroom. He scraped a hand over his mug and breathed out a laugh. Shoulda never told her he loved her. It gave her all kinds of leverage over him, and she sure took advantage. Maybe when she came back to bed, he'd take a little advantage of his own. Not a lot, no. She got the heebies too often for them to go too far and...

He smacked himself in the forehead and rolled out of bed. What an idiot he was. She was in there with his cum all over her skin, probably having flashbacks, and he was sitting there all lovesick and shit.

He tapped on the bathroom door. "You ok?"

"Um, fine. Just a sec."

He wiggled the door handle. Locked. His gut knotted into a wad and sank like a stone. "Open the door, baby."

"I need a minute, Drew."

"Are you on the potty?"

"No."

"Then open the goddamn door."

"I... I can't."

Fuck that. He slammed his shoulder into the door, once, twice. "I'm not leaving you in there by yourself."

"Drew."

Her voice cracked and broke, and fear rammed his heart into his throat. He slammed into the door. The wood creaked under his blow and held like the goddamn oak slab barrier it was. Why in hell had he put a solid wooden door on this one room? He banged into it again, cursing himself for being a moron and a half. Ok, so, paranoia had insisted he have one room in the house that was hard to get into until he could build a safe room, but not this one. Not when his Jaybird was in there, hurting.

He threw all his weight into the wood and the frame gave way, crunching into fragmented splinters as the door popped open. Jerusha was standing at the sink scrubbing her hands under running water, her skin ashen under its natural, brown-gold hue.

Drew shoved the door out of the way and was at her side in two long strides. He enfolded her in his arms, sheltering her from the pain in her mind, and rocked her back and forth. "Ssh, baby. I've got you. It's ok now."

"I was ok," she said, her voice shaky and weak. "I was ok until I saw it, and now I can't get it off."

"Let me help."

She sniffed and panted a sob into his chest. "It won't come off."

"I know, baby. Here." He shifted her back to his chest, lathered soap in his palms, and rubbed his fingers over her skin. "Watch, baby. See? I'm getting it off for you, same way I did the night you came home. You fell asleep on me, remember?"

"I'm sorry."

"Don't be. You needed the rest." He rinsed their hands off,

lathered up again, and started all over, beginning with her wrists, working his way down over her fingers and back up. "You trusted me to get you clean, and I did, didn't I?"

The tension drained out of her muscles. "Yeah, you really did."

"And that's what I'm gonna do now. When I'm done, you'll be sparkly clean, good as new."

Her gaze met his in the mirror. "You must think I'm as weak as a kitten."

"No, baby. I think you're human." He splashed the last of the soap away and cut off the water. "There. How'd I do?"

She flexed her fingers under his. "Nothing but Drew left."

"I was aiming for nothing but Jerusha, but that'll do."

"Just do me a favor."

"Anything, baby."

"Cut the light on the next time."

He kissed her temple, squeezed her tight. "We're gonna wait a while for the next time."

"Not too long, I hope."

"Tell you what. How about the next time, I do that to you and we'll go from there. Been a while since I used my trigger finger."

She sputtered out a laugh. "I already pulled your trigger."

He smiled into her hair. "Yeah, I guess you did. You're pretty damn good at it, too."

"I like doing it. You're so responsive, so beautiful." Her laughter faded and her eyelids fluttered shut. "Will you say it?"

"What?"

"How you feel. I know it's not fair for me to ask. I just...need to know."

"I love you," he said softly. "If you need to hear it, I'll tell you every chance I get."

"Even if I can never say it back?"

"I'm hoping someday you can." He snagged a towel, dried their hands off. "Go to bed. I'll be there soon as I get this mess cleaned up."

"I can—"

He picked her up, cradling her high against his chest. "'Fraid not, baby."

She scowled. "Might doesn't make right, Drew."

"It does in this house." He picked his way through the ruin he'd made of the bathroom door and tucked her into bed. "Cuddle time in ten."

"I'll be here, pretending I'm the little woman."

"Jaybird, you are the little woman."

He smacked a kiss to her mouth and went to scrounge up a box. When he fixed the door, he was by God not putting a lock on it again. They'd learn to knock and that would do just fine, but as long as Jerusha wanted him, he'd never allow her to hide her pain from him again.

Nineteen

THE DOORBELL roused Jerusha out of a deep sleep. Drew grunted and tucked her closer under his arm, and she sighed. He had one arm wrapped around her and a leg over both of hers, and was practically sleeping on top of her.

She hated to wiggle away from his toasty warmth, especially after last night. He hadn't blinked an eye when she'd freaked out. Ok, breaking down the door was a little much, but if he hadn't, she was pretty sure she'd still be in the bathroom scrubbing her hands raw trying to get Marco's ejaculate off her skin, days after Drew had cleaned it off of her. She should've listened to him, would've if she hadn't been so stubbornly intent on getting them over the hurdle of what had happened to her. How had he known she wasn't ready when she'd believed herself to be? Did he know her that well after such a short time?

She snuggled deeper into the rightness of his embrace. This was good. Maybe whoever it was would go away and she wouldn't have to get up.

The doorbell's chime echoed through the house.

Jerusha buried her face in the pillow. Well, crap. They weren't going away.

She snuck out of bed, grabbed a handgun out of the nightstand, and padded to the door on bare feet. Jet lag was the pits. She squinted at the bright sunlight streaming in around the blinds covering the windows. Wasn't it night in Turkey right now? Shouldn't she be asleep now, or was it still afternoon there?

She yawned and stumbled to the front door. Whatever. Hopefully, getting rid of their visitor wouldn't take long and she could sneak back into bed with Drew.

She stood on tiptoes and checked the peephole, then unlocked the door and threw it wide open. "Mom. What are you doing here?"

Rebecca crossed the threshold into the house and bussed Jerusha's cheek. "The two of you arrived so late last night, I thought I'd drop by this morning and save you a trip into Tellowee."

Jerusha shut the door, reached for her mother's coat, and remembered the gun in her hand. "Um, whoops. Let me put this up."

"Don't rush on my account. I'm quite happy to witness at least one of my daughters exercising prudence."

"I'd love to say I deliberately got it out, but I didn't. Just picked it up out of habit."

Drew entered the room, gun in hand, his bare feet shuffling quietly across the floor. He cupped Rebecca's shoulder, then draped a casual arm around Jerusha's waist. "Hey, Rebecca. We were coming by later to drop off the bones and touch base before we head to Boston."

"There's been a change of plans." Rebecca's mouth pursed. "Drew, darling, would you mind if I spoke to Jerusha alone for a moment?"

"Not a bit. I'll just go grab a shower." He dropped a kiss onto Jerusha's shoulder. "When you guys are finished, how about we grab some lunch at Rabbittown Café?"

Jerusha smiled and handed him her gun. "Sure, sweetie."

He padded back out of the room, his gun in his left hand, hers in his right, his glutes flexing under the thin knit material of his underwear. If Dave was Dani's Poseidon, what did that make Drew? Ares? Yeah, exactly. Drew was Ares, god of war, all around badass hottie.

Rebecca sighed. "That's the third man I've seen in his underwear in the past week and only one was my husband."

Jerusha whipped around and grinned at her mother. "You naughty devil, you."

"Hardly." Rebecca pulled off her gloves, shrugged off her coat, and hung them on the coatrack by the door. "Shall we?"

"Sure. The living room ok?"

"Of course. We have our best discussions cuddled up on the sofa, don't we?" Rebecca followed Jerusha into Drew's living room and sank sideways into one cushion, facing Jerusha settling into the adjacent one. "I've made other arrangements for the retrieval of the Sister's bones held at Boston University."

Jerusha sat straight up. "What? That's *our* mission, Mom. You can't just give it away."

"I already have." Rebecca cupped her hands over Jerusha's. "I made one promise to your father, Jerusha, just one. I swore I'd never throw you unnecessarily into harm's path and I've done my best to fulfill that oath."

"You send me on dangerous missions all the time."

"When you're clear-headed and rational. Can you honestly assure me you are now?"

Jerusha slumped into the sofa. "I'm doing ok, Mom."

"If you're doing so well, please explain how Drew received the bruises on his shoulder."

Jerusha dropped her gaze to her hands. "Mom."

"Tell me, darling."

"We were, ah..."

"Having sex?"

"Yeah, sort of. I went into the bathroom to wash my hands and I saw his ejaculate on my skin and I..." Jerusha closed her eyes and shuddered. "He broke the door down trying to get to me."

Rebecca chafed her palms over Jerusha's hands. "You're ok? No permanent damage to either one of you?"

"No, thank Ki, but if he hadn't helped me, I don't know what I would've done."

"You're in a relationship with him."

Jerusha glanced at the door leading into his bedroom. Relationship wasn't exactly the word. Drew was quickly becoming the closest friend she'd ever had, a vital part of her life, and she couldn't imagine not having him there every day. His laughter, his love, his strength. How could she ever live without those things?

She sighed and leaned her head against the back of the sofa. "I care about him."

"Only care?"

"I don't know, Mom. I just don't know. When we're together, everything's so perfect, even when we argue, and I feel so safe with him, like no matter how hard I fall, he'll always be there to catch me." She breathed out a laugh. "Sounds kinda silly, right? I mean, I'm a Daughter. What do I need with a man, even if he is beautiful and patient and kind, and he lets me win at Go Fish?"

Rebecca's smile was gentle. "Being a Daughter doesn't grant you immunity from love."

"But it makes it harder for us, doesn't it?"

"Often, yes. I think you're closer to it than you know. The way you talk about Drew, the way you look at him. That's very like the way Robert and I are with one another."

"So this is what love feels like, this urgent need to be around him all the time, this raging fear that if I let him out of my sight, he'll disappear on me and I'll lose everything good and right in my life?"

"I can't answer that, Jerusha. Love is different for everyone. You have to find your own path with Drew." Rebecca tucked a stray strand of Jerusha's hair behind her ear. "I don't want to influence you unduly, but I would be very happy to have Drew as a son."

Tears clogged Jerusha's throat and she sniffed them back.

Daughters didn't cry. Honestly, what was wrong with her lately? Just because her mother approved of the man in her life...

Wait. Her mother approved of the man in her life? "Really, Mom?"

"He's a good man. Hiro, too. I couldn't be happier with Bobby's choices in friendship." Rebecca cocked her head and a calculating gleam entered her pale blue eyes. "Should I begin drawing up the mating contracts? I will, of course, negotiate on his behalf."

"Great. There go my savings."

"And well spent, yes?" Rebecca rose and kissed Jerusha's forehead. "The two of you have earned some time off. Rest, relax, have some fun. We'll have a welcome home dinner this weekend. Say, Sunday at lunch?"

"We'll be there."

"Excellent. Now, go see to your man. I can find my own way out."

Jerusha wrapped her arms around her knees as Rebecca gathered her coat and gloves and left.

Could Drew really be the one?

She closed her eyes and rested her forehead on her arms. Her mother was right. He was a good man, the best kind, really. Look at the way he'd come after her, the way he'd helped her, how patient he'd been. And she trusted him, didn't she? More than she'd ever trusted a man, even her own family, and there, she trusted implicitly.

So she cared about him and she trusted him and she didn't want their time to end, now that their mission was over, but what did it all really mean? Had those feelings been caused by what had happened to her in Turkey?

No, she'd started falling for him long before then, maybe even before they'd left the States. They'd always had an easy rapport between them, had worked well together from day one. If she loved him, and maybe she did, it wasn't because of the way he'd saved her or the way he continued to save her every time

215

she went loony. They'd found something special. *Drew* was something special, whether he believed it or not, and she'd be a pure damn fool to let him go without at least trying to love him.

He strode into the living room squeaky clean and fully clothed, and plopped down on the sofa beside her. "Where's Rebecca?'

"She went back to work."

Jerusha opened her eyes and stared at him, absorbing everything, the faint tang of soap drifting off his skin, the soft smile in his cognac eyes, the casual way he hovered over her, protecting her even though she was fully capable of protecting herself. A tiny thread of hope shimmered to life inside her. She cupped her hand over his knee, just to feel him, just to have that simple connection.

"Mom's taken us off the mission and assigned somebody else to retrieve Eleni's remains."

He grunted. "I'm not surprised."

Well, that made one of them. "We have some time off, if you're ready for that vacation."

"Yeah, I might just be. Gotta take care of a few things first." He rested his hand over hers, enclosing her in his warmth. "When are you going back to London?"

"Not anytime soon. My identity's burned, thanks to the fiasco in Nevşehir, so I'm pretty much useless there." She flipped her hand over in his, meeting him palm to palm. "I thought I might hang out here for a while."

A slow smile curved his mouth. "I wasn't really planning on letting you go."

"Oh? And how did you think you were going to stop me?"

"Forget it, Jaybird. I'm not giving away my offense so you can prepare a defense. Besides, telling you takes all the fun out of it."

She narrowed her eyes at him. "Does this offense have anything to do with triggers and other gun metaphors?"

"Wait and see, baby." He smacked a kiss to her cheek.

"Hurry up and get ready. My belly's about to eat a hole in my spine."

She rolled her eyes, but she scooted off the couch. "You're so melodramatic."

"Hey, I ain't the drama queen, Jaybird."

She laughed and tucked her hand through his arm, and they bickered and joked all the way into his bedroom.

THE OMEGA was packed to the gills. Drew slouched into a chair and sipped a Brooklyn Lager, one ear on Bobby and Hiro's conversation, his gaze locked on Jerusha cutting up with her sisters and Indigo on the far side of the bar. The women were playing pool together, on teams, looked like. Jerusha's turn was about to roll around and he didn't wanna miss it. Every time she took a shot, she bent over and wiggled her ass at him.

He spread his knees a little wider and shifted in his seat. A couple more wiggles and he'd be ready to drag her home and test her readiness for full-on sex. Last night, after a full day spent doing nothing except being with her, he'd kissed every inch of her skin, then sent her soaring so high, he was pretty sure she hadn't come down yet.

He sure as hell hadn't.

Hadn't wanted to poke his head out of his house today either, wouldn't have if Bobby hadn't called and asked him and Jerusha if they wanted to get together with the gang that night in Tellowee's lone bar. Fuck all. He'd just talked Jerusha into staying, probably the closest thing to a commitment he'd ever get out of her. It was like their honeymoon or something. Who in their right mind bothered a couple on their honeymoon?

At least Jerusha was having a good time, and Drew didn't mind an hour or two touching base with Hiro and Bobby, even if they were stuck with that fucker Dave Winstead as a fourth.

Bobby nudged Drew's foot with the toe of his boot. "Saw where you put in for some leave."

Jerusha walked around the pool table, studying the spread. She bent over, wiggled her gorgeous ass, and shot. Drew sipped his lager. Oh, yeah. Best fucking view in the house. "Me and Jaybird are gonna hit the beach, maybe take in a game or something."

"So you're getting along with her pretty good."

Drew narrowed his eyes on Bobby. "Is that my best friend speaking or her brother?"

Bobby spread his hands wide. "Hey, I can be both, at the same time, even."

"Uh-huh."

"I'm worried, Drew, about both of you. You're not getting in too deep with her, are you? Because I love my sister, but she's an immortal Daughter. They don't let go of their hearts easily."

Drew studied his friend. Bobby would know all about the way an immortal Daughter held on to her heart. He'd fallen in love with his fiancée, Indigo, as a teenager and gotten his heart broken right in two for his troubles. It had all worked out, but not before him and Indigo were both dragged through the coals.

"I know what she is," Drew said.

Bobby exchanged a glance with Hiro, sitting on his other side, then focused on Drew. "You're in love with her."

Drew rubbed his earlobe between his thumb and forefinger. "You know, maybe you could say it a little friggin' louder. Not sure if they heard you outside."

Hiro hid a smile behind a sip of beer. "Friggin'?"

"Yeah, well. Jerusha's kinda strict about me cussing in public."

Bobby sighed. "Well, damn. I guess you're a goner." He fished his wallet out of the back pocket of his jeans and jerked a twenty out. "Wait. Who initiated sex first, her or you?"

"Her." And he still got hot just thinking about it.

Bobby pulled out another twenty and handed both to Hiro. "That's the last time I bet on one of my sisters."

"What're you doing betting against Hiro, anyhow? He

always wins."

"And he never learns," Hiro said.

Bobby grinned. "Good times."

Drew lifted his bottle. "The best."

Hiro propped his elbows on the arms of his chair. "What's with the ring? You two get hitched?"

Drew thumbed the underside of his wedding ring. Damn thing had grown on him, like it was a part of him or something. Every morning when he got up, he put it on, didn't even think not to. Jerusha hadn't questioned it. Hell, she was wearing hers, too. "Naw. Want to, though, if she'll have me."

Bobby rolled his hazel eyes toward the ceiling. "Sweet Goddess, I'm gonna have the two of you as brothers-in-law."

Drew cocked an eyebrow. "Say again?"

Hiro glanced down at the table. "Bobby, don't."

"He's your best friend, Hiro. You need to tell him."

"Tell me what?" Drew asked.

Bobby waggled his thumb at Hiro. "Our good buddy here has shacked up with India."

Hiro's black eyebrows snapped down over his dark eyes. "Don't cheapen it, Bobby. I care about her."

Drew barked out a hard laugh. "You care about the bitch that tried to cut your brother open? How the fuck does that work, exactly?"

Hiro stood slowly, his muscles rigid, his dark gaze a quiet threat. "Be careful how you speak about her. Whatever she's done in the past is behind her. She deserves a second chance."

Drew studied his friend, placid Hiro whose temper was so slow to rile, he might as well not have one. It was the first time Drew had ever seen the man get close to losing it. Pray to God that never actually happened. Hiro might look like a calm Japanese-American businessman out for a drink with his buddies, but he sure as hell could tear his way through whatever was put in front of him, whenever he wanted to.

Drew glanced at Bobby. "What's your take on this?"

"She's Indigo's sister," Bobby said quietly. "If Hiro can help her find some peace, maybe India can reconcile with her family. She about broke Indigo's heart when she went after me."

And Bobby would hate not being able to help his woman. Drew understood that all too fucking well. "All righty, then."

Hiro sat down and picked up his beer. "She's not a bad woman, just a hard one."

Drew zeroed in on the faint thread of emotion underscoring Hiro's words. "You've found something with her."

"Something I never thought I'd have."

Drew's gaze slid to Jerusha. "Yeah, I get that. Really, man. Just be careful. India ain't exactly known for her gentle nature."

One corner of Hiro's mouth lifted. "It's what I love about her."

"You would. Shit. Guess we're all toast."

Bobby tapped his beer bottle against the table. "To the women we love."

Drew snorted out a laugh. "Let's hope we live through whatever they throw at us."

Dave pulled a chair out and sat down across from Bobby. "What did I miss?"

Bobby scowled. "Not enough."

"Cut it out, Bobby," Hiro said. "He's practically family now."

"Fucking FBI," Drew muttered. On the other hand, an ex-FBI agent with an in on the Alexious could come in handy. "Say, Dave, ol' buddy, ol' pal. How's it hangin'?"

Dave grunted. "Somebody figured out a use for me. Must've taken a miracle."

Hiro choked on his beer, and Bobby reached over and smacked him in the arm, knocking the smaller man sideways.

"So sue me if you're useful," Drew said. "I was thinking. Before me and Jaybird take off, how would you guys like to deliver a little payback to Marco Alexiou?"

Bobby plopped his beer down. "Hell, yeah."

Hiro nodded. "I'm in."

"Marco's a little shit." Dave scrubbed a massive palm over his close-cropped hair and his stoic expression twisted into a scowl. "Lukas was not happy about the incident in Turkey. Can't promise anything, but he might be willing to help, too."

Drew smiled and slouched into his chair. "I was hoping you'd say that."

"When do we leave?" Bobby asked.

"Soon as we can make the plans." Drew glanced at Jerusha. She winked and grinned, and the funniest feeling clamped down on his heart, something an awful lot like forever. "What'll it take to fool the women?"

Bobby snorted. "Yeah, there ain't no fooling them. No matter what we tell them, they're gonna know we're up to something."

"Long as they don't come after us," Drew said.

"Basketball game?" Hiro suggested.

"Might work," Bobby said. "I'll check the schedules."

The four of them hunkered down over a plan to visit upstate New York and make sure Marco Alexiou never laid a wrong hand on another woman again. Dave was surprisingly well informed about Marco's whereabouts. Drew didn't question it too close. Dani's fiancé had spent a coupla years undercover with the Shadow and had maintained those ties, who knew why. Drew didn't give a fuck. Dave's inside knowledge was a big help now and that's what counted. Who cared how he got the info?

Half an hour into planning, the tempo of the overhead music changed and the lights dimmed. The women set down their pool cues and drifted toward the men.

"That's my cue. India's expecting me to call about now. Might as well do it from home." Hiro stood up, flopped cash onto the table, and cut a hard stare at its occupants. "The first man that utters the words *pussy whipped* can meet me on the mat when we get back from New York."

Drew held his hands up, palms out, and leaned back into his

chair. "Hey, man. I ain't no hypocrite."

Bobby snickered into his fist, and Dave shook his head.

Jerusha kissed Drew's cheek. "Who called you a hypocrite? I'll kick his ass to Atlanta and back."

"Nobody, baby. We were just being men, bullshitting each other."

She brushed the tip of her nose against his. "I like your manliness. Wanna see how it fits with my womanliness on the dance floor?"

"Great minds, Jaybird." He stood and stretched, and slung an arm around her shoulders. "God, it's good to be home."

"It really is." She wrapped an arm around his waist and guided him onto the dance floor, then curled up in his embrace. "Y'all looked like you were having a serious conversation."

Drew's heart skipped a beat. Fuck all. In his rush to avenge her, he'd forgotten how observant she was. "We're thinking about going to a basketball game. You know, guys' night out in New York. Dave's getting us tickets. He's got an in or something."

"Hmm. Bobby hates Dave."

And then there was that. "Naw, babe. They're trying to get along, for the sake of the family and all."

She rolled her eyes. "Yeah, those two know how to put aside their personal differences."

"Nobody likes a wise ass, Jaybird."

"Which is why you're one all the time." She leaned back and caught his gaze with hers. "What's going on?"

"Nothing, I swear. Just man stuff." He slid a hand under her hair and gripped her nape, massaging it gently. "You be ok for a coupla days this weekend?"

"I'm fine, Drew. Just make sure you're back by Sunday for lunch. Mom wants to have a family get together."

"Maybe we could move that to supper time."

"Drew, you really need to tell me—"

He dragged her close and captured her mouth with his,

shushing her the best way he knew how. God, he loved her sharp mind, but the last thing he needed was her figuring out what he was up to and interfering. A man had a right to beat the shit out of the bastard that hurt his woman. It was a hard and fast rule the female half of the species just didn't get, even the immortal, badass ones. Damned if he'd give up the privilege of making Marco bleed for what he'd done to her just 'cause the love of his life got nosey on him.

Twenty

JERUSHA SCROUNGED through Drew's cupboards for a bowl big enough to hold popcorn for six immortal women. Honestly, the man was thirty-one years old and had a cereal bowl. Just one, and it didn't match the rest of his dishes. She stared at a stack of plates, then moved on to the next cupboard. Even his dishes didn't match his dishes. No two were alike. What had he done, gotten them one at a time at dozens of different yard sales?

She shook her head and searched the cupboards under the counters. She'd always hated women who took over a man's life, rearranging everything, throwing out their old stuff in favor of color coordination, but in Drew's case, maybe it was justified. She pushed past a beat up blender, a shiny, new toaster, and a wok, and wiggled a good-sized, plastic bowl out. Surely he wouldn't mind if she switched out his stuff for hers once the movers packed and shipped her household goods.

Would he?

She frowned down at the plastic bowl. They hadn't gotten around to sorting that kind of thing out yet. In fact, they'd talked about everything except how and to what depth they were going to integrate their lives. Drew hadn't even questioned her staying, but he loved her. She hugged the bowl to her stomach. He loved her, told her every day at least once, and it was so good to hear.

Margaret poked her head into the kitchen. "Stop mooning over the boy and get your ass in gear. You've got a load of hungry women out here."

Jerusha rolled her eyes. And she'd thought Drew was bad. "I'm coming, I'm coming. Sheesh, Maggie May."

"Watch how you talk to your elders, little girl."

"Yeah, I'm so scared."

"Drew's been a bad influence on you. First, he teaches you to be a smart ass, and then, he convinces you to let him fight your battles for you."

Jerusha yanked the popcorn out of the microwave and dumped it into the bowl. "A, I was already a smart ass, thanks much, and b, it's kinda stupid for a lone Daughter to seek revenge against the Alexious, especially when the Shadow himself is practically living in Tellowee."

"He's just visiting, hopefully not for long." Margaret leaned a shoulder against the doorframe. "You don't seem upset about what happened to you."

Jerusha shrugged. "Did it bother me? Yes, but I'm getting over it a little at a time. And really, it was gross and, yeah, really gross, but it didn't hurt me."

"So you let Drew go after him."

"Nobody lets Drew do anything." Jerusha stared at the popcorn, dozens of yellow and white morsels just sitting there, doing nothing. No thinking, no planning, no looking over their shoulders, waiting to be got. "This is gonna sound crazy."

"We're immortal descendants of cursed warriors. How much crazier can it be?"

"Good point." Jerusha sighed and jostled the bowl of popcorn, evening the white and yellow mass out. "I think he feels like he needs to do something. I mean, he's never helpless when I go off course. He's always there for me, talking me down, so calm and loving and kind. But this whole vengeance thing is, I don't know. Maybe it's his way of atoning for my getting caught."

"He couldn't have prevented it."

"I tried telling him that, but he's a man and he feels responsible. Stupid, really."

Not that she'd say that to Drew, not exactly like that, anyway. He already had a complex about his intelligence. She had no clue why, either. He was sharp as a tack, quick on his feet. Had a good trigger finger. She ducked her head, hiding a smile. Boy, did he have a good trigger finger.

"Anyway, I figured, why not? He's got Bobby and Hiro and Dave with him. Between the four of them, they're safe enough."

"They're a small army on their own," Margaret agreed. "Now that you're finished mooning, can we start the movie?"

Jerusha huffed out a laugh. "Here, take the popcorn. I'll get the cookies."

She left the cookies in the packaging. They wouldn't last long anyway, not with all her sisters gathered in Drew's living room. Good thing he had a big couch and two recliners. Their place was the biggest, except for Charlotte's, but at Charlotte's, they'd never get any peace, what with three kids and a husband underfoot. So everybody had met at Drew's, Margaret and Moira and Charlotte, the eldest of Jerusha's sisters, Dani, their younger, adopted sister, and Indigo, Bobby's beloved.

Drew had told her to treat his house like it was hers. Maybe he wouldn't have said that if he'd known they were planning a girls' night in his living room.

She dropped the cookies onto the coffee table and squeezed into the couch between Indigo and Dani. Margaret had taken one of the recliners, Moira the other, and Charlotte was on the other side of Dani. Margaret had already put the movie in, thank goodness not a monster movie. Drew had already threatened Jerusha with that. She didn't need two in a row.

Indigo tucked her arm through Jerusha's. "It's so good to have you home."

"It's good to be back."

"Are you staying a while?"

"Probably a good long while." Jerusha plucked at an

imaginary speck of lint on her Yoga tights. "I was thinking about buying a house in Tellowee."

"Really?" Indigo lowered her voice and leaned closer, touching her midnight head to Jerusha's. "What did Drew say when you asked him?"

"Haven't yet. We're still kinda feeling our way through the whole relationship thing."

Dani snickered. "Yeah, y'all are feeling your way through something, all right. I saw the way he was looking at you at The Omega the other night."

Charlotte elbowed Dani. "Cut it out, Dani Do-Right. You can tease her after the movie."

Indigo tugged on Jerusha's arm. "Did he give you that line about a basketball game?"

"Like I didn't see right through that one."

"Very flimsy. I thought Bobby was more creative than that."

Dani leaned around Jerusha and her green eyes sparkled. "Blame it on Dave. He's probably the one that thought it up. I love him, but sometimes he's a little too straight."

Indigo clucked her tongue. "You'll solve that problem, won't you?"

"Already working on it," Dani said, grinning.

Margaret stabbed them with an icy stare. "Are we chatting or watching a movie?"

"Leave 'em alone, Maggie May," Moira said. "I was enjoying the gossip."

"You're just pissed 'cause Tom didn't get asked to go beat up an Alexiou," Dani said.

Moira threaded her fingers together over her stomach and the tiny fetus resting there. "Tom is good at many a thing. I'm happy to have him do them right at home, thank ye kindly."

Charlotte pressed the pad of her thumb against her thigh. "That's where she's got the poor man."

"That's where men are supposed to be," Margaret said.

"And that's why you'll never have one," Dani retorted.

"Honestly, the two of you are practically medieval."

Moira twisted her mouth into a quick smile. "Margaret's literally medieval. I skirted the edge of that one, by the Lady's grace and with her infinite wisdom."

Jerusha patted Dani's thigh. "Don't worry. They'll get what's coming to them."

"Ooo, she cursed ye good, Maggie," Moira said. "Me Tom's a saint compared to the man that'll snag yer heart."

"Have you seen Tom and Moira together?" Indigo whispered to Jerusha. "Charlotte's not even close to being right. He's got her exactly where he wants her, and she just thinks it's where she wants to be."

"Oy, there. 'Tis where I want to be, Indigo fair. No point in giving in too easy, though, is there?"

Jerusha settled in, content to surround herself with her sisters' easy jibes. She'd missed her family, but now that she was back close to home, she could immerse herself in their lives again. Drew wouldn't mind. Maybe he'd even want to buy a house close to Bobby and Indigo when they settled on one. Drew didn't seem to want children, but that was ok. They'd have her nieces and nephews and the other children in Tellowee running in and out of their house at all hours, making perfect nuisances of themselves, and they'd have each other.

It would be enough.

Now all she had to do was tell Drew that's what she wanted, and she was going to, as soon as he got home from the trip up north to see a *basketball game.*

She slouched down in the couch, grinning, and started working on the best way to tease him about where he'd been as soon as he got home.

SNEAKING ONTO Lukas Alexiou's compound in upstate New York was a lot easier than sneaking into Pinico Alexiou's estate in Turkey had been. Having Dave along helped a lot, especially since he'd called ahead and asked security to deliberately leave gaps, with Lukas' permission.

Handy guy to have in your corner, was Dave, even if he was a fucking Feebi.

Drew left his sidearm holstered as they crept through a little used gate tucked into the wall surrounding the backyard. Turned out January in New York was even colder than January in Turkey. He should've remembered that. It wasn't like he hadn't grown up in the northeast. Boston had its share of harsh winters, same as any other New England town. They were just a helluva lot harder to bear now that he'd spent years in the South, first in the Army, and then building a business with his closest friends.

And now, he'd probably live out his life there, hopefully at Jerusha's side.

Dave took point and led Drew, Bobby, and Hiro through the snow covered landscape to the main house, an imposing Gothic Revival mansion straight out of a horror flick. Marco and his family lived in one wing, Lukas in the other. Marco's son was in Tellowee with his uncle, the biggest impetus behind hitting asap. Drew wanted revenge, yeah, just not so bad he'd inflict it on a kid. Seeing that kind of thing damaged the mind in ways it took years to sort out. He'd gone through that after Sean had died. If it hadn't been for stealing the wrong car from the right man, Drew would've spent a good chunk of his life paying his dues to society behind bars.

They reached the house minutes after going through the gate. Dave unlocked a side door and turned off the alarm, then up they went, through winding passages toward Marco's half of the house. His wife was an invalid, apparently due to a run in with a Daughter a few years back, and slept separately. Dave's contact on household security had called as soon as Marco retired to his room for the night, paving the way for their little rendezvous.

Get in, beat the shit out of the asshole, get out, a lot like his and Jerusha's mission in Turkey should've been. This time, nothing would go wrong, and if it did, oh, well. Drew had a lot of anger to spread around on Jaybird's behalf. If things went according to plan, and no reason why they shouldn't, him and the three men who'd tagged along would all be home in time to enjoy Rebecca's good home cooking and the company of their women.

Marco was exactly where he was supposed to be, sound asleep in his bed in the room across the hall from his wife. The men crept in one by one, Dave, Bobby, Hiro, Drew. Dave closed the door behind them and leaned his back against it, arms crossed over his broad chest. Drew positioned himself at the foot of the bed, Hiro and Drew on either side.

The room was dark, lit only by the moonlight streaming through the thinly curtained windows. Hard to make out who was who and impossible to catch a peek at what was about to go down.

Good enough.

Drew nodded, and Hiro yanked the covers off of a nearly nude Marco. Bobby slapped a gloved hand over the man's mouth and jerked him off the bed. Marco's eyes popped open. To his credit, he didn't scream, but he did fight and try to squirm out of Bobby's grasp.

Drew's mouth stretched into a thin, cold smile. Out of all the Daughters Marco could've picked on, he'd chosen the Enforcer's favorite sister. Nobody got away from Bobby once he made up his mind to snare somebody. Wasn't that just Marco's bad luck?

Hiro strolled casually around the side of the bed and stopped beside Drew. Bobby dragged Marco into the middle of the floor, in between the massive canopy bed and the sitting area arranged around a fireplace on the other side of the room.

Drew pulled his toboggan off and stepped into the moonlight in front of Marco, and Marco's eyes widened. Drew grinned. Oh, yeah. This was gonna be fun. "You know who I am."

Marco nodded slowly.

"That's good. I'd hate to have to explain why I'm here. But you already know, right?"

Marco blinked. Drew took that as a yes, or maybe an *oh, fuck, I'm in trouble now*. Either one was fine by him.

"Thing is, you hurt a good woman. My woman, as a matter of fact, and don't none of us here take too kindly to that." He pointed at Bobby, then jerked his thumb over his shoulder at Dave. "That man there is her brother and that hulking brute is her future brother-in-law. And this guy beside me? He makes death look like a walk in the park."

Drew jerked his chin at Bobby. Hiro stepped forward and snagged one of Marco's arms. Bobby pulled his hand away from Marco's mouth and grabbed the other arm.

Marco grimaced and spat onto the floor. "If you kill me, you'll start a war the likes of which the People have never seen."

"Oh, I'm not gonna kill you," Drew said. "I'm just gonna ball up my fist and hit you one time for every bite mark you left on my baby's skin. You know how many there were?"

Marco's eyelids slid shut and he sagged into Bobby and Hiro's grips on his arms. "Seventy-four," he whispered. "Some of them faded and I had to bite her again. It was so beautiful."

Drew shook his head. "You're one sick mother fucker."

"Pinico wants her. I had to break her. She had to be ready for him."

Drew stuck his face close to Marco's. "He better not ever come near her again, you hear me?"

"One man won't stop him."

"Yeah? Try a whole army of 'em. You want war? See what happens if he lays a hand on another Daughter."

Marco laughed, cold and malicious. "Don't confuse me with my brother. I want to see the People slaughtered. I want every, single last Daughter crushed under the Shadow's heel."

"And you think you'll be the one to wear the shoe, is that it?"

Drew glanced around at Dave. The other man shook his

head. Yeah, that's what Drew thought. Lukas wasn't giving up control of the Shadow anytime soon. Looked like little brother was gonna have to bide his time in the wings.

Drew stripped off his gloves and stuffed them into his back pocket with his toboggan, then twisted his ring off and tucked it deep inside his front pocket. "Somebody count for me. I'm too pissed off to keep track."

"Seventy-four," Bobby said. "Save some for me."

"Plenty to go around," Drew said, and slammed his fist into Marco's cheek, relishing the pain rocketing through his bones as skin met skin and vengeance was exacted, one solid blow at a time.

JERUSHA WANDERED around Drew's house, sweeping up popcorn, throwing empty cookie wrappers in the trash. Indigo was right. It was good to be among family again, good to have a home near the heart that had nurtured her.

And it was good to have her sisters around. Recent events had thrown them together a lot over the past few months. The theft of the artifacts from Sandby borg, India's attack on Bobby, the ever-present quest to protect the People. Family pulled each other through the hard times and celebrated every bit of the good.

Jerusha hugged her arms around her waist over the odd contentment filling her. Drew was going to be her family. They were already friends, already lovers, but he needed her to be his family, exactly the way she wanted him to be hers.

Why hadn't her immortality broken? Was she not meant to give her heart to Drew or was she simply rushing the process in her hurry to bind him to her?

She gnawed on her lower lip as she locked the house up and switched the lights off one by one. They'd only known each other a couple of months, excepting the one time they'd met in Reno.

He'd never forgotten her. Hadn't he told her as much when

he'd shared the story about his bird feeders, how they'd reminded him of something? Her eyes. He'd remembered them half a decade later, not because his memory was mystically sharp as hers was, but because they were beautiful to him. *She* was beautiful to him.

She flopped onto the bed back first and something wondrous bubbled through her, carrying her heart along in its wake. It was huge, filling her from stem to stern with the love he held for her, and she sighed it out, sharing it with the air around her.

Was that what love felt like?

She squinched her eyes closed and waited. Surely this happiness bursting through her was love. Surely the Lady Ki would lift her curse now. Surely She would never allow one of her Daughters to suffer through eternity without her heart.

Nothing happened.

Jerusha opened one eye and peeked at the ceiling. "Please?"

A vehicle roared by on the street outside, the furnace kicked on. Jerusha's happiness gradually ebbed away. She trusted Drew, she suspected she loved him. Sheesh, she'd even let him take vengeance in her place, like the little woman he pretended she was. What else did she have to do to break the wretched curse? Wasn't it enough to crave him, to yearn for his presence, to find refuge in his touch? Did she have to grovel, too? Did she have to scream and demand and rage against her fate, the way the Seven Sisters must've done so long ago?

Or was he simply not the man she was destined to love?

She pushed herself upright and shoved her hair away from her face. No, she could love Drew. It was there in the quiet ache in her heart, in the bone deep knowledge that she could count on him no matter what curves life pitched at them, in the satisfaction of knowing he loved her so much, he'd stick with her even if she never aged another day.

That was love, the steadfast hand of a man, the solid beat of his heart, the gentle laughter and the burning passion and a

233

lifetime of friendship, built day by day, one kiss at a time. How could she ever give that up?

She used the bathroom, set the ring he'd given her by the sink, and washed her hands and face. Brushed her teeth and pulled on one of his t-shirts. She flipped the bedroom lights off and crawled into the middle of his gargantuan bed, and buried her face in his pillow.

"Drew," she whispered. "Come home to me. I need you so much."

A suffocating weight pressed her into the mattress, and she choked on the breath whooshing out of her lungs. Sweet Mother, what was happening to her?

The weight lifted, sucking the strength out of her marrow, sapping her will, and she arched off the bed, gasping for air. Darkness crowded around the edges of her vision, and she fell into it, drifting along the plains of nothingness, Drew's roughhewn face etched firmly into her mind.

Twenty-One

THE HARTSFIELD-JACKSON International Airport was packed with people, loud as hell, and so bright, Drew flinched away from the sunlight pouring into the building through the plate glass walls. Sunglasses weren't cutting it. The hangover jackknifing through his skull didn't help and neither did the dull throb in his bruised knuckles.

It had been so fucking worth it.

He hitched his backpack over his shoulder and followed Bobby out to the car they'd left there for the return trip home. The day was balmy and clear skied, a perfect antidote to New York's freezing chill, but God, did the sun have to burn so bright?

Beside him, Hiro tugged his ball cap lower, shielding his eyes. "Tell me why I helped you again?"

"'Cause you're my bestie," Drew said.

Dave grunted. "Girls."

Drew elbowed him in the ribs, hard. Helping them take Marco down a notch or seventy-four didn't make Dave one of the guys. He'd have to earn that rank the agonizingly slow way the same as everybody else, through sweat and blood and the screams of their enemies.

Come to think on it, Dave had gone through that gauntlet once, not eighteen hours past. Now he only had about a hundred more times to go before he could be a bestie, too.

Drew's phone buzzed against his hip. He pulled it out, thumbed into the text, and grinned. Jerusha. Her first message that morning had been his name followed by a tiny, pink heart. The second message had contained a picture of endless sapphire water lapping onto a white, sandy beach. This one simply said, *Miss you.*

He texted her a quick, *Home soon, baby,* and stuck his phone in his pocket. Now that he was back, they could figure out where they were headed. Him? He was all for her moving into his house, lock, stock, and barrel. She could do whatever with it. Women liked that kinda thing, right? And without her, it was just a place to rest his head at night, maybe catch a game between assignments.

He ducked into the backseat of Dani's Jeep, slouched down in the seat, and closed his eyes. They could talk about the future and stuff, his job, hers, the family they'd make between them. And he could get one of those tattoos. Whatsit? Like the one Bobby had inked into the skin covering his shoulder blade, so everybody would know who Drew loved.

"Hey, Bobby. What's that thing on your back called?"

The front passenger's seat creaked. "An *aenkanien.* You gonna get one?"

"Thinking about it."

"Me, too," Hiro said softly.

Drew cracked an eyelid. "Ya don't say."

Hiro was slouched into the backseat, mirroring Drew's casual slump, his eyes hidden behind his sunglasses, the brim of his cap pulled low. "Just thinking about it."

Drew closed his eyes and leaned his head against the seat. "Reckon if we get 'em at the same time, we can get a discount?"

Bobby snorted out a laugh.

"I'm getting one," Dave said. "Music, maybe."

"Well, hell," Drew said. "If he's getting one, we gotta."

"It would be a crying shame to let the Feebi win," Hiro

agreed.

Drew's phone buzzed. He wiggled around on the seat and pulled it out of his pocket. Jerusha had sent him another text.

Have something to tell you when you get home.

What?, he texted back.

A surprise.

His heart flipped over in his chest. A surprise, huh? Maybe she was pregnant. Oh, yeah, that was one he could handle, about the way he'd handled putting the baby there in the first place. He didn't mind waiting until she was completely healed to have sex with her again. He'd wait as long as she needed him to, but God, he missed being in her.

He smiled and rubbed a fist over the hammering beat of his heart. A baby. Jerusha's blue eyes smiling up at him out of his daughter's face. Fuck, yeah.

No, wait. She'd told him she couldn't get pregnant right around the first time they'd made love. He swallowed down his disappointment and let his hand slide to the seat. He didn't even know how it was possible for a woman to have sex as much as they'd been at it and not get pregnant.

He kneed the back of Bobby's seat. "How exactly do Daughters get pregnant, anyhow?"

"The needing. Three or four days of her being so horny, she wears her man out." Bobby sighed and sank lower in his seat. "Indigo's gonna go through it soon. We're hoping she'll get pregnant."

Hiro popped upright and poked his head between the front seats. "Did you say three or four *days?*"

"Depends on the woman, but yeah. Never been with a Daughter during her needing, but I've heard the rumors. Non-stop sex, her so wild and greedy, sometimes it takes two men to satisfy her."

"Fuck that," Drew said. "Ain't nobody else gonna lay a hand on my Jaybird."

Bobby twisted around in his seat. "Don't worry. She'll only

want you, but you better lay in supplies now."

"Yeah, man. Only, I don't even know when hers is."

Hiro cleared his throat. "So, India and Indigo's would probably be around the same time."

"Not necessarily," Bobby said. "Why?"

Hiro huffed out a laugh. "Do you really have to ask?"

Bobby turned around and thumped his back into the seat. "Right. Stupid question."

Drew eyed his phone. Three or four days in bed with Jerusha, trying to satisfy her every sexual whim? Molten need screamed through his blood and his dick hardened. He opened her last message and texted, *When is your needing?*

A minute later, her reply popped onto the screen. *Early fall, why?*

Curious.

Drew dropped the phone into his lap, grinning like a damn fool. Early fall was, what? Eight months away? Sounded like a good excuse to take a vacay and, yeah, he'd sure as hell lay in enough supplies to last him and Jaybird through at least a week.

"Hunh." Hiro tucked his phone away and sank into the seat, his skin unnaturally pale. "Hey, uh, Winstead. Mind going a little faster?"

"Yeah, Winstead," Drew said. "I got things to do."

"You and me both, pal," Dave said, and the car leapt forward, carrying the four men toward the women they loved.

JERUSHA PACED a circuit around Drew's living room from the front entrance of his house to the bedroom doorway to the windows overlooking his back yard and back again. How was she going to tell Drew what had happened to her? Would he be happy that she loved him or would he be pissed because he was stuck with her?

She frowned at the bird feeders hanging all over his backyard, along the fence, from the eaves of the house, on freestanding posts cutting a jagged line through the brown grass. He wasn't exactly stuck with her. Men were always free to leave a mortal Daughter, but a Daughter's heart could only be given once. She'd never loved another man the way she did Drew. That love would only grow over time, becoming so huge, she'd never survive the loss of him in her life, and wouldn't want to.

Stupid, stupid. She'd *asked* the Lady to break her immortality, begged for it so hard, Ki had listened. How could she have succumbed so easily after knowing him such a short time?

His key turned in the lock. She whirled around and hurried toward the front door, and skidded to a stop half a dozen feet away. She could do this. Drew would listen. He might be rough and rowdy, but he had a big heart, a kind one. How could she have fallen in love with him if he didn't? How could he be disappointed when he loved her, too?

He stepped inside, shut the door, and smiled, and her heart sank. His eyes were bloodshot. Why were his eyes bloodshot?

He bent down and kissed her cheek. "Hey, baby. Sorry it took so long. We got hung up in traffic on the way out of Atlanta."

She crossed her arms over her chest. "Why do you smell like alcohol?"

He hunched his shoulders around his ears. "Ah, we got a little carried away last night celebrating."

"After the basketball game."

"Uh, yeah. You know how men are, Jaybird. One toast led to two and before we knew it, we were drunk as skunks."

"The game was that good, huh." She narrowed her eyes at him. "Who won?"

He winced. "Ok, you got me, baby. We didn't really go to a game."

"I know you were at Marco's, Drew."

"Don't be mad," he said softly.

She wrapped her arms around his waist and rested her

cheek over the steady thump of his heart. "I'm not. I was trying to give you a hard time. It's just not coming out right today."

"You can save it up and give me two hard times tomorrow." He squeezed her closer to him. "You said you had a surprise."

"Kind of." She squinched her eyes tight and blurted, "I love you."

His heart stuttered under her skin and he went deathly still. "You love me."

"And I'm mortal."

"You, ah..." His knees buckled and he swayed. "Oh, God. You really love me."

"Didn't I just tell you?"

"Yeah, you did. Never thought I'd hear you say it, though." He hooked his hands around her waist and picked her up, whirling her through the air, a huge grin on his face. "I love you so much, Jaybird."

She clutched his shoulders and held on for the ride, laughing with him, and wound her arms around his neck as he slowed and stopped. "Well, that was fun."

"It's just the start, baby. Me and you, together." He touched his forehead to hers and brushed his fingertips over her stomach. "A family. Bobby told us about the needing. We don't have to the next time you go through it, but maybe the time after that, we could try for a kid."

She searched his eyes and marveled at the tender need shining out of him. "I thought you didn't want kids. You said as much, the night you told me about your brother."

"I said I didn't think I'd be a good dad, and sure as shit, Jaybird, I probably won't be. I'll try real hard, though, I swear it." He pressed butterfly kisses across her skin, buried his face in her throat. "Marry me, Jaybird. Live with me forever as trigger and triggeree."

Laughter sputtered out of her. "I am *not* vowing to be your triggeree."

"It was worth a shot. Will you marry me?"

"Yes, Drew, I will, whenever you want." She sighed and eased away from him. "We can talk about it while I tend these cuts on your hands. Did you really have to hit him with both fists?"

"Left hand got tired. You swear you love me?"

"I don't let just anybody fight my battles for me, Drew."

"And you're positive you don't wanna be my triggeree?"

She took his hand gently in her own and led him into the bedroom and the bathroom beyond. "Forget it, sweetie. There are some lines a woman can't cross."

"How about Micky and Minnie?

"Your ears are too small."

"Popeye and Olive Oyl?"

"Do I really look like Olive Oyl?"

"Naw. Your ass ain't scrawny enough, thank God. Speaking of."

She laughed and kissed him and bandaged up his hands, and after, they fell into bed together and practiced making a family in the shelter of each other's love.

Epilogue

F AMILY TRICKLED into the Upton house in clusters and spurts. Nearly all of Rebecca's living children had made it with their beloveds. Not all her grandchildren, no. Margaret's daughters were still abroad working for the benefit of the People, as were Rebecca's immortal granddaughters by her eldest child, Mina, now deceased, killed on a battlefield before she'd found her heart.

Rebecca rubbed her fingertips in slow circles over her temples. Mina would've loved having the family gathered around her. She would've adored the men her sisters had found love with and she would've spared nothing to protect them all.

Jerusha slipped into the house, followed closely by Drew.

Rebecca rose to meet her. "There you are, darling."

"Sorry we're late."

"I've heard that more than once today." Rebecca gripped Jerusha's elbow and guided her into the living room where the family had gathered. "You're glowing."

"I'm mortal," Jerusha whispered. "We're getting married."

"Two pieces of good news, right when I needed them. Congratulations, darling." Rebecca turned to Drew and bussed his cheek. "No more fighting, Drew. You're a family man now."

Drew's mouth twisted into a frown. "Who spilled the beans?"

"I didn't get where I am by ignoring what's going on around me."

He tugged his earlobe and glanced beyond her into the living room. "Yeah, uh, think I'll go watch the game."

He wended his way through the crowded room and flopped onto the floor next to Charlotte's children. Jerusha threaded her fingers through her mother's. "I really have to remember that one, especially if it keeps him in line."

"I have dozens more exactly like it, though none of them ever worked on your stepfather. He knows me too well."

"I have a feeling Drew's going to know me that well, too. So, how's the Boston bone expedition going?"

"Eleni's remains are on their way here as we speak, thanks to you and Drew."

Jerusha glanced at the floor. "We didn't having anything to do with retrieving them."

"But you figured out where they were. Without that knowledge, we would never have been able to find them." Rebecca tugged Jerusha closer. "I wish you'd been able to find Sanctuary."

"We found the Lost City. I know it's not the same, but at least we know where it is now."

"And someday, we'll be able to visit and perhaps return the remains of the Seven to their rightful place, and the Prophecy can at last be fulfilled."

Jerusha frowned and dug the tip of one boot into the floor. "Listen, about that. What was it the Prophecy said about the Sisters and their bones?"

Rebecca had studied the refrain so often, the words danced in front of her eyes while she slept. " 'Daughters and Sons will gather where the bones of the Sisters shall lie.' Why?"

"How many of the Sisters' remains do we have here?"

"Soon to be three, the ones found at Bones the day Dani killed Lilith, the ones you and Drew smuggled out of Turkey, and the ones being brought here from Boston."

Jerusha's gaze lifted slowly and met her mother's. "We have three here. What if we found the other four sets? What if instead of returning them to the City of the Sisters or Sanctuary or wherever, they're supposed to be here in Tellowee, with the People who are alive now?"

A giant fist caught Rebecca in its grip and the blood rushed out of her head. "What makes you think that?"

"The Prophecy never mentioned *where* the Sisters' remains would lie. It only said that they had to be together, I'm assuming before the Prophecy could be fulfilled. What if we've been chasing a dead end trying to find Sanctuary? What if the answer to this part of the riddle has been under our noses the whole time?"

"Oh, sweet merciful Mother," Rebecca breathed. "Why didn't I see this before?"

"Maybe you just needed a fresh set of eyes, a different perspective. I don't know." Jerusha knuckled her forehead. "In fact, I don't even know why I'm thinking about it. I've been a little wonky since the mortality whammy hit me last night."

"While Drew was gone?"

"Yes, but other than scaring the life out of me, it wasn't a big deal. I woke up safe and sound this morning, and I swear, it was like little hearts were floating in circles around my head."

Rebecca laughed. "When I told you to find your own path, I didn't think it would literally be lined with hearts."

"That's life with Drew." Jerusha lowered her voice. "He asked me to be his triggeree this morning when he asked me to marry him."

"His what?"

"Long story."

"Sounds like a good one." Rebecca glanced over the heads of her family, the many hearts she'd been privileged to love in her long life. "Come into the kitchen. You can tell me all about it over a nice cup of hot cocoa."

They strolled hand in hand through the house, their heads

bent close together, enjoying the bonds of mother and daughter. Rebecca couldn't quite forget the possibilities Jerusha had proposed or their implications to the path the People had stepped onto the moment the Prophecy of Light had been unearthed in a grave halfway around the world, but today was for family. Tomorrow was soon enough to worry about the rest.

About the Author:
Lucy Varna lives in the Blue Ridge Mountains of northeast
Georgia, surrounded by her large, extended family.
Visit her online at:

www.lucyvarna.com
www.daughtersofthepeople.com

The adventure continues...

The Gathering Storm
(Daughters of the People, Book 6)

Coming soon!

www.ingramcontent.com/pod-product-compliance
Lightning Source LLC
Chambersburg PA
CBHW060421180626
46817CB00007B/2614